ALL AMONG THE BARLEY

ALL AMONG
THE BARLEY

Melissa Harrison

BLOOMSBURY PUBLISHING
LONDON · OXFORD · NEW YORK · NEW DELHI · SYDNEY

BLOOMSBURY, BLOOMSBURY PUBLISHING and the Diana logo
are trademarks of Bloomsbury Publishing Plc

First published in Great Britain 2018

ISBN: HB: 978-1-4088-9799-7; TPB: 978-1-4088-9798-0; EBOOK: 978-1-4088-9801-7

2 4 6 8 10 9 7 5 3 1

Typeset by Integra Software Services Pvt. Ltd.
Printed and bound in Great Britain by CPI Group (UK) Ltd, Croydon CR0 4YY

MIX
Paper from
responsible sources
FSC
www.fsc.org   FSC® C020056

To find out more about our authors and books visit www.bloomsbury.com
and sign up for our newsletters

The past is not dead, but is living in us,
and will be alive in the future which we are
now helping to make.

~ WILLIAM MORRIS

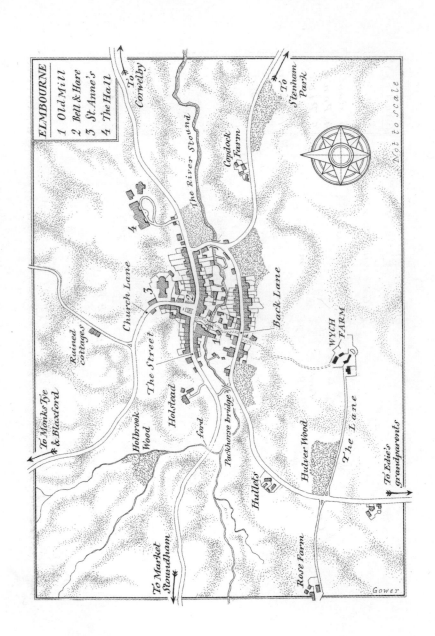

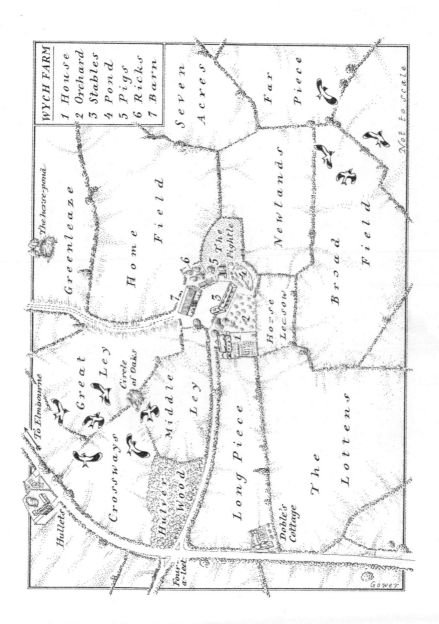

WYCH FARM

1 House
2 Orchard
3 Stables
4 Pond
5 Pigs
6 Ricks
7 Barn

Not to scale

The horse-pond

Greenleaze

Home   Field

Seven   Acres

Far   Piece

Newlands

The Tightle

6   5   4

7   3   1   Horse   Lezow

1   2

Great   Ley

Circle of Oaks

Middle   Ley

Broad   Field

To Elmbourne

Crossways

Hulver   Wood

Long   Piece

The   Lottens

Hullets

Four-a-lees

Doble's Cottage

Gower

Prologue

Last night I lay awake again, remembering the day
the Hunt ran me down in Hulver Wood when I was
just a girl. It was December, as it is now, and I had
ventured out into the icy afternoon to cut some
green boughs for the house. None of the others
minded much about decorations, but I loved the way
the firelight flickered on the glossy leaves of holly
I always hung above the parlour hearth.

Frost had hardened the furrows of the ploughland
and at the fields' margins ice stood in the cart ruts,
bubbled and opaque. I had a sack, and a set of
pruning-shears, and I wore a pair of my brother's
old work gloves on my chilled and clumsy hands.
As I walked, a white owl kept pace with me, drifting
silently at head-height on the other side of the hedge;
perhaps it hoped I would startle some blood-warm
creatures from its tangled base.

It was dim that afternoon in Hulver Wood, and no
birds sang. I pushed deeper and deeper in, stopping
at the jill hollies with their blood-red berries and

wriggling my toes inside my boots to keep off the frozen ache of the ground.

The sound of the 'gone away', blown close, cleaved the still December air. Heart pounding, I crushed the prickly leaves down into the hessian and twisted a rough knot with trembling hands. But they were far too close already, and from the top of the wood bank I saw them streaming towards me from The Lottens into Long Piece: the hounds ahead and questing in full cry, the pink- and red-coated riders urging the thundering horses on behind.

'Get on! Go!' shouted the Master of Hounds as the first of the baying dogs reached the trees. 'For God's sake, girl, *will you move!*'

But trembling, I froze, and the pack broke around me like water before my legs could carry me out of the way.

I

My name is Edith June Mather and I was born not long after the end of the Great War. My father, George Mather, had sixty acres of arable land known as Wych Farm; it is somewhere not far from here, I believe. Before him my grandfather Albert farmed the same fields, and his father before him, who ploughed with a team of oxen and sowed by hand. I would like to think that my brother Frank, or perhaps one of his sons, has the living of it now; but a lifetime has passed since I was last on its acres, and because of everything that happened I have been prevented from finding out.

I was an odd child, I can see now – certainly by the phlegmatic, practical standards of the farming families thereabouts. I preferred the company of books to other children, and was frequently chided by my parents after leaving my tasks half-done, distracted by the richer, more vivid world within my head. And sometimes I talked to myself out loud without meaning to, usually as a way of drowning out a thought or a memory I didn't want to have. Father would some-times tap his head and call me 'touched' – only in fun, I'm sure – but perhaps, looking back, he was right.

I was thirteen in 1933, the year our district began to endure its famous – or infamous – drought. It crept up on us: the hay came in well, and when the rick was thatched Father was pleased, because he knew it was dry and wouldn't spoil; this meant that the horses would have enough fodder to last the winter, and he would not have to buy any in. But without any rain the field drains ran dry and by August even the horse-pond by the house had shrunk to a thick green scum. I remember John Hurlock, our horseman, taking buckets of well-water to Moses and Malachi when they came in from the fields at three o'clock; I can see as though it were yesterday how greed-ily and noisily the great horses drank, how at last he would fill the buckets again and fling the water over their twitching flanks, washing away the white rime of sweat from their chestnut coats. Oh, my beloved creatures, how they must have missed walking into the cool horse-pond, as they always had, and drink-ing their fill.

Frank was sixteen by then, and doing a man's work on the farm; Father was starting to rely on him almost as much as he did on John. My sister Mary, who had married Clive that spring, already had a baby boy, and although Mother harnessed our little pony Meg to the trap and drove over to Monks Tye once a week with a

loaf or a suet pudding, we saw little of her at Wych
Farm. With Mary gone I felt strangely suspended, as
though awaiting what would come next – although I
couldn't have told you what that was. It was like hide-
and-seek, when you're waiting for someone to find
you; but the game had gone on for too long.

Of course, the drought meant that the cornfields
suffered, and that year the harvest was down, our
wheat barely sixteen bushels to the acre.

'Seven Acres will lie fallow next year,' Father said
as John and Doble, our yardman, came in for their
supper after the last of the corn was in. It wasn't what
you might call a Harvest Home, but there was ale,
and a ham, and boiled batter pudding, and Mother
had twisted a few ears of barley into a rough figure
and set it on the kitchen table. Opposite me Frank
glanced up, alert, at Father's words. The men took
their places, and John remarked that Seven Acres had
lain fallow only the year before.

'Do you think to tell me how to farm?' asked
Father; but John did not reply. Mother sat down, I
mumbled Grace, and we began to eat.

The autumn of that year was the most beautiful I can
remember. For weeks after harvest-tide the weather
stayed fine, and only slowly that year did summer's
warmth leave the earth.

In October, Wych Farm's trees turned quickly
and all at once, blazing into oranges and reds and

burnished golds; with little wind to strip them the woods and spinneys lay on our land like treasure, the massy hedgerows filigreed with old-man's-beard and enamelled with rosehips and black sloes. Along the winding course of the River Stound the alder carrs were studded with earthstars and chanterelles and dense with the rich, autumnal stink of rot; but crossing Long Piece towards The Lottens the sky opened into austere, equinoctial blue, where flocks of peewits wheeled and turned, flashing their broad wings black and white.

At dawn, dew silvered the spiders' silk strung between the grass blades in our pastures so that the horses left trails where they walked, like the wakes of slow vessels in still water. At last, wintering fieldfares and thrushes stripped the berries from the lanes, and at night the four tall elms for which the farm was named welcomed their cold-weather congregations of rooks.

The dew dampened the stubble in the parched cornfields, drawing from it a mocking green aftermath that had Grandfather recalling the flock of purebred ewes that once were overwintered on the land.

'It's not worth the shearing of them these days,' Father said. 'I've told you that.'

'I wholly mislike good fodder going to waste,' the old man replied, banging his stick upon the floor, 'and that's a fact.'

The year wore on, the leaves torn from our elms by autumn gales until the branches were stark. I read *The Midnight Folk* and spent my days pretending to be Kay Harker and embarking on imaginary adventures involving knights, smugglers and highwaymen, Rollicum Bitem Lightfoot the fox and a coven of witches so terrifying I eventually wrapped the book in a feed-sack and buried it under the dung-heap in case they should burst from its pages and carry me away, so consuming had my enthusiasm become.

Father sent Doble out with a billhook to brash the hedges of their summer growth, and as he worked his way around the farm his bonfires sent columns of smoke into the winter sky. Stenham Park, a few miles away, held a pheasant shoot, and Father and John were beaters; they returned with two couples each and a brace of hares John shot near Hulver Wood on the way back.

We threshed in late November. Woken at dawn by the roar of an engine, I watched from my bedroom window as the huge and curious contraption processed along the lane towards the farm, helmed by the machinist and trailing its ragtag crew. Its wheels seemed nearly to top the hedges, and I was glad that we had not had rain; one year it had become stuck in the lane's deep mud and was only dug out in the afternoon. There had been rough words between Father and the engine driver over who would pay for the lost time.

Downstairs, Mother was making tea and frying bacon.

'I expected you down half an hour ago, child. Cut some bread, enough for the threshers; the men have already eaten. And wash your face.'

I fetched two loaves from the pantry. They were round and dense and wrapped in white cloths; Mother could never get the bake as light as she wanted and blamed the range, but I loved the way her bread always stuck to your back teeth and made you feel fed. Father often told her that she should use the brick bread oven in the hearth, but she said it was old-fashioned and dirty and took up too much of her time.

When breakfast was ready she went to the back door, wiping her hands on the blue apron that was always tied around her waist, and called to the machinist and his crew; they took off their caps as they came in, and sat awkwardly at the kitchen table. Shy of their strangeness and the deep accents of their speech, I made myself some bread and jam and took it outside.

Doble was in the barn making it ready for the grain, the terrier that travelled with the threshing crew busy about his feet after rats. In the rick-yard the thatch had already been stripped from the ricks; Father and John were by the engine, helping to check that the drum was level. Frank was up on the first rick, pitching the first sheaves down to the platform, his breath pluming white in the morning air; I wished that I could be up there with him, pitching sheaves, but although I helped with haymaking and weeding and standing the cut corn into stooks to dry in the fields, threshing was men's work.

All day, while I was bent over my school-work and breathing the odour of damp books and ink and chalk, the ricks diminished steadily. When I returned at four they were nearly gone, the engine still clanking and roaring, the men serving it as though it were some kind of heathen god. In the barn the new yellow straw was beginning to stack up, and there were sacks of chaff and seed-corn and two piles of the precious grain, ready for the merchant's lorry that would soon come to take it away.

'What a mess, what a mess,' Doble muttered to himself, stooping to collect the stakes and wooden spars that he called 'springles', which had helped hold the sheltering thatch on the ricks. He hated the barn to be in disorder, as though the storing of grain were an imposition and not its true purpose.

I went to find the cats, for I felt I should be useful and surely they would be needed to keep the mice out of the barn until the lorry came. Nibbins, the matriarch, was sleeping in the stable, but her grown-up kittens, feral and unpredictable, were nowhere to be found. I clapped my cold hands in their rough wool gloves and she raised her head and regarded me, but wouldn't stir. She knew the little terrier was at the farm, no doubt.

'Another day of it,' Mother said, inside. She looked weary; even more so than usual. 'That's what your father says.'

'Just two days?' I asked, taking my satchel from my shoulder and hanging it on the back of a kitchen chair. 'Are we keeping some over? John says wheat often fetches a better price come summertime.'

'No, your father means to thresh it all now. It's just — there isn't much. It saves the wages, I suppose.'

Christmas came and went more quietly now that Mary had left home. As he always did, John brought in two huge ash faggots from where they had been seasoning in the dairy, and Mother lit them with kindling she had kept back from last year's fire. But we had no green boughs to dress the house with that year.

The fields were always rested until Plough Monday, which that year fell on the eighth of January. We'd had no snow, but the earth was frozen; it wasn't wet, which was a blessing, for a wet winter was hard on all of us, especially if the lane to the village became impassable with mud.

The light failed at around three each day, and the nights were cold and long. A few days into the new year I ran out of books to read, and one morning defied Mother's dire warnings about pneumonia, slipping out while she was busy baking to go and see the trees.

At the junction of the two meadows with Crossways was what had long been the Mather children's special place: a tight circle of stunted oaks that Father said had sprung from the same coppice tree, many centuries ago. What made it magical were the vast flints they gripped in their roots, or that seemed to grow from their gnarled trunks; one was a hag-stone with a hole through, the largest by far on our land. When I was really little I believed the ancient oaks had drawn the flints up from the earth and were showing them to us for some mysterious reason of their own, and I counted these trees among my most particular friends.

Of course, there were any number of old stories about the place: that it was a fairy dell, and that any horse led past it would hear their music and be dragged down to their silver halls; that a Saxon queen had been baptised there in a long-gone spring that had washed the soil away from the oaks' exposed roots; that an oak had been split into six by the Devil, enraged that he had lost a scything contest with Beowa, who we called John Barleycorn. One trunk held a couple of links of an iron chain, sunk deep in the living bark; when I was little, Frank had loved to frighten me by telling me it was where a murderer had been manacled and left to die, and that at midwinter his ghost returned, only permitted to move towards the graveyard by one cock-stride a year. It was complete and utter nonsense, of course. The oak had merely been a hitching-post at one time.

Generations of Mather children had played there; Father and his younger brothers when they were little boys, and Grandfather and his siblings, no doubt. Frank and his friend Alfred Rose made it their camp when they played Cowboys and Indians; Mary and I played shop among the roots, read our books, or simply went there to escape. Not long before she got married I discovered that Mary had taken Clive there when they were courting, something I struggled to forgive her for.

I hadn't been to see the oaks for nearly a whole month, and I couldn't bear the thought of them out there in the cold fields, alone. To me, several of the trees on our land were alive, by which I meant that they had thoughts and feelings of their own. The big oak in the lane, for example, loved me and greeted me warmly when I passed, keen to know how I was and what I was up to; and the four strong elms that sheltered the house liked me best of my siblings, and disliked Alfred Rose very much.

Now I laid a gloved hand on each oak's trunk and whispered a 'hello', and then I stood in the circle of trees for a while, glad to have comforted them in their bare winter solitude and feeling their loneliness ease.

The trees may have been lonely, but I would never have agreed that I was. Loneliness was something that happened to old people, but I was young and had all my family around me, so it couldn't very well have been that.

When I was little and still shared a bed with Mary, I would sometimes ask her to tell me stories before we went to sleep: about the balls that had once been held at Ixham Hall, about a local girl who was said to have run away with the gipsies, or my favourite story, the one about the end of the Great War. Looking out over our bleak, muddy land that winter's day brought it once again to mind.

I don't suppose Mary truly remembered every detail as perfectly as she told it, but over the years what she did recall became embroidered, I suppose, and fixed into place, so that in time it was as though I remembered it, too. She would describe how she and Frank, who was only a baby, were in the barn with Doble one afternoon. Frank was grizzling so Doble was dandling him on a hay-bale while she played on the threshing floor with her peg dolls. Then she looked out to the yard and saw a strange man bringing in the horses: a man in uniform, holding the two bridles, leading the tired team home. 'Look, Doble, a soldier!' she said, and he cried out and rushed to the barn door; but of course it wasn't his son Tipper but John Hurlock our horseman, and Doble stood with his arms hanging at his sides and sobbed then, like a child.

The War must have been over for weeks, although Mary had no memory of hearing about it – or of the armistice celebrations I presume the village held. And Doble must have known by the time John returned that his son was dead, his body smashed into Flanders mud by a shell. I suppose it was just the sight of John, in uniform, with no Tipper or Uncle Harry: our sole survivor a man from another county, all that Wych Farm had been spared.

Of course, Doble mastered himself and fetched baby Frank and Mary, and Father and Grandfather appeared from wherever they had been working to welcome John home. Mary would tell me how poor Doble grasped John's hand in both of his, how he shook it and shook it and wouldn't let go. And then came the part about John taking the horses to the stable, how he insisted upon it, and asked to be let alone with them for a while, saying to Father that he'd thought of this moment every day since joining up two years before.

What's missing from the tale, though, is Mother. John must have walked across-country from the railway station at Market Stoundham to go straight to the horses in the fields; and if they were in the fields and Father at the farm, Mother must have been working them, for as the daughter of a horseman that's what she did in the long War years. So, unlike Mary, when I picture the end of the War I picture something I didn't see and cannot fully imagine: John in his filthy uniform stumbling over thick winter clods to where my mother guides the plough behind the straining team; then, as she sees him approaching and halts the horses, something is said between them that however hard I try, I cannot hear.

II

Constance FitzAllen arrived at Wych Farm five months later, on a bright red bicycle. It was a June day, dry and warm, and we were haymaking.

Ours was the first of the farms in the valley to cut our hay each year. We usually began on the sixth of June, unless of course it was a Sunday; Grandfather held that the first week in June was always dry. At one time Hullets, with more south-facing land than us, had cut three days before, but now the house, orchard and outbuildings stood abandoned, the roof of the old black-timbered barn half falling in.

Our little Fordson had come from Hullets; John said the farmer there had bought it brand new with the money they got when their horses were sent to the Front. Apart from a brief trial, though, we didn't much use it, for our land was too heavy and petrol too dear. Like most small farmers in the district, we cut our hay with a horse-drawn mower, as we had since the olden days when men scythed the fields by hand.

We had a spring-tined harrow for breaking up clods, a broadcast sower, and a red Albion reaper-binder we relied upon at harvest-time, all of them horse-drawn; Father had bought them just after the War, believing, as many had, that prices would stay high.

I wasn't allowed to help ready the mower with its long sickle-bar blade, nor to walk too close to it while it worked. Instead I had been tasked with looking after the whetstone, lest it fall out of John's pocket on the jouncing iron seat, and at his shout running to shoo away any birds, like partridges or larks, that were brooding eggs in the long grass and wouldn't stir. Only the previous day we'd found the nest of a landrail with three deep-blotched eggs; John had said the mother bird wouldn't return, they never did, and so I'd picked them up gently and slipped them under one of our hens to brood.

I first laid eyes on Constance as we turned at the headland; she had leant her bicycle up against the gate and was sitting on its top bar. She wore loose trousers held in by bicycle clips at the ankles, a man's shirt, sleeves rolled, and no hat; she held up a hand to shield her eyes from the morning sun, and she was smiling. It was all so long ago now; yet I will never forget the sight of her there.

John saw her at the same moment I did; I could tell by the set of his back, although he gave no sign. Moses and Malachi walked steadily on, the mower whirring, the sweet scent of cut grass rising all around. As we neared the gate she jumped down, and I wondered if she and John knew one another; but it was my name, not John's, that she called.

'Edith – it *is* Edith, isn't it? How d'you do – I'm Constance FitzAllen. I was told you were making hay.'

I remember thinking how tall she was: quite the tallest woman I had ever met. She stuck out a hand, and after a moment I took it; it was larger than mine and strong, like Frank's but without Frank's calluses. My own hand was hot and damp and I wished I had thought to wipe it on my skirt. She was still smiling.

'I heard in the village that you'd started, and I bicycled straight over,' she said. 'I promise I won't get in your way.'

'Yes, of course,' I said idiotically, although I hadn't the least idea what she meant. John had turned the horses and was heading away from us up the meadow; I hoped he wouldn't break a mower blade on a flint, or put up a bird. I couldn't see Frank anywhere; I presumed he was opening up the next field by hand, or perhaps had gone back to see to the pigs. Our sow was not far off farrowing.

'So that's John,' Constance said, shielding her eyes again. 'John of the horse magic. How marvellous! You must introduce me.'

'He's ... he won't like being disturbed,' I managed.

'Of course! Of course – I don't mean now. This evening, perhaps, or tomorrow. There's plenty of time. May I leave my bicycle here, or will it be in the way? Thank you. So tell me, Edith: you've just finished with school; won't you miss it?'

I shook my head. I knew that when September came I would be sorry not to see Miss Carter, who had lent me books from her own home, but generally it was a relief not to have to go back to school. I had no especial friends to miss; the other children all knew that I was clever, and coupled with my lack of skill at playground games it meant that I was at best ignored, at worst disliked. This was something I tried very hard not to mind, telling myself that I preferred my own company, but if truth be told it never ceased to smart. Sometimes, when I was younger, I would imagine I had secret powers and pretend to curse the other children, visiting boils and sickness on them with a glance.

I nearly died of diphtheria when I was four, spending weeks in bed with nothing, not even books, to overexcite me, and Mother always held that after that I was a very different child. She believed my illness had left me with a weak constitution, so that at school I wasn't allowed to play rough games or run about. Instead I remained in the classroom at playtime, reading, or walked around the schoolyard by myself if I wanted some fresh air. Being the youngest child at home, and us not having any near neighbours, as the people in the village did, I grew up used to my own company, I suppose.

Constance had begun to walk slowly along the field margin, and I followed; I felt that I must know her but had forgotten, or perhaps Mother had told me about her coming and I hadn't taken it in. How did she know me, and what on earth did she want?

'So what's next – further study, perhaps? I hear you're quite the scholar.' She picked a pink dog-rose from the hedge and sniffed it, then began to twirl it quickly and deftly between her fingers, first one way, and then the other, until it was a blur.

'Miss Carter – my teacher, that is – she wanted me to train to be a teacher. But Father says I'm needed at home for now.'

'Ah, of course, of course. Anyway, I've put up in the village Elmbourne,' she said airily, and as if it needed to be explained. 'I thought a month, but perhaps longer. Everyone's been so welcoming, although I must say my lodgings are a little … austere.'

'At the inn?' I said. The Bell & Hare was the only place I knew of that let rooms – mostly to commercial travellers, though it wasn't entirely impossible, I supposed, that someone should come for a holiday. A woman in britches on her own, though? How the village would talk.

'Oh no – I'm boarding at the draper's for now, with a widow, a Mrs Eleigh.' It was as though she had read my mind. 'I wrote ahead; it's all very proper. We shall see, though. It may not suit me. *She* may not suit.'

She turned and really grinned at me then, and I was dazzled; I smiled back at her, I couldn't help it.

'Why are you here?' I blurted out, and felt myself blush. 'I'm – I'm sorry, I don't mean to be rude –'

She just laughed. 'Oh! Not at all. It's I who should apologise, Edith; in the last few days I've grown so used to the people in the village knowing my business that I presumed the news would have travelled here – such as it is. I'm making a study of country ways: folklore, cottage crafts, dialect words, recipes – that kind of thing. The War – well, that's when everything began to change, don't you agree? And it's such a dreadful shame to see it all being forgotten. So I mean to preserve it – or some of it, at least – for future generations. We simply *must* celebrate places like this.'

I stored that away to think about later. It was the first time I had ever heard anyone talk like that; the first time, I suppose, that I had glimpsed my little world from the outside: as something worthy of note, and subject to change. It unsettled me, but there was something else about it too, something interesting; and I liked being addressed as though I were a grown-up, too. It hadn't happened to me before.

'Do you mean – are you writing a book? You're an author?'

'Oh no. Well, I'd like to think I might be, one day.' She had turned almost coquettish, which made me oddly uncomfortable. 'I've had a little sketch in *Blackwood's* and interest from one of the weekly magazines. One day, yes, a book of some kind, if it can be managed. And not one of these elegies for a lost world, either! No, the English are already far too much in love with the past. Something more practical, something that makes a difference – we must remake the country entirely, I feel; set it back on the right course. Don't you agree?'

John was turning the horses again; the sun glinted off their head brasses, and I heard him curse as a partridge exploded clucking and flapping from under Moses' hooves.

'Anyway, that's why I'm here – to learn all your secrets!'

She linked her arm through mine and squeezed, and I saw that the dog-rose she had plucked had lost two of its five pink petals.

'Now, tell me all about haymaking,' she said.

I loved our two meadows, Great Ley and Middle Ley, and I was always half sorry when they were cut. In April and May the grass grew tall and was thick with buttercups and sorrel and jack-go-to-bed-at-noon; later in the year they were alive with butterflies, snakes and grasshoppers, and starred on August nights with the tiny green lights of glow-worms. We never manured them, yet they were so rich, so reliable, that we would sometimes take a second cut of hay in September, depending on the weather and how much new grass had grown.

It was wonderful, of course, to see the tall rick safely made, and to know that John would cut slabs of sweet-smelling fodder from it even in the depths of winter. But the meadows looked so bald and bare when at last the long windrows of grass had been turned and cocked and then carted away. I wished each year, when the grass was tall, that we could somehow let them be.

Of course, it was a silly thing to wish for – I understood that. Far from being a paradise, the unmown meadows at Hullets were thick with thistles and hogweed as tall as a man, while brambles and scrub stole further into them every year. Owls and kestrels hunted them, and the paths of foxes and badgers burrowed through the tangled grass, but even to children like me and Frank the meadows had quickly become almost impassable. Hullets was proof that nature needed husbandry; that if it wasn't put to work, it went to ruin.

'Land is like a woman, John,' I'd heard Father say once. 'You may love her, but she must produce; it does her no good to be idle.'

I could remember Hullets the very first year it was empty. I can only have been seven or eight, I suppose, and although I knew little of the family who farmed it, or why they were suddenly gone, I had grasped that their meadows would not be mown and I could not keep away. In the weeks after ours had been cut, until school began again, I would run there and lie in the tall grass with its feathery seed-heads and read *Little Black Sambo*, or *Bevis*, which was missing its binding, or Frank's copy of *Treasure Island*, until my shins and elbows itched where the grass pressed in. At last I would hear Mother calling me in exasperation, but it has always been my habit never to close a book unless I have reached a sentence of seven words exactly in case something dreadful should happen to the farm, or to my family; so I would delay, and often go home to a hiding, because we were expected to work in the fields when we weren't at school and not to waste time reading books. Yet the following afternoon I would be back in the meadows again, glorying in their luxurious, uncut wildness, my tasks neglected, I couldn't help it, somehow.

'I've a mind to mow 'em myself,' Father muttered, more than once. 'We could do with the feed.'

'George, you can't,' said Mother. 'What if it's sold? That hay isn't yours to take, you know that.'

But Hullets didn't sell, and although after that first year Father stopped eyeing the land, we none of us quite grew accustomed to it lying unused.

I walked with Constance to the top of Great Ley, where a deep hedge of oaks and field maple separated it from the cornfields, and from Hullets further on. It was full of the wheezing demands of newly fledged birds, the sky above us a hard blue vault where larks invisibly sang; perspiration beaded my forehead, although Constance seemed barely to feel the heat. The mower whirred in the distance, its sound rising and falling not with the breeze, for there was none, but with its changing distance from us. I touched the whetstone in the pocket of my skirt, feeling its roughness against the sensitive tips of my fingers and my badly bitten nails.

Constance asked me questions, and I answered; but all the while my mind was turning over the simple fact of this strange woman, here on the farm, and trying to understand what it meant. Would she be here all summer? Every day? What would Father and Mother think about it? And for that matter, what did I?

'I suppose it's the grain harvest that's the main thing, rather than the hay,' she mused at the headland. 'Such a shame the old traditions are passing away, like choosing a harvest lord. Do you still "cry the neck"?'

'Cry the neck?'

'Yes – the neck, or the knack. When the last sheaf is cut. Isn't that right?'

I tried to think; already, I found, I didn't want to disappoint her. More than that, I wanted her to like me, and I felt from her ready smile as though perhaps she might.

'I – I don't know; I don't think so. I can ask John; perhaps he'll know what you mean. Or Grandfather.'

'Oh! Does your grandfather live here on the farm with you, Edith?'

'Oh yes – Father's father. Didn't you meet him at the house?'

'Gosh, I had no idea. No, I met your mother, but she didn't ask me in. There was a colourful old character sweeping the yard – that can't have been him, though?'

'Oh no, that'll be Doble. We've had him forever.'

'Your foreman?'

'No – he's just yardman now. His son, Tipper, was foreman, but he died in the War. John saw him get blown up,' I said, unnecessarily.

The War was a somewhat hazy idea to me, it all having happened before I was even born and Father having been excused on account of being a farmer – but despite John never speaking of it to us children we had somehow got hold of that one detail, and it fascinated us far more than it should. Really it was a kindness of my father to allow old Doble to resume work after Tipper's death; there were plenty of young, healthy men who would have taken his place, and been glad of the cottage, too, which was tied. But there had long been Dobles at Wych Farm, just as there had long been Mathers, and Lyttletons at Ixham Hall to whom we paid rent. It was the way of things.

'He's a wonderful example – Doble, I mean. Positively an archetype, in those antique clothes – I do believe his trousers were actually knotted at the ankle with string!'

If that was the case he must have been cutting chaff, or dealing with rats; but there didn't seem much reason to explain. He often made himself a sort of cloak from old grain sacks, too; but then, nearly everyone did when it rained.

'It's so sad to think of his type disappearing,' Constance continued, with a dramatic sigh. '*Landflucht*, you know. Soon the true peasant class will all be gone, with hardly anything to even show that they were here.'

'Would you like to meet Grandfather?' I asked, to change the subject, for something about the way she spoke of Doble was making me feel uncomfortable, though I couldn't have said what.

'Oh yes! Very much. Nowadays it really is the ancients who are the true keepers of wisdom, don't you think?'

I wondered what Father would say to that. I adored him, as girls do their fathers, and was as grateful for his good favour as a puppy that wants to please; but at the same time I knew that he was not perfect, for he was testy when it came to matters touching on his authority, and unpredictable at times, too. But the farm was a heavy responsibility, so it was hardly surprising; and I felt secretly that I understood him even when he was in a temper – perhaps even better than Mother did.

Constance stood and gazed at the corn in the next field, the one we called Crossways; it was only about a foot high and looked thin to me, and I knew that unless it rained soon the harvest would be poor again. Seven Acres, far away on the other side of the farm buildings, was fallow as Father had instructed – something that wasn't spoken of at Wych Farm. Of course, she wouldn't know any of that.

Frank was checking the snares in the ditch on the far side of Middle Ley, where it met Hulver Wood. He straightened up as he saw us approach, shading his eyes against the mid-morning sun. The elders were in bloom, holding the creamy plates of their flowers up to the sky; somewhere deep in their dense green foliage wood-pigeons clattered and fought.

'Is that your father?' Constance asked, raising an arm to wave. It wasn't such a strange question; Frank was tall and broad for seventeen, and he wore long trousers. He had recently begun, a little clumsily, to shave.

'No, that's Frank, my brother,' I said as we drew closer. 'Frank, this is Constance –'

'Constance FitzAllen,' she called, striding forward and pumping his hand firmly in hers. 'So: behold the heir apparent! I'm here to learn all your secrets, as you've probably heard.'

Frank said nothing, just looked from one of us to the other. I found that for some reason I couldn't quite meet his eye.

'Secrets?' he said at last.

'Why, yes: your country wisdom and ways. But I'm afraid I've rather distracted your sister from her duties.'

She stood with her hands in her pockets, quite at ease and smiling. 'I'm ever so sorry; it won't happen again.'

'Likely it will,' he replied. 'She's a rare one for it.'

I took the whetstone from my pocket and gave it to him.

'Constance has asked to meet Grandfather. Can you take over from me in Great Ley? I think John's already put up a bird.'

'Nice to meet you, Miss FitzAllen.' Then, nodding at me, 'These rabbits are a regular plague. I shall get Doble to fetch up some sulphur cartridges,' he said.

Our farmhouse was old and timber-framed, with a long, crooked thatch roof, small, deep-set casement windows and a brick chimney leading up from two huge hearths scratched, if you knew where to look, with the mysterious circular patterns we called 'witch-marks', drawn with compasses many hundreds of years ago. Downstairs the floors were of yellow brick laid in a herringbone pattern and covered, in the parlour only, with threadbare Turkey rugs; upstairs there were wide elm boards. From the kitchen, a set of steep stairs with shallow treads led up in a half-turn; at its foot was a heavy, faded curtain against draughts. We had a coal-fired range, a fifteen-gallon copper for heating water and a pump at the back-house sink, but no electric supply or refrigerator; we washed once weekly in a zinc bath, and there was an outdoor privy with a tin of Keating's Powder to keep the flies down. Wych Farm was draughty and ramshackle, and little had changed there in five long centuries – certainly not what Grandfather called our 'loving' clay, which wore out horses and men and in winter made our mother curse. But despite its privations I was happy to grow up there because I loved our land fiercely, every single inch of it – and because I knew nothing else.

There was nobody in the yard and I could see that the pony and trap were gone; the back door was closed and Mother nowhere to be seen. She had probably gone to visit Mary, or perhaps Doble had taken the trap somewhere and she was working in the vegetable-garden, or in the orchard seeing to the bees.

I asked Constance to wait at the door, because I didn't want to surprise Grandfather with a stranger in the house. I suppose I was worried what he would make of her. I hardly knew myself.

He was seated in one of the two wing chairs in the parlour, which meant that he must have heard us cross the yard. He turned his face with its sunken eye sockets towards me as I came in.

'Well, child?'

His tone was curious, not scolding, and I went to him and laid one hand on his shoulder so that he would know I was there.

'She's called Constance FitzAllen and she's staying in the village,' I said. 'She's come to learn about farming, and – well, about the old ways.'

'She were here an hour or so ago, is that right? Your mother sent her off with a flea in her ear.'

'Did she?'

'Oh yes, that she did. Sent her packing. Looks like she's got her own ideas, though. Do you bring her in.'

I found Constance in the backhouse peering inside our copper, which was just then empty of water and unlit. 'It's such a shame you don't make your own butter and cheese here,' she said. 'I told your mother as much earlier. We simply *must* keep the old skills alive.'

So that was what had made Mother take against her. 'I'll – I'll introduce you to Grandfather now, if you like,' I said.

'Oh, yes please! What a treat. Yes, lead the way!'

Grandfather was standing, leaning on his stick. I had forgotten to tell her he was blind, but I could see that she understood it straight away, which was a relief.

'Mr Mather, I'm Constance. Constance FitzAllen. It is such a pleasure to meet you,' she said, taking his hand in both of hers. 'Thank you so much for sparing me your time.'

Indoors, her voice was softer than it had been, and she herself seemed smaller, or perhaps gentler somehow.

'No, no, missy,' he said. 'Sit yourself down. Edith, let's have some tea, shall us? Your mother's gone to the village with Doble. She won't be back for an hour.'

30

In the kitchen I moved about quietly, setting the kettle to boil on the range and reaching down teapot and cups from the dresser. I strained to hear what the two of them were saying, but I could make out nothing above a low murmur. I cut some slabs of ginger cake and found three good plates, feeling a stab of irritation that I should have to play mother and miss out on the talk. Already I felt that Constance belonged to me and not to Grandfather, or anyone else at the farm.

I set the tray down on the little walnut table by Grandfather's chair. But before I could do anything further, Constance took the lid from the teapot and peered into it, and then began to pour.

'Yes, those were hard years – hard years,' Grandfather was saying. 'We shall never see the like again, God be praised.'

'They say in the village –'

'This? It's nothing hard work won't remedy, you mark my words.'

Grandfather had farmed through what the old men of the village called 'the coming-down years', and although he would not often speak of those times we knew that thistles had grown head-high on Seven Acres and Far Piece, and that, despairing and half-starved, his two brothers had left for New Zealand – where perhaps, we sometimes speculated, they lived on still. 'Buy nothing and sell nothing!' he would sometimes say to our father, and bang his stick upon the floor.

Now, Constance picked up Grandfather's cup and saucer as though to hand them to him, then put them down again and looked to me. I took the cup, set it on the arm of the wing chair and guided his hand to it. Through the open window came the distant whirr of the mower in Great Ley.

'Thank you, Edith,' he said.

I poured my own tea, took a slice of cake and went to the window seat. It was my favourite place to sit, as I liked to look out at the yard and feel myself at the heart of the farm; I'd picture the way the fields and lanes stretched out from me to the other farms and woods and villages beyond. It felt like the way I wrote our address in my notebooks, beginning 'Wych Farm' and ending 'The Universe'. Yet sitting there now I felt dismissed from the visit, as though I were a child again – despite the fact that I was fourteen years of age now, with school behind me for good.

'What delicious cake, Edith,' Constance said brightly. 'Is it your mother's recipe?'

'Oh no, we buy it from the shop in the village,' I said. 'But – Mother makes her own honey cake,' I added hurriedly, blushing red; 'and we make preserves, of course – I help with that – and we bake. Mother doesn't hold with shop-bought bread.'

'But you've no mill hereabouts any more, have you?'

'It is a great shame that we lost the mill in Elmbourne, a great shame,' Grandfather said. 'No, the railway put paid to it. Our corn is taken away in a lorry now, and it goes all the way to – to – well, my son can tell you all about that. Ada buys her flour in the village, and who knows who grew the wheat for it, or where! Such times we live in.' Lightly, he tapped his stick upon the floor.

'I suppose you've brought in a good many harvests, Mr Mather?'

'That I have.'

'It must worry you to see all the changes.'

'Worry me? It don't worry me. We must have change. We must have it! I didn't farm like my father, and George don't farm the same as me. That's the way of it. You can't stand still, not if you want to get on.'

I smiled to myself. Constance was wrong if she'd thought he was the type to praise the olden days and set his face against anything new.

'What about the horses?'

'Well, what do you mean?'

'Most farms are using tractors these days; I read an article about it in a magazine.'

'We've got a Fordson,' I interjected. 'It's in the barn.'

'Oh, they're all very well on light land, but they're no good here, we found that out. No, they engines shan't ever replace horsepower,' Grandfather said.

Frank's friend Alf had his supper with us that evening, for he had walked over in the afternoon to help Frank on our land. The two of them had been in the same class all through school, and used to go egg-collecting and hunting sparrows with catapults together. Now they were both seventeen, and men, they had given up such childish things, instead playing darts at the Bell & Hare, going rabbiting with Alf's four ferrets and helping on one another's farms from time to time.

I'd known Alf and his elder brother Sidney all my life. Sid had a stutter, and a palsy that caused his head to pull sharply to the left as he spoke and rather spoiled his looks; Alf, though, I'd been a little sweet on when I was a very young girl. For he was a nice lad: everyone said so. He was taller than Frank and less stocky, with dark hair and eyes; I don't think anyone would have called him handsome, exactly, but he had a pleasant face. He was funny, too: 'Alfie Rose could get a laugh out of a wet hen,' Mother sometimes said. He smiled a lot, and his teeth were good; he had an easy way with people, and was generally well liked. He wasn't book-clever, perhaps, but that didn't matter; he was what the old men of the village called 'knacky', which mattered much more on a farm.

By the time I left school no traces of my childish pash remained, for I had experienced greater loves by then – Percy Bysshe Shelley; John from *Swallows and Amazons*; Miss Carter, my teacher, too. Yet there must have been something left of it in me that he, with his more worldly eyes, could discern, for why else would he behave as though I was still sweet on him, a conviction I didn't have the first idea how to shake?

After we had eaten that evening I carried the plates to the backhouse to wash up. Frank and Father had gone to the barn with Doble to see to something or other; John and Mother sat on at the table discussing Malachi, who had that morning cast a shoe. Mother was the only person with whom John would discuss the horses, for while he was at the Front she had been seen to plough and harrow and drill from foredawn to sunset, despite having Mary to look after, and then Frank coming along. I sometimes wondered if she missed those days now.

Alf crept up close behind me as I stood at the sink, his warm breath sudden on the back of my neck. He made me jump.

'Can I do anything? John's gone to the stables.'

I felt his hands at my waist.

'Please let me, Edie,' he muttered, moving his hands to the front of my ribcage and letting them creep up. I could feel his thing pressing against the small of my back.

It seems strange to me now, but I felt nothing but a blank whenever Alf Rose touched me – although I usually thought about a lot of things very fast. I thought about whether I was clean, and whether, up close, I smelled of sweat; that possibility tormented me a great deal in those years. I wondered what I was expected to say and do – what other girls did – and sometimes at night I would find myself consumed with worry about the trouble I would be in if someone found out. As I stood there at the sink that evening I could see us as though through someone else's eyes rather than my own: Alf shuffling up close behind me, me staring down at my wrists where they were lapped by the warm, greasy water. Of course, it was tremendously flattering that he liked me so much.

Then he stepped back quickly and picked up a plate and dish-cloth, and I turned to see that Mother had come in with the last of the things to wash up.

'Oh Alfie, you are a good boy,' she said.

III

My diary that summer was a green Silvine exercise book, one of four that Miss Carter had given me on my last day of school so that I might compose poetry, or keep up my penmanship, or copy out improving passages from books. I did try to write poems for a time, but they came out horribly imitative – feeble versions of Shakespearean sonnets, or John Clare's verses, or Keats. Clearly I hadn't a voice of my own, and so quickly gave it up as a bad job and decided to use the exercise books as diaries instead.

Yet even this I found that I failed at; for instead of sparkling aphorisms, fascinating conversation and news of current affairs, all the pages revealed each week was that I saw to the hens twice daily and grudgingly fulfilled my other tasks, was pleased when Mother made jam roly-poly and petulant when it was liver, read greedily, said my prayers dutifully, was chided frequently for mooning about and once a month suffered the Curse.

Now and again I tried to scribble down something of my fears for the future, in an attempt, I suppose, to clarify the deadening vagueness of my thoughts. But while I was starting to know what I didn't want from life, I had no idea yet what I did; or – more pertinently – what I might and might not be allowed. I knew only, at fourteen, that I wanted to matter to the world in some way.

I wrote nothing of Alf Rose in my diary, and for that I am glad – for who knows where that book is now, or in whose hands. But I did write about Connie in it, and about everything that happened, as far as I understood it. And for a little while, at least, I think it helped.

Frank and I went upriver: we went for the whole day. It was a Monday, I remember, because I should have been helping Mother; but Father had given us leave because the hay was nearly in and he allowed that we had worked hard.

Mother had objected: 'It's wash-day on Monday, I can't spare Edie.' We were in Great Ley then, all of us together; Mother and I had brought cold tea and meat pies and laid a rag rug in the shade of a hedgerow oak, and Doble, in waistcoat and shirtsleeves, had brought Grandfather with him over the fields to feel the June sun on his face. Only John was missing; he had gone to fetch water so that the horses might drink.

My heart had sunk at Mother's words. I hated wash-day almost as much as she did, and what's more

I hadn't had a day away from the farm in weeks. I looked to Frank for help, but he was gazing out at the meadow before us, its mown grass left where it lay to wither; under the bright sun the new hay was already fading from green to gold, and it smelled sweet. Probably Frank would be granted a day's holiday, I thought. It wasn't fair.

Doble helped Grandfather into a canvas chair while Mother poured the tea. Father and John planned to mow Middle Ley after we had eaten, and then between us we would take our wooden rakes and ted it all into haycocks to parch. We would rest on Sunday, and on Monday, if Father judged it dry, the men would cart it back to the yard and build the rick.

Father lay back on the rug and tipped his hat over his eyes.

'You can manage one wash-day by yourself, Ada,' he said. 'God knows you'll have to when we get Edie wed and off our hands.'

And so, on Monday, after I had seen to the hens and helped Mother strip the beds, Frank and I set out. Straight away, it was as though we were little children again: Frank turned as he opened the farm gate and grinned at me and I couldn't help but grin back, I don't know why; perhaps the sheer rarity of it, for we hardly ever spent time together now unless we were working in the same field. He started to run up the lane, and I ran after him, and we raced one another, laughing at the prospect of the day-long river and the blue sky above.

At the four-a-leet with its white-painted finger-post Frank stopped running and I helped him buckle the knapsack properly onto his back. He was one of those boys who do everything slapdash-fashion; at home I could tell where he'd been by the drawers and cupboards standing open, the lids left off jars and the lamps burning in empty rooms, a carelessness Mary or I, as girls, would never have been allowed. His work on the farm was meticulous, however; Father and John saw to that.

'Shall we go by the road, Ed, or walk across the fields?'

'Let's go by the fields.'

Some say that ours is a flat county, but that isn't quite true: it undulates gently, unlike the level land-scape of the Fens, and dips to the winding course of the River Stound; but the skies are huge, and the views, from any slight rise, go on for miles. The lanes are narrow, the fields small and deeply hedged, sometimes in double rows, tree-high: oak and ash, field maple, and dog-roses twining through. Because our part of the country was never reshaped as other places were, by prosperity or the railways or indus-try, a great many of its dwellings have survived to a great age. The farmhouses are often sway-backed, with deep thatch and crooked timber frames; the black barns are brick-footed, with tall gables and great doors. Our churches are of knapped flint gleaned from the fields, the land itself raised up in prayer; and everywhere the corn reaches right up to the village edges, as I have been told the vineyards do in France.

We walked along the margin of a long, narrow field on the other side of Hullets, land that Bob Rose farmed with the help of his two sons. A few years ago he'd let ninety acres down to grass and was breeding red polls for beef, and he was now trying his hand at market gardening, too – though he couldn't quite give up his feeling for corn.

'I see Rose's bit of barley's addling well,' Frank said. 'I wager this'll run ten coomb an acre.' He looked out thoughtfully across the breeze-rippled field, the barley's green beards giving it a soft nap, like a dog's fur.

A good barley crop is, in corn country, the pride of every farmer, for it is so exact in its requirements: it will not forgive poor weather, and to please the maltster, and not be sold for pig-meal, it must be cut when perfectly ripe – a matter sometimes of a single day – and carted immediately rather than being left in stooks in the field, for even light rain then may set the kernels to sprout fine hairs and spoil the crop. Yet despite its demands it takes less out of the land than wheat, and a good malting sample will see it fetch a high price. Most of our neighbours risked some portion of their land to barley, for a good year filled their coffers as well as redounding to their credit among their friends. It was why Father had sown about half of our own land down to it that year.

'Rose's land's wonderful light compared to ours,' continued Frank. 'More heart in it, too, somehow. But see, Ed, this barley was nursemaid to the grass Rose sowed last April, so he'll have to harvest carefully or the butts of the sheaves will be green.'

'He keeps it tidy, though – don't you think? There's hardly a weed, to my eye, and he keeps his ditches clear.'

Frank bridled a little. 'Well, he can afford to pay for extra hands – he makes a fair profit on that young beef he's got. Oh yes, he's rich as Croesus, is old Rose.'

'Where did he get the money to turn over to beef, though?'

'Oh, he did well out of oats just after the War.'

'How do you know that?'

'Everyone knows – well, 'cept you.'

I wondered whether Sid or Alf had told Frank about their father's money, but it didn't seem likely. Apart from the cost of feed and wages, and the prices fetched for beasts and corn at market, money in the abstract – profit and loss, their balance sheet, the future – was something farmers never discussed outside of their families, and neither would their sons; so that often, the first the district knew about a man in real trouble was when a notice of sale appeared in the *Gazette*, as seemed to happen more and more often in those hard years. No, it seemed to me that wherever they were said to have come from, Rose's fabled riches could be no more than village gossip, which as often as not was wide of the mark.

On the other side of the field we left Rose Farm and ducked through a gap in a tall hedge to where a straight path ran west for a mile, flanked on each side by hazels and young oaks. Father said that before the War it had been a lane of rolled stone with a good, deep ditch on each side for drainage; now, though, it was just a narrow path overarched by trees. The hazels had not been coppiced for many years and had grown and spread to form huge stools, and cow parsley stood thick around them; the ground was covered in dog's mercury and ramsons, dying back. The dauby clay that was now the path's surface made a *click-click* sound under our feet as though in the heat it were dry-mouthed; on each side of the cool path, through gaps in the rampant June growth, the green barley blazed.

As we walked I thought about wealth and what it might mean to have it — beyond the chance to pay for outside labour to keep your cornfields free of weeds. Mrs Rose still scrubbed the floors, for they had no char; Mr Rose's black Sunday jacket was so old it looked green in certain lights, and apart from the fact that they were allowed comics, his sons had been raised no differently to Frank. Perhaps it was about the future rather than the present, though — not having to concern yourself with what was to come, or worry about having a bad year, as we did.

I wondered if we were poor – if we were getting poorer. It was impossible to say. I knew, of course, that last year's harvest had been bad and that Father feared that it would be so again, but how far his worry was out of the common run of things I couldn't yet tell. Farmers must always worry, for whether they prosper is subject to God, and the weather – and to the government, now.

'Farming from Whitehall, that's what it is,' Father would say at the announcement of yet more tinkering with wages, or prices, or agricultural policy. 'A man should be able to farm his own land as he likes' – and he would fling the newspaper down in disgust. He had never forgiven Lloyd George for repealing the Corn Production Act in 1921, and never trusted a politician after. Although he said he was a Conservative, in line with the Lyttletons to whom we paid rent, he didn't vote, but paid his N.F.U. dues and expected them to represent him. Mary told me that when he discovered that Mother had cast a ballot for Stanley Baldwin he caught her a slap that split her lip – though it would have been the same, I now believe, had she voted the other way.

When at last we emerged from the shade of the trees, the light on the river was blinding. I was wearing my bathing costume under my clothes, and while Frank took off his knapsack and began to unpack it I unbuttoned my blouse and kicked off my shoes.

'Are you going straight in?' Frank asked, looking up from where he knelt on the riverbank, shielding his eyes.

'Yes, I'm roasting. Aren't you?'

'All right. But be careful, Ed. I'm not fishing you out if you drown.'

The back of his shirt was dark with sweat where the knapsack had rested, and he took it off and spread it on the grass for the sun to dry. His forearms and neck were nut-brown, the rest of his body pale and strong. I passed him his trunks and he stepped into them and fastened the belt at his waist; then he looked for a moment at the bright river, and turned to grin at me. 'Last one in's a sissy!' he yelled, and jumped in

God, the way it can fizz up through you some-times – happiness, I mean. The sun, and dear Frank in the Stound there, laughing; the cold river-water making my heart rise in my chest as I waded cautiously in. My feet sank into silt as black and fine as a powder pigment; it plumed up so softly and treacherously that I took a breath and quickly leaned forward into my usual awkward breaststroke.

'Isn't it rare!' Frank shouted. His hair was plastered down and he looked foolish; with both hands he flung a furl of bright water at me, splashing my face and making me gasp.

'Beast!' I shouted back, laughing.

We floated on our backs for a few minutes, and then Frank swam downstream to look for moorhen nests.

After a while I hauled myself out and sat on the bank waiting for the river mud to dry on my legs so I could brush it off. It was hot, and I lay back on my elbows and saw through half-closed eyes a cobalt kingfisher shoot upstream, calling *peep*. It was low over the water, and almost close enough for me to touch.

When Frank returned we ate our sandwiches and drank warm lemonade. He belched and wiped his mouth with the back of his hand, and I began to tell him off but belched too, and then I was helpless with laughter. Every time it began to subside Frank belched, and set me off again. Once he would have tickled me until I begged him to stop, but we didn't do that any more.

'You know, Ed, you could be pretty if you tried,' he said at last. He was lying back on his elbows and watching the river slip by, green weeds starred with little flowers trailing in the current like the picture of Ophelia that Miss Carter had shown us in school.

'Oh, give over, Frank.'

I sat up and began to drag a comb through my wet hair. What he had said was categorically untrue; while Mary had always been pretty, and took after Mother, I had inherited far more of Father's looks – and I had his short, stout legs and broad shoulders, too.

'It doesn't matter what I look like, does it?'

'Well, it might do. Happen it will, soon.'

'What do you mean?'

'Well, you know. You might want a sweetheart one day.'

I stared at him. 'A sweetheart? Frank, I've only just finished with school.'

'Mary was walking out with Clive at fourteen.'

'I'm not Mary. Why, do you have a sweetheart? I suppose you do. Who is it? Tell me!' I lay back down again and pinched his arm.

'Ow, get off. And never you mind about me. Just – don't let Mother keep you at home, that's all. If you don't want to marry yet, you could study. You could be a teacher, or a nurse, or – or something. Lord knows you're brainy enough.'

I knew then that he wasn't teasing, that this was something he had thought about, and planned to say.

'Mother doesn't keep me at home, Frank. Whatever do you mean?'

'Well, you've never even been to a dance. You don't have any proper grown-up clothes. She keeps it from you, Ed, that's what I mean. She keeps you at the farm, but you can't stay at home forever. Something will happen next, and you should choose it – that's all.'

I knew he was right, and yet my mind shied away from his words as it always did when I tried to picture myself as an adult, living far away from the farm. I knew that I didn't want to be a teacher, for I thought children were exasperating, with their helplessness and neediness and inability to endure their own company, as I had learned to do. It was true I hadn't been to a dance, but then I'd never wanted to; I wasn't interested in frocks or fashions the way Mary had been, but that was hardly Mother's doing. Was it?

The mud was tightening and turning grey around the fine hairs on my calves, and I began to pick it off. Frank was eating an apple; I knew already that he would eat the core in two bites, and then flick the stem into the river.

'Alfie Rose would take you to a dance, Ed. If you wanted to go.'

I pictured the way Alf looked at me when he made me go and meet him in the barn, or behind the elms. 'I don't want to,' I said.

'Think about it.'

'I already have. And why are you so interested all of a sudden, anyway?'

'I'm not! It's all the same to me. Now, I'm going to fish – unless you're planning to swim again.'

'I might have a dip in a bit. Why?'

'Mother said I'm to stay with you if you swim in case you get a cramp, that's all.'

'Oh, for goodness' sakes, Frank. I'm not delicate any more.'

I had *Lolly Willowes* in my bag, and I took it out and rolled onto my front to read. But after a while my eyelids grew heavy, and without even waiting for a line of seven words I laid my head down on my arms and slept.

I have no memory of having had diphtheria, but something Frank once said has always stuck in my mind. He called me over to a bucket in the yard one morning when I was about eight or nine years old to show me a frog that had fallen in overnight and got stuck. It floated on its back in the morning sun, white and cold and bloated.

'That's what you looked like,' he said, dunking it with a stick. We watched it bob back up, and I knew straight away what he meant.

'All puffed up, like you were drowning.'

He scooped the frog out in both hands, gently, and we carried it to the garden and buried it under the raspberry canes, where Frank muttered some solemn words over the grave that he said were holy and Latin and that I was too stupid to understand.

He was right about the frog in a way, for I had been drowning: diphtheria strangles children, slowly swelling their throats and stopping their speech and breath. I don't know why I was spared, or how Mother got me through it — what bargains or sacrifices she made. She was haunted, perhaps, by her other dead children: the first-born boy she lost in infancy, and the baby before me that was born dead. Neither do I know why I should have been struck down with diphtheria in the first place, when neither Frank nor Mary ever had a day's illness bar the usual childhood cuts and scrapes, and I don't recall Mother or Father ever being laid up, there being always too much to do. I do know that John spread straw in the yard so that I wouldn't be disturbed by the sound of hooves and cart-wheels; and when the crisis was past and I at last regained my voice he was the only grown-up at Wych Farm who didn't continue to treat me as though I was in some way helpless – something I eventually began to believe myself.

'Leave her be, Ada,' he'd tell Mother as she wrapped me in scarves on a mild September morning, or slapped the back of my legs for climbing the big oak in the lane with Frank. 'She'll outlast the rest of us, you mark my words.'

Frank and I set off to walk home at about four. It was still hot and bright, but the sun was no longer over-head and the yellow irises by the water were casting shadows like black swords on the bank. We walked with the sun behind us and I felt it warm on my calves where the skin had begun to turn red as I slept. There was calamine lotion at home, pink and chalky and soothing. When we got back I would ask Mother where it was.

'When's that woman coming back? Constance FitzAllen, I mean,' Frank asked.

'I don't know.'

'Didn't you ask?'

'No, I – I didn't get the chance, somehow.'

He laughed. 'No, she's a bossy one, and that's a fact! No wonder she can't catch a man.'

'She's going to be an author, you know. That's why she's here – she wants to write about the countryside.'

'She'll tire of it soon enough, I'll wager. You know she's a neurasthenic? That's what they're saying in the village, anyway.'

'What's that?'

'It's a rich person's condition. It just means they're bored, or they've got a case of nerves, from what I can make out. They go to the country to get better – like a rest cure.'

I couldn't help but laugh at that. 'Rest? On a farm?'

'Oh, you know – fresh air, going back to the land: "I'm Happy When I'm Hiking" and the Woodcraft Folk. Father says it's all Socialist nonsense, anyway.'

'Do you think she's rich, then?' I asked.

'Course she is. She's from London.'

'Not everyone in London is rich, Frank. They've got slums, you know; it's not all – not all debs and jazz and the Ritz.'

'If you think Constance FitzAllen is from a slum, Ed, you've got even less sense than I've been giving you credit for.'

'I don't! Oh, never mind. You're probably right – if she can afford to board with Mrs Eleigh for weeks on end she can't be short a bob or two. Anyway' – I took his arm – 'I don't mind her. Do you?'

'I don't know her well enough to mind her,' he said. 'I just hope she's got enough sense not to get in the way.'

_____

We joined the road again by Hullets' ruined barn, its once-black timbers grey and gaping, the catastrophe of its roof even more shocking up close. Its horse-pond was entirely choked with yellow flag irises, with barely even a twinkle of water showing through the mass of tall green spears. The house's black, rotten thatch sagged with the weight of the weeds and house-leeks growing from it, all the glass in the windows was gone, and chunks of pargeting were dropping out from between the timbers like spoiled icing from a cake. It brought to mind the carcass of an animal – and yet I couldn't look away.

I suppose that's why it was me who saw it, and not Frank: a movement at one of the downstairs windows as though someone had been watching us pass through the derelict farm buildings, and had quickly withdrawn from view. I stopped and shaded my eyes, but it didn't come again, and after a few moments I decided it must have been a trick of the light and hurried to catch up with Frank where he was turning into the lane.

Back on our own land at last, the summer evening opened itself around us, warm and soft and still. Hulver Wood was loud with throstles and blackbirds and spinks calling one after another after another; there were whitethroats and yellow buntings and all the countless other birds that flocked to the farm and built their nests and raised their young and left, as our barley-birds already had that year – the last year that I would ever hear them sing. Most of the time I hardly noticed the birds, so many were there; but that evening I remember listening to them as we walked down Great Ley in the twilight, their song rising around us from the hedges and thickets and joining with the faint conversation of swallows in the warm air overhead.

Before going inside I shut up the hens for the night. A few years before, at the advice of a neighbour, Elisabeth Allingham, we had bought four dozen Leghorns and six modern wheeled huts. They were mine and Mary's responsibility – mine alone now, of course – and poultry proved in those years to be a good investment, despite Father's scorn.

In the coop, where I'd left them, two of the land-rail's eggs were cold, but there was a tiny, coal-black chick, downy and awkward, struggling in the nest. I fetched the hen and settled her with it, hoping she'd at least keep it warm for the night.

IV

John was not a tall man. He was a full head shorter
than Father and a little bow-legged, but he was very
strong, his brown arms corded from all his years at
the plough. His hair under his cap was sandy and his
eyes a pale grey-blue, and he was both utterly familiar
to us and yet a mystery – although it's fair to say that I
wondered very little about him in those days, because
the world of your childhood is one of fixed points
and certainties, or so it seems.

And John was a fixed point, always level, always
kind, but always remote. It was he who found me the
day I went missing, when I can't have been more than
two years old. The whole place was in uproar, the way
Mother told it; all the farmhouse's rooms, and the yard
and the barn, had been searched. At last John discovered
me in the stables, where I had somehow clambered
up onto one of the draught horses and fallen soundly
to sleep on its back. He did not touch me, but went to
fetch Mother; and whenever the story was told he

marvelled anew at how I could have done it: 'And her only a baby!' he'd say. I remembered nothing, of course, and so could offer nothing by way of explanation, but I loved to hear my one adventure retold.

Unlike Doble, whose family had been tied to ours for generations, John was what we in the village called a 'furriner', having been born sixty miles or more north of us, where our clay gave way to flat, rich peat. He came from a long line of horsemen, and although he would say nothing of it we knew he had been initiated into their secrets when he'd left school at fourteen, the age that I was now. His own father being hale and strong, and there being several brothers, he had left home not long after to seek work and apart from the War he had been with us ever since. 'A farmer is no good twenty miles from his own land', the saying went; but John proved it wrong, for he came to know our land better than any of us by the sheer working of it: by walking the horses across it day in and day out.

It was Grandfather who had originally taken him on, he to whom John had first answered at Wych Farm, and sometimes still did. But should he have wished to, John could easily have countermanded him, or Father, without saying a word, because he could charm the horses, which meant that nothing could proceed without him.

I never once saw John and Father drink together at the Bell & Hare, or discuss anything personal beyond the daily running of the farm. Perhaps that is simply how it must be between man and master, or perhaps it was due to the difference in their politics, for when I was quite small I do remember hearing rough words between them, and that was when all the lorry drivers and railwaymen had come out on strike. 'Damn you, man, you sound like a bloody Bolshevik!' Father had shouted. 'Well, happen I am, for all that,' John had replied.

The yard, the sheds and barn were Doble's responsibility, but the stable belonged to John. He slept in a room above the loose-boxes so as to be on hand at all times for the horses, and he kept a little flower-garden, edged with stones, near the vegetable patch; he said he'd learned about flowers in the trenches, which seemed to me a strange thing. Father said it was a waste of good growing earth, but when Mother watered our vegetables she'd also water his roses, larkspur, hollyhocks and forget-me-nots, and sometimes a few blooms found their way into her yellow vase on the kitchen table, where they looked very well.

It fell to John to keep the trap, the wagons and the tumbril in good repair, as well as the Fordson in case it should be called upon. And it was he who took Moses, Malachi and Meg to be shod, and who saw to them when they were ill, consulting a book the rest of us were not allowed to see.

'It's nothing but some silly old superstition, like those hag-stones he's got hanging up over the stable door,' Frank told me once, when I conceived a scheme to get a look at his mysterious book. 'He probably can't even read very well, Ed.'

'Well, it won't do any harm, then,' I replied. 'If it's not black magic or anything.' But Frank flat-out refused to climb the ladder to John's lodging when he wasn't there, and I lacked the courage, and so let the matter drop.

It was John I thought of when I found the land-rail chick floppy and nearly lifeless in the coop on only its second day hatched. It struggled a little as I cupped it in my hands, its huge feet working, but it was clearly very weak. John was good with animals of all kinds, not just the horses; he'd helped Frank rear a leveret one year, and had bound up the leg of a deer that had been hit by a motor-car in the lane, keeping it in an old sheep pen and feeding it hay and linseed cake until at last it could be let go. For all that, he had no compunction about shooting rooks, rabbits and pigeons, or anything else that threatened our crops.

'It's half-starved, poor mite,' he told me that morning, holding a hand out for the landrail chick. He was eating breakfast in the kitchen, where I had rushed back after feeding the chickens. He set down the old bone-handled knife he brought to every meal and gently lifted the bird's stubby wings to see the frail body beneath.

'Edie, you must find it something – quickly, now. And some water. Perhaps your mother could lend us that eye-dropper of hers.'

Mother, washing lettuces, dried her hands on her apron and went to fetch the dropper from upstairs.

'What can it eat, John?' I asked.

'Go and find some worms, or slugs, insects – anything like that. You'll need to mash them up and feed them to it on the end of a match.'

'I'll do it, if you can't bear to kill them,' said Frank, finishing his porridge and pushing his bowl and spoon away from him for Mother to wash up.

'That's all right, I can manage – honestly I can.'

'Suit yourself.'

Beside the barn, what had long ago been a sheep pen and dip was now a place where old and half-broken things were kept, in case a use should be found for them: a broken churn, the iron seat from a mower, a pair of end ladders from a wagon, a half-rotted spinning-wheel and some elm paddles whose long-ago use I could only guess at. It was shady there, and cool, and lifting the old, discarded things I picked slug after slug from their damp undersides until I had a dozen or so curled and cold in my hot palm. I ran with them back to the yard, where Doble was leaning over the piggery wall. We had promised a piglet to Mother's parents, and she and I would be visiting them that afternoon.

'This one, I do believe, Edith,' Doble said, indicating the animal in question with his stick. 'He mayn't look much now, but he'll fatten up all right.'

'Doble, what can I mash these up with?' I asked, showing him the slugs.

'Have you a carbuncle? My mother allus swore by a poultice of slugs.'

'No, it's for a chick to eat, a landrail. It mustn't die.'

Doble laughed. 'Do you put they down on the step there, and I'll do it. That's right.' He pressed on them firmly with his stick. 'Does John aim to help it eat?'

'Yes. He's giving it water inside.'

'It'll be right as rain, then, Edith. You'll see. That man's a dab hand with God's creatures, and all manner o' what.'

I picked a dock leaf from by the gate and scooped up the slugs.

'Now, don't let your mother catch you taking that mess inside,' he said, and winked.

By noon the chick looked stronger. John made it a nest of straw in a box and set it on the back windowsill out of the sun. Later that afternoon it sat up, its eyes open, and whenever I drew near, its beak became an urgent pink gape. John showed me how to drop a little water in – not too much, in case it choked – and how to give it bits of food on the end of a match.

'Will it live?' I asked him.

'Perhaps; perhaps not,' he said. 'It'll only want feeding like this for a day or two, then it'll be up and about. You'll have to keep an eye on it for a little while, though, and see that it can find food.'

'I'm going to see Granfer and Grandma this afternoon; should I take it with me?'

'Best leave it here. Your brother can look after it,' he said.

To visit my mother's mother and father was to travel back in time to the olden days. It was as though everything modern – motor-transport, tar-macadam roads, the wireless – didn't exist for them, and never would. I see now that they were the last of the Victorians, inhabiting a world that had long passed away, and so to be with them was to be granted a temporary reprieve from all the anxieties of the modern age, the sense of things speeding up and going wrong that dogged us all invisibly in those years – even me. The War had touched them, of course, in the shape of Harry's death; but despite the hand-tinted photograph in its oval frame it was never spoken of: an aberration that had happened once, was in the past, and would never be allowed to occur again.

I climbed down from the trap to be held briefly at arm's length by Grandma, her one good eye scanning me closely but kindly so that she might understand how I was; then came a light embrace during which I inhaled the smell of rue and King's Empire tobacco that clung to her shawl before I was passed to my grandfather and wrapped in his still-strong arms.

'Hullo, lass. Oh, but it's a treat to have you here.'

Doble had wrapped the piglet in a grain sack with its feet tied. I went to lift it from the cart, but Mother reached past me and swung it easily out, handing the squealing bundle to Grandma, who took it to the little pen behind their dwelling and released it. Granfer uncoupled Meg from the trap and led her past neat rows of vegetables to their little paddock, where a piebald goat was tethered.

'Do you come inside, the both of you,' Grandma called to us from the step.

The cottage my mother had grown up in had been tied, like Doble's, but Granfer had saved all his working life and when he retired as head horseman he'd bought a railway carriage with a little strip of land two miles from Wych Farm, one of six carriages all inhabited by the elderly. A pot-bellied stove kept their two rooms warm in winter; they grew or traded most of what they needed, as the others did, and bought items such as tea and tobacco from the carrier when he came. Granfer missed the horses, naturally, and talked of them often; but they were entirely content with their lot.

Mary had walked over from Monks Tye and was sitting in Granfer's rocking chair nursing the baby, which was then five months old; she smiled as we came in, but didn't rise.

For a long time, when we were children, Mary and I were inseparable. We shared a bed until she was twelve; not for lack of space, for the farmhouse had more than enough rooms to go around, but because we liked to be with one another – and because of the drowning nightmares I had as a very small child, from which I would surface gasping and choking for air, and which meant that for a long while I feared being left alone. We would wait for sleep spooning, and if I had a bad dream Mary would comfort me; we became so used to one another's movements and the rhythm of our hearts and breath that it was almost as though we were one child, our long hair tangled together as we slept. It meant that even our worst fights were bracketed by closeness, for in those years I don't think we ever once went to sleep back-to-back. And then one morning Father said that it was high time Mary had her own room to sleep in, and that was that.

And yet I remained linked with her somehow, I felt, for my monthlies had arrived during her marriage service – though I didn't discover it until we had arrived back at the newly empty-seeming farm. Shut in the dim privy, rigid with fright, I'd hoped that perhaps the blood having begun in St Anne's meant God was protecting me; but with Mary gone there was nobody for me to ask. Mother found out the next day, which was wash-day, but she said little to me beyond giving me a box of necessaries and a wordless embrace, and I asked nothing back.

Grandma took her place in her chair by the stove and once we had kissed Mary she gestured me and Mother towards the little milking stools they brought out for company. On an oak dresser pewter gleamed dully in the June sun: two tankards, a pepper-pot and salt, a jug, a wide, flat charger and two candlesticks. This Grandma called her 'garnish', and along with the lovely old lace mats made long ago by her own grandmother, the pewter pieces were the pride of her home. The walls were hung with horse ornaments: bosses, ear-bells, fly-terrets and face-pieces showing the rose, the fleur-de-lis, the star, three crescents, and one – my favourite – with a lion rampant. These were my grandfather's, and I loved to hear how he'd come by each: some he'd won at ploughing contests, but others had been handed down from one horseman to another and were who knew how many generations old.

'Here, Edie, do you have some fudge while your granddaddy makes tea.' Grandma retrieved an old cocoa tin from somewhere beneath her chair and held it out, and I took a golden square from it, crumbly and soft. 'Now, Ada. I've heard from Mary, so do you tell me your news now,' she said, fishing a matchbox from her apron pocket and lighting her little clay pipe. 'How are Frank and George?'

'Frank's well. He's moving the hens to Great Ley now the hay's made. The manure will do it good.'

'And George? We expected him here with you to-day.'

'He's – a little indisposed.'

There was a pause that I didn't know how to interpret; I looked at Mary, but she seemed entirely engrossed by the baby at her swollen breast. A red-faced boy with masses of black hair, she'd called him Terence, which I thought rather a horrible name.

'And the men?'

This meant John and Doble.

'Yes, tolerable. I'll take some more of that liniment for Doble, if you've made any of late. He sends his thanks and says it fair loosens his back.'

'Yes, I have some. John mustn't use it, though – it won't do him any good. Besides, the horses.'

'I know, Mother.'

Granfer brought the tea over on a japanned tray and set it on a little table. The cups and saucers were fine bone-china painted with blowsy cabbage roses; they were the kind the sun glows through, and quite the most valuable thing in the little dwelling. I never really remarked on them at the time, although I have wondered since how they came to be there and how they remained unbroken, given Grandma's wall eye and Granfer's hands, twisted like roots from decades of guiding the plough. Even the cups' gold rims were bright and intact, as though they were new. Perhaps they had been given to Grandma when she was in service; or perhaps they were payment for a favour of some kind.

'All my lovely girls,' said Granfer, taking the chair opposite Grandma and smiling. 'How are you both?'

Mother smiled. 'We're well, aren't we, Edie? Yes, we're well enough, I'd say.'

'The hay is made?'

'The men will be thatching the rick to-day.'

'Ah, that's rare news. Haven't we had the weather for it! We were saying so just yesterday, weren't we, my dear,' and he reached across and took Grandma's hand.

'It seems there are people living over at Hullets,' Mother said then. I felt my mouth fall open with the surprise of it; so I *had* seen someone at the window when I was passing its ruins with Frank.

'At Hullets?' asked Mary. 'Who?'

'A family.'

'Do you mean … so it's been sold? At last?'

'No. They're – well, they're trespassing, from what we can make out.'

This was troubling. I suppose in many ways I was something of a prig; certainly I was interested in what the law said, and felt that everyone should abide by it, because it had not yet occurred to me that the law might ever be wrong, or unfair. The idea that some people might break the law, just do what they wanted in life – it made me afraid, I suppose, and I turned that fear into a high-minded kind of recti-tude, a far nicer feeling to have.

'Well, the police must make them leave,' I said robustly.

'We haven't told the police.'

'Why not? They're not allowed to be there!'

'Because, Edie … because they're poor.'

'Lots of people are poor,' said Mary. 'Why don't they apply for poor relief?'

'I don't know. Perhaps because they're not from our parish. They're – from somewhere else.'

'Why have they come here, then?'

'They'll be looking for work,' said Granfer; 'there's always folk on the road at harvest-time, child, you know that. Bob Rose will have a few extra shillings for hired hands, I expect.'

'But there are plenty of village people who'll work for Bob Rose! And anyway, they can't just move in anywhere they want. Can they? I mean, Hullets isn't *theirs*. Someone should tell Lord Lyttleton,' I said.

'There are children to think of, Edie,' said Mother. 'Now, listen to me: I won't have you talking of this to anyone, do you hear me? Is that understood?'

I looked to Mary, who raised an eyebrow, but it seemed the subject was closed.

'Now, tell me,' said Granfer after a moment, 'how're they 'osses?'

This was what he most wanted to know, and as he and my mother talked I looked across to Grandma, whose left eye looked at Mother, the right into the middle distance, her given name of Clarity seeming something of a cruel joke. Although their neighbours now were kind, Mother could recall women turning away superstitiously lest Grandma overlooked them or their animals or children. It was the reason that Mother had, like me, had few friends at school.

'The creature will live,' she said suddenly, turning her good eye on me. 'What manner of bird is it, child?'

I had long ceased to wonder how she knew such things before we told her; she always had, it was just her way.

'It's a landrail, Grandma,' I answered. 'We found three eggs in Great Ley, but the others didn't hatch.'

'And what other news have you?'

'Frank and I went to the river for the whole day yesterday, and swam. It was marvellous. Oh, and Frank caught a huge tench.'

Mother and Granfer talked on; Grandma simply looked at me and waited, her head cocked to one side, like a wren.

'Oh yes! I nearly forgot,' I said, hoping to head her off before she guessed that there was anything bothering me, or – heaven forbid – asked about Alf Rose. 'A woman came. She's called Constance FitzAllen and she dresses like a man. She's writing a book, and she's staying with Mrs Eleigh at the draper's. She'll be here all summer.'

Grandma nodded. 'That she will. From which direction did you say she came?'

'Which direction?'

'This Constance brings weather with her, child, as the wind does.'

'Oh – I'm not sure which direction. She just appeared.'

Baby Terence had finished feeding and was now beginning to grizzle. I knew I should offer to take him from Mary, and perhaps walk up and down with him outside to give her a break, but I didn't want to. I might have warmed to him more had everyone not examined me so openly for signs of motherliness every time I was in the same room as him; but they made me feel as though I was being tested, and it set me against him somehow.

Grandma stood at the sound of Terence's opening wail. 'Let me take him, girl – there, that's right.'

Mary passed the baby to her, and she settled him easily onto her hip and began to show him the brasses on the wall.

'So. How's the farm, Ed?' Mary asked. 'How are the apple trees, and the horse-ponds? And are the swallows nesting in the thatch this year?'

'Oh – yes, I think so.'

'How lovely! I miss the sound of them, you know – I was telling Clive about them only the other night.'

The truth was, I hadn't paid much heed to the swallows; after all, they built near Mary's bedroom window, not mine. But Mary had begun to talk rather elegiacally about home since she'd left, as though it were a lost paradise, and I sometimes hardly recognised the place she talked of as the workaday farm where I lived.

Clive sold vacuum cleaners and other appliances door-to-door, and was considered to be on his way up in the world. He and Mary had rented one of a row of brick houses that had been built in Monks Tye just after the War, very smart and clean, with indoor plumbing, a back boiler and electric lights; they had a moquette settee and matching armchair that they had got on the H.P., and even a Frigidaire. Mother rather envied the little house's modernity, but I would have felt cooped up in its blank rooms all day long.

'Why don't you come and visit? You could come back in the trap with us to-day – there'll be room,' I said. 'Come and stay the night.'

'Oh, Ed – I couldn't.'

'Why not? You never come.'

'It's just – well, Clive wouldn't like it, for one thing.'

'But Terence hasn't ever seen the baby swallows, and they'll fledge soon,' I tried. 'Oh *do* come. You can sleep in my room – it'll be just like the old days!'

She looked at me then with a sympathy I couldn't bear. 'Ed, I'm ever so sorry – all Terence's things are at home, and there's Clive's supper to think of. I can't just ... do whatever I like, you know. I'm a married woman now.'

After tea Granfer and I set out for a walk, leaving the women talking together in low voices. It was a warm June day, not so hot as it had been for haysel, but close; the sky was flat and white and a breeze knickled the oats on the far-distant slope beyond the smallholdings and the water meadows where a herd of red polls grazed.

'Shall we have rain?' I asked, shading my eyes.

'No, lass. Not yet.'

'The clouds are a little darker over there, though – look.'

'We don't get rain from that way. We allus get our rain from Corwelby way.'

At home Grandfather had already told me it wouldn't rain; I only asked Granfer for the pleasure of it, for the way his words sounded so certain about what was to come, and made me feel certain, too.

'Now, who's this lady writer who's got your mother in a bate?'

'Oh, Constance FitzAllen. She told Mother she should make butter, I think – no matter that we don't even keep a cow. She believes in local sufficiency, and she says it's a shame that the traditional skills are all passing away.'

'Good riddance to 'em, I say. I take it she's not the type for to do any dairying herself?'

I laughed and shook my head.

'And she's a spinster? How old, would you say?'

I tried to picture her, but it was hard; she was more of a series of vivid impressions in my mind then, with none of the detail that came later.

'I don't know. Mother's age, or thereabouts?'

'Well, perhaps she lost a sweetheart. The War made a lot of spare women, you know, child. What's she like? Is she a nuisance?'

71

'I don't think so – although I've only met her once. She seems rather cheerful. It's just – she says exactly what she means.'

'Aha!' he chuckled. 'Like your mother. Well, that do explain it.'

I thought about that. It didn't seem to me as though the two were anything alike: Constance with her man's attire and her easy manner, Mother with her chapped red hands and constant fatigue. And yet I could dimly perceive something in it, for despite their wildly differing situations they were in some way evenly matched.

'Now, do you walk ahead and open that gate for me. I find they latches wonderful stiff these days,' the old man said.

We had brought two bales of hay and some ash hurdles with us, and before we left I helped Mother unload them from the cart and stack them by the gate to the little paddock. Then I led Meg from the paddock back to the trap, the little goat bleating at the loss. Granfer began buckling her back into the traces, and I smiled to see the sun glint off a pretty brass chain that lay across her forehead.

'I see she has a new bridle, Granfer. Howsoever did that happen?'

'Ah, well. Your'n was rotted clear through, nearly, and one of they blinkers gaped. Don't she look smart for it!'

'She does.' I touched the smooth, close-grained leather of the harness, which was stamped on the brow-band with the letters M, C and P.

'From the old place,' he said. 'The mistress died in child-bed, you see. We weren't ever to use her things again after that – it all had to go. I took the tack to the saddler, but he said it were bad luck, wouldn't even give me a shilling for it; in the end I'd to drive her barouche clear out of the county to sell it. But it looks well on your girl, and I'll not see good leather go to waste.'

Mary came to the door of the carriage to wave us off, for she meant to stay a little longer. As we got into the cart Grandma handed up a basket heaped with herbs, goat's cheese wrapped in muslin and a dark, stoppered bottle of liniment, and I took it on my lap, inhaling the fragrance the sun drew from it.

'Go safely, child,' she said, taking Granfer's hand where they stood.

'I will, Grandma,' I replied. Then Mother shook the reins, the axles creaked and we were on our way.

V

One morning I came back from Middle Ley, where I had taken the little landrail chick to learn to forage, and found Constance in the kitchen with Mother. I stopped in the doorway in surprise; Mother was kneading dough and talking, and Constance was leaning up against the dresser and listening respectfully. Her eyes flicked over to where I stood and she winked theatrically and grinned. I knew she'd been at the farm the day before and had spent some hours with Grandfather, but it was wash-day and she'd gone by the time I'd finished helping Mother hang out the sheets and clothes to dry.

I smiled back, and realised that I was glad to see her. I felt as though she perceived me more clearly than my family did, for they all took me for granted, whereas she seemed curious about who I was and what I thought. Although I did not know her well yet, I felt more real, more interesting even, when I saw myself through Constance's eyes.

'No, I don't mind a tin loaf now and again, they are so good for sandwiches,' Mother was saying. 'But really, I prefer proper bread. Even if I use a tin I make it church and chapel.'

'Church and chapel?' Constance asked, licking her pencil and returning her attention to the little notebook she held. 'Whatever's that?'

'Oh, you know. Neither one thing nor the other. I take a small tin and fill it right to the top so the crust rises over, like a mushroom. Look –' and she handed Constance a top-heavy loaf which she turned over to see the square shape of its base.

'Oh no – you mustn't –' said Mother, reaching out and turning the loaf back the right way up. 'It's – well, it's bad luck to turn a loaf. If you believe in that kind of thing, of course,' and she laughed.

'Fascinating,' said Constance, scribbling minutely in her notebook. I began to climb the stairs.

'Is that you, child?' Mother called as the old oak treads creaked. I turned and came back down.

'Yes, Mother. Hello, Constance.'

'And how's the little one to-day?' Mother asked, setting the dough on its board on the kitchen windowsill to rise. 'Are you managing? I do think perhaps it would be better if John –'

'It's doing rather well, actually, Mother. Look –' and I scooped the chick gently from my skirt pocket and set it on the kitchen table. It wobbled briefly, then settled its downy feathers and began to look about.

'Oh, how charming!' said Constance, leaning forward with her hands in her pockets and peering at it. 'What is it?'

'A landrail. Corncrakes, I think some people call them.'

'Is it an orphan?'

'Yes. Well, the mother might still be about somewhere, but we don't know where. We found the nest when we were haymaking, and hatched it from an egg under one of the hens.'

'How marvellous. Will you keep it as a pet?'

'Oh no – it'll be gone in a week or two, I should think. Off to find its friends.'

'There's certainly no shortage,' said Mother. 'The sound of them fair keeps me awake this time of year.'

'What are your plans for the rest of the day, Edie?' asked Constance.

I shrugged, and looked at Mother. 'I'm not sure. Why?'

'I thought a bicycle tour of the valley might be in order; Ada's been telling me about some fascinating places – some interesting people, too. What do you think? Will you show me around?'

Where exactly did we go that warm June afternoon – which roads, which lanes did we take? I can't be sure, now, if we cycled up to the ridge that day or on another afternoon, or whether we went as far as Monks Tye, where Mary lived. That summer we spent so much time together that it seems to me now as though we were out bicycling every day, she with the wind whipping at her hair, calling to me over her shoulder as though I was an old friend of hers, as though I could understand everything she said.

In reality, of course, Connie and I can't have cycled out more than a dozen times, for there were many afternoons she spent at other farms, other houses; days when we saw nothing of her, because she was out with her notebook elsewhere. She changed in those weeks, began to ask better questions, ones that didn't already contain what she believed the answer might be; she learned, too, to rein some of her brashness in. And people took to her; even at the start, even with all her opinions and her tactlessness. She was, despite everything, somehow innocent – that's the only way I can describe it. There was something about her that wasn't pretence.

'So you and Mother are friends now,' I called out that afternoon as we reached the end of the lane. Swallows swooped around us, hawking for clegs and crane flies; the air was full of their chatter. The day was warm and still.

'Of course we're friends! Now, which way?' She asked, slowing at the four-a-leet.

'Right – let's go through the village. What happened?'

'What do you mean?'

It struck me that she had perhaps not realised that she had ever given offence. 'Well –'

'Oh, you mean the butter! Oh no, that's quite forgotten. She's a dear, your mother, really she is. I wouldn't offend her for worlds.'

I thought it best to let it drop; perhaps Mother would throw some light on their reconciliation later.

'Do you have any brothers and sisters, Connie?'

'Just Jeffrey. He's a year and a half older than I am.'

'And have you always lived in London?'

'Well, we were born in Sussex, where my mother's people are from. My father – he was a schoolmaster, you know – he preferred to teach the deserving poor rather than seek advancement at the better schools in the area. He took up an invitation to help set up a new school for the sons of clergymen which also admitted forty poor boys each year, and that's how we came to Tooting.'

'Your father sounds very admirable.'

'Oh, he's quite, quite brilliant, but very much a man of principle. Of course, Mother wasn't happy about it at all.'

'Why not?'

'She thought he should have more ambition – and earn a few more readies, of course. And she hated London, after sleepy old Sussex; she still does, as a matter of fact. No-one will ever persuade her it isn't as bad as all that. I mean, cities are an abomination, obviously: dreadfully devitalising and artificial. But we lived on a garden estate – one of the very first, in fact, and rather elegant. "Rational architecture" and all that, you know?'

I didn't; in fact I couldn't picture it at all. When I thought of London it was either one thing or the other: dazzle or slums. I had very little to relate it to other than Market Stoundham, and I knew that was far wide of the mark. It seemed clear, though, that however decent and well appointed the houses, her family's circumstances must have been reduced compared to their earlier situation. I was beginning to understand that although she wasn't like most of the people I knew in the village, she wasn't gentry either. Perhaps a lack of funds was behind her writing ambitions – she'd mentioned that she lived in a boarding-house when in London, rather than with her family, and I supposed that couldn't have come cheap.

'Have you ever done any teaching?' I asked. 'Like your father?'

I asked because a few days earlier, a letter had arrived from my old teacher, Miss Carter, asking if she might put my name forward for a position as nursery-maid to two small children in nearby Blaxford; I had replied to say that I didn't much like children, but I hadn't quite stopped worrying that I had done the wrong thing.

'Oh goodness, no. I couldn't bear it,' she replied. 'Jeffrey's a private tutor, but other than helping my cousin Olive with her violin practice I've never taught anyone a thing in my life – unless of course you count the War.'

'The War?'

'I was a V.A.D. – you know, with the Red Cross – and by the second time I went out I knew the ropes well enough to help the new girls settle in. Now, I feel I already know Elmbourne well – though I would like to call in at the wheelwright's one day and watch him work, and I want to talk to the black-smith, too. But not to-day, I think. Where shall we go, Edie? I'm in your hands.'

The village's main thoroughfare, The Street, ran along the north side of the river, which was only a stream here really, and slow. There was a post office and general stores, our little schoolroom, a grocer, a butcher, two smithies – one with a crim-son petrol pump outside – the wheelwright Connie had mentioned, who was also a cabinet-maker and undertaker, a draper, a sweet shop and the Bell & Hare; once there had been an inn called the Cock, too, but that was no more. We had nearly everything we needed, excepting a bank and a doctor, both of which could be found in Market Stoundham, where the cattle and grain markets were held. There was little need to travel any further, and most people didn't; likewise, new people rarely moved to the district, and so our day-to-day world was composed almost entirely of people we knew.

Church Lane turned north off The Street to St Anne's and the rectory, and then west towards Monks Tye; on the corner, across from the Bell & Hare, was our little village green and the pump. Back Lane, which ran parallel to The Street but on the south side of the water, was lined with old cottages and a short brick terrace; there was a fine old half-timbered wool merchant's house there too, sagging somewhat, but a reminder of a long-ago time when there had been money in sheep. Back Lane had once been part of a separate hamlet, long since absorbed but still marked on the old tithe map on the wall in St Anne's; a path led through tangled willows and alders between Back Lane and The Street, crossing the river near the old mill by a set of broad stepping-stones.

We pedalled slowly along The Street and left into Church Lane, then turned right towards the peas and beanfields of the valley's gentle, south-facing slopes. Tall beeches grew here, and the road was white and deep-sunk between shady banks; flints gleamed in the fields on either side. I pointed out a row of three cottages half-ruined; two had been gutted by fire, while on the third moss grew rich and green on the clay pantiles of its roof.

'Another ten years and those will have gone home,' I called out to her as we sailed past. 'That's what Father says.'

'Gone home?'

'Oh, you know, become a ruin. That's what we say here when the old cob houses sink away into the ground.'

'But why let them go – why aren't they being repaired? Close to the village, and so pretty – surely someone would like to live there? I'm sure I know people who would.'

'Really? Who'd want to live somewhere like that, with damp walls and no pump in the kitchen, just a shared well and a shared privy?' I said, pedalling hard in an attempt to draw level with her. 'Mother says those old places are dark and unsanitary; they should pull them all down, she says. I dare say they would, but there's an old couple clinging on.'

'No, Edie! Really?' She braked suddenly and craned back over her shoulder; I had to pull up pretty sharpish so as not to crash into her. 'People are living there, now?'

It surprised me that she was so taken aback. 'Yes – but they're ancient, they won't move. They've lived there all their lives, and they'll die indoors if they can. That's the way of it, you see; and it's either that or the Poor Law – that means the workhouse, or whatever it is they say we must call it these days.'

Connie took out her notebook and wrote something in it; I think she planned to go back and call on the old couple another day. Whether she did or did not I don't know, for I never read her book, which came out five or more years from the day we last saw one another, and which was kept from me for reasons I have since come to understand.

Perhaps her writing was the reason she seemed to learn so much about us all, and so quickly; even things we did not know ourselves. For it was she who told me about my grandmother – Father's mother – and what had happened to her in her last years. This was some weeks later, I think; I'd mentioned the fact that I had had diphtheria, and she'd told me about a new inoculation, and then she went on to describe the modern therapies being used to treat lunatics, like giving them convulsions instead of endless cold baths.

'Of course, it's all come too late for your poor old grandmother. Who knows, she might have been cured!'

'Grandma? Whatever do you mean?'

'No – Albert's wife; your father's mother.'

I felt a shiver come over me, like the blind surfacing of a buried memory, or the passing shadow of a premonition. 'Did someone walk over your grave, Ed?' Mary would have laughed.

'Do you mean she was a lunatic?'

'Well – yes, darling. Quite insane. She died in the county asylum, apparently. Surely you knew?'

We must have visited nearly all of the valley's farms that day, Connie writing down notes in her book in her elegant copperplate hand. I know I introduced her to the Coopers at Holstead, with its fine timbered house and fashionable tennis court, and old Elisabeth Allingham, who farmed alone, growing peas and field beans at Copdock; I showed her the Summersby's flock of sheep grazing the rough pasture near Holbrook Wood. And I pointed out the distant sugar-beet factory and the vast new open fields that were farmed from who knows where, their owners half a county away.

I showed Connie the woods and copses, too, and pointed out which ones had been planted as cover for foxes – like Hulver Wood, at the end of our lane. Father didn't like the Hunt coming onto our land, I explained, but as a tenant farmer he had little choice. They compensated him for any spoiled hedges and the chickens that upped and died if the hounds came too near, but beyond that there wasn't a great deal he could do. I told her how once, years before, a whipper-in had told Father to open a gate for him, and Father had done as he was bid – although Frank, who was there, told me he didn't reply to the man, or drop his gaze. Doble touched his cap to gentry – and to Connie, as she pointed out – but John always refused to. He said those days had ended with the War.

And then, at the end of our tour, I took her to see Ixham Hall. Built in Tudor times of warm red brick, and topped with tall octagonal chimneys, it was set at the end of a long carriage ride amid some fine landscaping that was at that time beginning to overgrow. There was an enormous barn of the usual black timber, where Grandfather could remember having the Harvest Home, and a private chapel built with stone from a long-gone Norman keep. Fifty years earlier the Hall had had nearly a thousand acres, nearly all of it tenanted, but since then much of the land had been sold.

The Lyttletons were our 'people' and had once been known as good landlords, endowing the village with a schoolroom and keeping the labourers' cottages decent and the roads in good repair. But the eldest of the two sons had died, and his father soon after; the younger son, Cecil, who lived in London, was rumoured to be part of a rather fast set – or so the village said. When Lady Lyttleton passed away, not long after I was born, the Hall was shuttered up; for as long as I could remember it had stood empty, and from time to time there was talk of its sale. The tenant farmers like Father found life harder under an absentee landlord, although Sir Cecil, via his agent, was not remiss in the collection of rents.

Every year, between haymaking and harvest, the village held a fete in the grounds of the Hall. Sir Cecil would return from London and take up residence for a week so that he could oversee the preparations; afterwards we wouldn't see him again until November, when he came back to hunt. It wasn't much, I suppose, but we enjoyed it: there was a flower show and a band, a coconut shy and a tombola, and all the village turned out for the day. I was half looking forward to it, half plagued by dread, because it was an event where groups of friends generally larked about together, and I didn't have anyone to walk around with. But perhaps Mary would walk over from Monks Tye for it this year, or we could always offer to fetch her in the trap; perhaps Mother would agree to mind the baby, and she and I could be sisters for a little while again.

Connie and I propped our bicycles against one of the stone gateposts and I showed her how easy it was, if you turned sideways, to slip through the ironwork gates.

'Gosh – I suppose all Elmbourne's young ne'er-do-wells must sneak in and get up to no good!' she said, angling her tall frame through.

'Actually, I've never seen another living soul in here – apart from at the fete, of course,' I replied. 'The sexton comes and cuts the grass and keeps an eye on things, but there never seems to be anybody about. At school everyone used to say it was haunted, you see.'

'Haunted? But how wonderful! You must tell me more – a black dog, or the Wild Hunt? It's fascinating to think how all these funny little folk tales spring up. I may well write something about them; they're the wellspring of the nation's character, I feel.'

We were walking up the carriage ride with its centre seam of weeds, which led in a sweeping curve to the big, blank-windowed Hall.

'No – it's Lord Lyttleton,' I said. 'He shot himself in his study after the telegram came saying his son had been killed at Ypres.'

When at last we arrived back in the village I thought we would bicycle to the draper's and part company there, but instead Connie dismounted outside the Bell & Hare. I stood uncertainly astride my bicycle as she raked her fingers through her hair in an attempt to tidy it. She was clearly intending to go in.

'Aren't you coming, Edie? You must be parched – I know I am.'

'Oh – no, I won't.'

'Really? Let me at least buy you a lemonade.'

I tried to picture it: the two of us standing at the bar of the inn, like men. She would drink beer, I was sure of it.

'I can't, Connie. I'm sorry. I should get back.'

She looked at me a long moment, and then stuck out her hand and grinned.

'Very well, darling. *Jusqu'à demain,*' she said.

Alf Rose was at the four-a-leet; I couldn't tell if he was waiting for me, or just happened to be walking over from Rose Farm. My heart sank a little; I stopped pedalling and let my bicycle slow, aware all of a sudden that my face was shiny with perspiration and my hair stringy and tangled. There were probably dark patches under my arms, and I felt my usual wash of shame.

'Hello, Edie,' he called, and I squeezed the brakes and dismounted. 'You look fair hot and bothered.'

We turned into the lane. I wheeled the bicycle between us, trying with my free hand to tuck my hair behind my ears.

'I've been out bicycling,' I said, unnecessarily. 'Showing Constance FitzAllen around.'

'The famous Miss FitzAllen! What's she like, then? Frank says she wears britches.'

I kept my eyes on the ground. 'Well, she's ... I like her,' I managed. I didn't know how to explain her to him, and anyway, it sounded from his tone as though he had already made up his mind.

'So where did you take her?' he asked, opening the gate to our farm. 'And why didn't you bring her to see us? You haven't been over in months.'

'Oh – we ran out of time,' I said, wheeling the bicycle through. He was right, though: I hadn't been to Rose Farm in a long while.

Until he left school, Frank used to wait for me after lessons every day so I could walk home with him and Alf – and when I was even younger, with Mary and Sid too. We Mathers would leave the Rose boys at the four-a-leet, usually, but sometimes we would have our tea at one another's houses and play for a while or look at comics, which were a much-admired feature of the Rose house, though not of our own.

It was a surprise the first time Alf kissed me; it was at Rose Farm and I can only have been ten or eleven years old. I had just come out of the privy and didn't realise that he was there, and he probably surprised himself as much as he did me. At any rate we laughed about it, and later he ragged me that if I said anything he would tell everyone I was fast. As it went on – well, I don't know how I felt about it, really. Alf was such a nice boy, and everyone liked him, and the attention made me feel as though I was important in some way, I suppose.

During my final two years at school I would walk home alone, and then I would usually take the quicker route to Wych Farm, down the field path, rather than taking the lane past Rose Farm; I wasn't avoiding Alf, exactly, I just preferred to walk that way. The kissing was a secret between us, and although there were times when I did think to ask Mary about him touching my chest and putting his hand up my skirt, I suppose I was in some way becoming quite wicked because I wasn't quite sure if I did really want it to stop. I'd picture how coldly he would look at me if he knew that I'd made such a fuss about nothing, and how I would be forever scorned by him and perhaps by Frank too, if he found out; and then I would tell myself that it was all right really, and quite natural. After all, everyone at home said I was babyish for my age, and so it probably did me good to be made to grow up.

'*Awful, awful,*' I muttered to myself involuntarily, and then cleared my throat to cover up the sound I'd made.

'I'd be happy to show her the calves, Edie, if you think she'd be interested,' Alf said; clearly he hadn't heard me, which was a relief. 'We could tell her what we mean to do to modernise; Father's got plans for a milking herd next year, you know. "Down corn, raise horn" and all that.'

'Oh – I don't think she'd be much interested in that.'

'Why not?' he said, bridling a little.

'She's interested in tradition and history; she says she wants to write about the old ways, not the new. She wants to preserve our ancient way of life here in the village – England is the country, and the country is England, she says.'

'Why, she sounds mazed. There's nothing round here that people would want to read about in a book.'

'It's about reconnecting people in towns to the land, she says – to their inheritance.'

'Their inheritance? How is it their inheritance if they haven't even been born in the country, if they've never worked a day in the fields?'

'As a *nation*. She says the English have become estranged from their birth-right, from the bonds of blood and soil or something. Oh, I don't know, Alf. I'm going to put my bicycle away.'

'It's the fete soon, Edie,' he called after me. 'Will I see you there?'

'Oh yes, we're all going,' I replied.

In my bedroom, the door latched, the landrail chick peeping in its box, I combed my hair, washed my face and changed out of my dirty dress. I was glad to have got away without him kissing me, but I felt rattled; I hadn't been ready to be Connie's mouthpiece, I wasn't equipped to defend her, or her ideas. Now it was as though I was allied with her somehow, and although I liked her, and enjoyed spending time with her, I wasn't yet sure what that meant.

VI

Connie went back to London at the week-end for some kind of 'political do', as she called it. On the Saturday night there was to be a dance at Monks Tye, to which Frank and the two Rose boys were going; I had stubbornly set myself against it – although if I was honest a part of me did want to go, and a couple of weeks beforehand I might well have said yes.

'She's like a half-broke horse,' Father said as he passed through the kitchen where Mother and I were talking on Saturday afternoon. 'You give her too much choice in the matter, Ada. She should go to the dance with her brother – it's high time she made some friends her own age. Make the girl see a bit of life.'

'She's a child yet, George. Let her go another time, when she's ready,' she replied, which made me feel relieved – although Frank's words to me by the river played somewhere at the back of my mind.

'Did you go to lots of dances, Mother? When you were my age?'

'No, child. You and I are alike in that,' she said, and smiled.

'Why didn't you?'

'Well, I met your father young, for one thing, and he was never much of a one for gallivanting.'

'But did you want to?'

She sighed. 'At the time, yes, if truth be told: I did feel as though I were missing out. But looking back it were probably just as well. The fact of it is, you don't know how young you are when you're young, and a pretty girl like I was in those days can get in all sorts of trouble.'

'What kind of trouble?' I asked, sitting down at the kitchen table. I wanted her to say the things out loud that were trouble; I wanted her to name them, so that I might understand what they were.

'Oh, I don't know. It's not something you need to worry your head about yet, child.'

Pollen had fallen from some of John's flowers in the yellow vase on the table, and I licked a forefinger and began to pick it up.

'Mother, did you used to have a best friend to talk to?'

'Lizzie Allingham was my friend, and still is, God bless her.'

'Did you talk to her about ... about dances, and sweethearts, and walking out?'

She laughed. 'Oh no, Lizzie never had any time for boys. She always said they were only ever after one thing.'

'And you didn't have any other friends?'

'You know I didn't, Edie. My mother – your grandmother – well, children can be cruel, and that's all I'll say about that.'

Mother wanted to see *Evergreen* with Jessie Matthews, which was playing at the Regal in Market Stoundham. So after supper on Saturday night we took the field path to the village and caught the 'bus from outside the Bell & Hare. Once we were seated and the 'bus had rattled off, she took a gilt powder compact from her bag, powdered her nose, and then applied a little lipstick. We didn't often go to town except on market days, and so it was a treat.

We had had a good meal of devilled kidneys – Father's favourite – and it wasn't long before I found myself dozing off. By the time Mother nudged me awake we were approaching our stop, the 'bus crawling up Sheepdrove amid motor-cars, horse cabs and men on bicycles; the pavements were thronged with girls in modish hats and here and there a tramp returning to the workhouse for the night. It was exciting, bustling; I liked the little town on market day, but I loved it even more in the evenings, when, instead of gathering in for the night, as the countryside did, everything seemed to come alive. It felt there as though anything might happen, which was intoxicating: for in contrast, the farm was a world of ancient and immovable rhythms and beliefs.

The picture was lavish and exciting, and I can still remember Mother's rapt face aglow in the flickering light from the screen. During the finale, as the lovely dancing girls kicked their legs, she leaned forward, her lips parted; when the lights went down she sat a while and dabbed at her eyes with her handkerchief, although the ending hadn't been in the least bit sad.

'Do you need to visit the ladies' room?' she asked as we got up and began to make our way to the exit. We had sat for so long that the National Anthem was over, the lights had come up and the usherette was doing the rounds with a canister of Flit.

I shook my head.

'Go on, now; you'll only fidget on the 'bus. I'll meet you on the steps.'

The ladies' room was full of young women chattering like sparrows. They reminded me a little of Mary before she was married, but of course they were town girls, and far more sophisticated; doubtless they would have found her rustic and quaint. They crowded the mirror, applying rouge and dabbing lipstick from their teeth. When I moved through them they parted, kindly; but I knew I made barely a ripple in the sparkling current of their night.

Mother was outside smoking a cigarette, something she did very rarely and only when we were away from the farm. I wondered where she had got it; I was sure she wouldn't dare keep a packet in her bag.

'Oh, I *do* so love the pictures. Don't you?' she said, taking my arm. 'To think of it all ... well. It makes me feel – I can't quite say. Oh Edie, do you know what I mean?'

'Oh yes,' I said, although I didn't; I just couldn't bear to disappoint her. I had liked the film well enough, and the newsreel had been very interesting, but I could see from her glowing expression that it meant something far greater to her. Once, I had recited Browning's 'Home-Thoughts, from Abroad' in the kitchen, which we had learned by rote in school and which I loved passionately for more than a year; but although she had stood by the range and listened closely I could see no answering feeling in her face. I wondered whether it was just now the same for her – whether she had hoped to share a feeling with me, and was now disappointed. Mary wouldn't have let her down, I reflected; they both loved going to the Regal. But it was hardly my fault that I preferred poetry to the pictures.

We didn't have long to wait for the 'bus, which was the last service back to Elmbourne. Frank was to meet us at the stop and walk home with us, and had been threatened with a hiding from Father if he wasn't there on time. I wondered what the dance had been like and whether I'd have enjoyed it; whether it would have mattered that I didn't have any clothes like the girls at the Regal, or whether, it only being a village dance, nobody would mind. I knew there would have been girls and boys my own age there, as well as older ones, and that Frank would have kept me company and not left me with nobody to talk to. Why was it, then, that I hadn't wanted to go?

The 'bus appeared, rattling and cheerful, and the other passengers began to climb on board. Mother, though, seemed barely to have noticed, and stood staring past it, up the street.

'What's the matter?' I asked, peering. 'Come on, or we'll miss it!'

We climbed on and took our seats, but as the driver pulled away Mother continued to stare out of the window, and it was then that I saw John on the steps of one of the public houses, and pressed up against him a woman in a moth-eaten fur stole, her décolletage on show. I said nothing, and neither did Mother, but the pale moon of her face was reflected, unblinking, in the dark glass of the 'bus window all the way back.

In Broad Field the beans began to flower and smell sweet. Along our lane and the road to the village hogweed took the place of the spent cow parsley, its creamy blooms busy with soldier beetles making love. Everywhere the paths were narrower now, choked by waist-high nettles, cleavers and meadow grass with its feathery seed-heads. The clover came out in the pastures, and the flat rosettes of plantain and the tiny yellow stars of lesser trefoil carpeted the bare soil at the margins of the wheat.

Whenever Hullets' ruined buildings were in view I found myself gazing over, hoping to catch a glimpse of the family living there. But I saw nothing and nobody, and Mother was tight-lipped on the subject, only reminding me, when I brought it up, not to gossip in the village or tell tales.

The landrail chick grew bigger every day, bright-eyed and constantly looking for food. I kept it in my room for fear of the cats that slunk about the yard, and when it wasn't sleeping it ran around after me, peeping and stumbling on the rag rugs, a dark ball of fluff more like a baby crow than the wheat-coloured, tapestried bird it would become. Each day, after I had seen to the hens, I took it to practise foraging at the field margins, where it would tentatively explore the hedge bottoms, never straying far from where I sat reading a book. Once, when a sparrow-hawk passed over us, I saw it clamp down into the grass; it seemed to have been born with an understanding of where danger might come from, and I wondered how many generations it would be until the mowing-machine would draw from it the same response.

When John judged that it was strong enough I let the landrail chick go in The Lottens, just near the hedge separating it from Broad Field. There was a ditch half-hidden by brambles and bryony, and at the bottom of it, water; there was plenty of cover, and all the young corn and field beans to explore. It crouched for a moment and seemed uncertain what to do with its new freedom; but when I looked back at the corner of the field, it was gone.

Connie was back from London and was fast becoming something of a fixture at Wych Farm, so that we no longer remarked much upon it when she rode her bicycle up the lane or knocked at the back door, looking for someone to talk to her about basketry, old-fashioned names of plants, or playground rhymes. She would sometimes find us where we sat at the kitchen table, or she'd pull back the heavy curtain and halloo up the stairs; if there was nobody indoors she'd look in the barn or the vegetable-garden, or try the fields. I became used to seeing her striding towards us, hatless and smiling; it was a welcome distraction from work. And she opened the farm up somehow, too – we became lighter, more genial, around her, as though we were being kindly looked upon by the outside world.

Only John seemed not to welcome her; he was never rude, but in the face of her questions he became even more taciturn and remote. Of course he told her nothing of the secrets of his trade, as I had warned her he would not; yet she continued, utterly unabashed by his refusals, in her attempt to charm.

Just once during that time did I see him roused to irritation, and that was when Connie bemoaned the increasing use of tractors on the land.

'I just feel that we're in danger of losing touch with the soil, and with all the lovely old traditions,' she'd said. 'And of course, all these clever machines will eventually put farm labourers out of work.'

'Tradition be damned, Constance,' he'd flashed back. 'I've seen good men crippled and broke by a life spent out in the fields, and farmers go under for lack of good hands. It may be a – a diversion to people like you, but farming in't some kind of a game.'

A familiar red bicycle was leaning by the gate when I returned from releasing the landrail, and I found Connie in the parlour with Grandfather, trying once more to coax him to sing. She had heard from some-one at the Bell & Hare that he was the last man in the district to remember all the old ballads, but I could have told her she would be unsuccessful, for according to Mother he had stopped singing the day my grandmother died. They enjoyed talking to one another, though, and so I let it be.

'Hello, Connie,' I said, sitting on the arm of Grandfather's chair and taking his hand. 'Are you with us for the day?'

'If you'll have me. I plan on making another attempt on your bread oven, if your mother will allow it.'

'Really? On a day like to-day?'

'Yes – I don't want to wait for winter. Elisabeth Allingham uses hers, did you know? And her house isn't hot. I was there only the other day.'

'They're modern, for all that,' Grandfather interjected.

'Brick bread ovens? Whatever can you mean, Albert?'

'It was my mother's mother had ours'n put it; it was never part of the original hearth. Acourse, back then you made most things in one great pot over the fire.'

'Yes indeed! I believe Florence White describes that very arrangement in *Good Things in England*; I'll get a copy for Ada if she doesn't have one – it's all the rage. I don't suppose your grandmother ever told you in detail about any of the dishes she made, did she? Is there anything in particular you recall?'

Connie's pencil was poised over her notebook; she was as alert as the thresher's terrier when it scented a rat. I stood up.

'I should get on, really – Father's asked me to pull ragwort to-day.'

'Nasty job,' said Grandfather. 'Do you give her a helping hand, Connie. And I'll speak to Ada about the bread.'

Connie was clever enough to know a deal when she saw one, and we left Grandfather where he sat by the parlour window, dappled light falling through the elm leaves onto his old face.

'You'll need some gloves,' I said, rifling through the coats and boots and bits of tack that had accumulated near the back door.

'Oh, don't worry about me, Edie – my hands are toughening up rather well.'

'Honestly, Connie, it's bad stuff. It can poison you through your skin, and it sickens the horses. That's why we pull it up.'

I found us a pair each, and we wheeled a barrow out to Horse Leasow. John had been grazing the horses on the Pightle of late, so the grass in the other pasture was growing tall.

'See those – with the yellow flowers? We must get rid of them all now, before they set seed.'

'Such a shame – it's awfully pretty,' she said. 'Do you know, in town they sell bunches of this at the railway stations? They call it "Summer Gold".'

I showed her how to grasp each plant at the base and tug it slowly so as not to leave any roots in the ground, and how to spot the young ones, too, that had not yet flowered. We began to walk slowly up the field next to one another, scanning the ground and pausing when one of us found a plant to pull up. One of the cats from the barn appeared, keeping its distance but alert for any harvest mice or voles we flushed from the grass.

Perhaps it was the fact that we had a job to do, or the way that we were walking in parallel, not looking at one another, but we began to talk of ourselves;

not in the way that we had before – an exchange of information, or gentle ribbing – but more seriously, more openly, as though there were not a quarter of a century between us.

'Why did you never marry, Connie?' I asked her. 'Was it the War?'

'I didn't lose a sweetheart, if that's what you mean. I suppose I never wanted to enough, or I would have made more effort, as all the other girls seemed to. I don't know. It all just seemed like such a frightful *faff*.'

'What was the War like? Was it dreadful? John says –'

'Oh darling, please don't make me talk about it. It was all such a long time ago.'

I decided not to be put out by the rebuff; after all, her tone was cheerful rather than abrupt.

'Well … were you ever in love?'

'Oh, masses of times. I find it passes quite quickly, as long as you keep your head.'

'What's it like?'

'Oh, well. A bit like champagne, and a bit like a bad case of influenza. It puts you on your back and turns you into a damned fool.'

I laughed. 'But don't you regret not getting married?'

'Not one bit.'

'Didn't you want babies?'

'I thought I did once, but now I think I just wanted them because you're supposed to. You know – because everyone does.'

There was something exhilarating about hearing her speak so forthrightly about the kind of things I hadn't even dared wonder about in my diary, let alone say out loud. It was irresistible somehow.

'But how can you tell the difference? You know, between wanting them because you really want them, and wanting them so as to fit in with everyone else?'

'Oh! Well, now you're asking.'

I thought for a moment. 'Perhaps – perhaps it's like being in love; Mary used to say you just *know*. Perhaps if you're even wondering whether you want to get married and have babies, it means that you don't.'

She laughed. 'Or perhaps it just means you're the kind of person who thinks too hard about things.'

I straightened up for a moment and tried to fasten my hair better, away from the perspiration on the back of my neck.

'I don't know how to stop, though.'

'Stop what?'

'Thinking too hard. I don't know how else to be.' I was surprised to feel my eyes swim with sudden tears.

'Oh Edie, you don't need to be any different at all, don't you know that?' She shaded her eyes to look at me, a fistful of ragwort limp in one glove. 'You're utterly exquisite just as you are.'

'No, I'm not, Connie, and you know it. If I was, I'd be popular like you, and I'm not.'

She didn't say 'But everyone likes you!', for which I was grateful. 'Look. Other people are fools, Edie – you can't use them as a measure. Especially around here.'

'What do you mean?'

'Oh, just that … in out-of-the-way places it's hard to be – different. You'd be quite normal in London, I promise you that.'

This seemed very unlikely to me, but I let it go, pondering instead her advice about not using other people's opinions as a measure. There was something valuable in it for me, I felt, if I could only work out how to apply it; but how else was one to learn about oneself other than by trying to perceive one's appearance, and one's character, through others' eyes?

'If it counts for anything, Edie, I think you're terrific. You're by far my favourite new friend.'

'Do you mean that?'

'By *miles*, darling. I'd be long gone, and probably bothering all the farmers at Blaxford and beyond by now, if you and I hadn't met. And then I wouldn't know ragwort from sowthistle, or speedwell from forget-me-nots; I wouldn't be able to say what a landrail sounded like, or a skylark; I wouldn't know any of the marvellous rhymes you've taught me, or the local legends, or *anything*.'

We worked in silence for a while as I cautiously turned over the kind things she'd said. I wanted to remember her words exactly, but I wasn't quite ready to believe them, so new a sensation had they brought. I had grown used to making do with my own company, and in any case it would have done me no good to realise that I was lonely – far better simply to 'buck up', as Frank would say whenever I looked glum. So the possibility that I had a friend who thought well of me was something I still felt a little cautious about.

'You miss your sister Mary, don't you?' Connie said after a while.

'All the time.'

'Doesn't she visit?'

'She's busy now, I suppose, with the house and the baby. And anyway, Mother says Clive doesn't like her to. He likes her to be at home. I see her at my grandparents' sometimes, and I go over with Mother to visit now and again – but it's not the same.'

'No, I can see that.'

'She used to be so much fun. And she was so excited to be getting married. Now she just looks tired.'

'You don't like this Clive much, do you?'

'No. Well – I don't know. Mother says I'm jealous.'

'And are you?'

'I suppose, a bit. He was always coming to the house and taking Mary out for walks or to the pictures, and I wasn't allowed to go. And now he has her all the time, and I can't ask her anything.'

'What do you want to ask her, Edie?'

'I – I don't know.'

By the time we had weeded about half of Horse Leasow the sun was reddening the backs of our necks and the barrow was heaped high. Together we pushed it back to the yard for Doble to burn, and went inside for something to eat. The men had already had their dinner, but Mother had left bread and cheese and a bowl of hard-boiled eggs on the table under a cloth.

We ate with the wireless on, and afterwards I carried our plates to the sink while Connie took the leftover food back to the pantry. A few of the bricks were broken in there and I could hear them clinking as her feet moved over them; could tell, in fact, that she had paused to scan our shelves of home-made preserves. I hoped she didn't linger over the tins of peas and tomato soup and condensed milk, which I could guess she wouldn't approve of; I tried to imagine Mother's face if Connie were ever to write anything critical of us in one of her magazines.

'Will you show me upstairs, Edie? I've never seen the rest of the house,' she said, emerging from the pantry as I was drying our plates.

'Haven't you really? Of course, come up. There's not much to see, though.'

'Oh, you know me. I like these old houses. There's something so magical about them.'

I wondered if she'd say the same in the depths of winter when the kitchen was the only room in the house where you didn't need to wear woollen gloves, or during a wet autumn when our clothes stank of mildew and storms tore hanks of old thatch from the roof.

We climbed the steep and creaking stairs, Connie stopping to remark on the wormy, battered oak of the treads smoothed by centuries of feet. She thought them rather lovely – though Mother wanted them replacing. 'One day one of us'll put a foot clear through,' she sometimes said.

The stairs led directly into the room where Mother and Father slept, and I hastily pulled the counterpane over their disordered bed and pushed the chamber pot out of sight. But Connie made straight for the fireplace, which had over it the traces of a painted pediment, very faded and incomplete where some of the plaster had flaked off to reveal the bricks beneath. I watched as she ran her fingertips over it; it was as though I was suddenly seeing the room, so familiar, so ordinary, through her eyes.

'Early seventeenth century, I'm sure of it!' she breathed.

I showed her the beam with an ornate 'G.M.' carved into it by my great-great-grandfather, and the rings on the floor of the empty chamber above the old dairy from the great wheels of cheese that had once been stored there. We peeked into Frank's untidy room with its giddily sloping floor, still with a kite pinned to the wall despite his age; and Mary's old room with its faded wallpaper, now the place where we kept spare blankets and linen and winter greatcoats, and still where I went to sleep if I was feeling particularly desolate, as I often did on the day or two just before the Curse.

'I suppose being small, with such tiny windows, helps keep the bedrooms warmer – after all, only your parents' room has a fireplace.'

'Oh, we hardly ever use it. Father says it's unhealthy to sleep in warm rooms. I expect really it would cost too much in firewood,' I said.

In my room she peered out through the little deep-set window, doubtless orientating her position in the house by the yard and horse-pond; and then she set to examining my books, which were set in piles on my writing desk, since the gable end of the house often became damp over winter and I didn't want them to spoil.

'*Swallows and Amazons*, yes, and Masefield, and dear old Jefferies, and John Clare. No Williamson ... You've read *Tarka*, though? Surely you have. Such a brilliant man, and with a lot of good ideas. I met him at a garden party once, raising funds for a political party. Oh, and what about Waugh? Though perhaps you're a little young – well, I'll write home for one or two of his, and you can see how you get on.'

I sat on the bed feeling backward and childish, something I rarely felt around Connie. I was the bookworm of the Mather family, the one real reader in the house, but just then I felt as though I knew nothing about literature at all.

'Do you know a lot of authors, Connie?'

'Oh no, not really. I wouldn't say I *know* Mr Williamson, we just had a chin-wag over a couple of gin slings. He probably wouldn't even remember me. I met Henry Massingham too, once. Such a fine man. It was his articles on rural crafts and home cultivation that helped me to see what my life's work should be. I told him so at the time.'

'Connie – when are you going back to London?'

She straightened up and turned around. 'Well – I'm not sure, darling. Don't say you're tired of me already; I'm not ready to return to Tooting just yet. In fact, do you know, I've rather grown to like it here. Perhaps I'll stay, and marry some ruddy-cheeked rural swain.'

I smiled at that. 'I'm not tired of you, Connie, of course not. But – could I come and visit, do you think? When you go back?'

'A trip to town? Marvellous idea! Am I to take it you've never visited London before?'

I shook my head. 'Market Stoundham's the furthest I've ever been.'

'Well, you must, in that case. After the harvest has been safely gathered in, perhaps? You could come on the train.'

I couldn't imagine being trusted to make the journey alone, but perhaps she could speak to Mother and persuade her. After all, Mary would doubtless have been allowed to go at my age.

'September can be a marvellous time to come, with the gas lamps lit in the evenings and the leaves on the plane trees turning yellow,' she continued. 'I'll ask Ada, too, shall I? We can make it a ladies' week-end.'

She must have seen something cross my face because she laughed then.

'Oh – just you and I, Edie? Yes, whyever not!'

Our barley was well along now, flaxen from a distance and with the beards tipping over almost as we watched. The wheat, too, was ripening: the stalks were still blue-green, but the tops of the ears were fading to a greenish-yellow, a tint that would become richer and spread down the ears as they fattened to finally gild the stalks and leaves. Then the sound of the cornfields would alter: dry, they would susurrate, whispering to Father and John that it was nearly time. The glory of the farm then, just before harvest: acres of gold like bullion, strewn with the sapphires of cornflowers and the garnets of corn poppies and watched over from on high by larks.

But not yet. We still needed more rain, for the land was thirsty from the year before and the streams and field drains were still low. And while we waited for it to ripen, the corn could become knee-sick, fall prey to wireworms, earcockle, stinking smut, take-all or a thousand other plagues. It could be laid low by storms, spoil in the barn or simply fail, times being what they were, to make a good price.

That evening at supper, Father held forth on the Wheat Act, which, he said, was merely a tariff in disguise, the money to guarantee prices coming from a tax on British flour at the mills. He had been to a Farmers' Union meeting in Monks Tye that afternoon, and his fettle was up.

'And who's to say they won't betray us again as they did before?' he said as he ate. 'They walk all over the little man, they allus have.'

'You can't trust politicians, George. They lie and lie,' Connie said. She had stayed on to eat with us, although I wasn't quite sure if she'd been invited or had simply not left. 'They'll tell you the sky is green if they think it'll win them a vote. We should have proper import controls to protect our native English farmers – it's the only way. There are advertisements in the newspapers now for Argentine beef, brought over in refrigerated ships.'

I glanced up to see how Father would take her interjection. None but John or Grandfather joined in with talk on farming matters; not Doble, not even Frank yet, and certainly not a woman. If he should reprimand her – well, I didn't think I could bear it. I felt the blood rush to my cheeks at the thought.

'Happen you're right, Constance,' Father said, looking at her speculatively. 'Wheat's less than five pound a tonne, yet we're bringing in flour from Canada now, and barley from Czechoslovakia's fetching double what ours is, straight off the boat. That can't be right.'

John had stopped eating and sat looking at Connie, his bone-handled knife and one of our old tin forks held lightly in his hands.

'They do say import controls would mean ordinary people would pay more in the shops for food, though,' he said.

'But this country *must* be able to feed itself without relying on imports,' Connie said, 'and that means ensuring decent, honest Englishmen like you, George, can continue to farm.'

Father nodded. 'Why, it was barely worth harvesting at all in '30; I might as well have let the corn rot in the fields for the little I got for it, and for all the work I put in. It'll take more than a few of their marketing boards to turn it around and make farming pay. It's enough to break a man's spirit, I'll tell you that straight.'

'That's true enough,' said John. 'But it seems to me you want what's not possible: you want the government not to meddle, but then again you want 'em to protect prices.'

Grandfather cleared his throat, and I wondered if he might interject. But whatever his opinion was on the matter, he kept it to himself.

'Whitehall simply cannot underwrite prices indefinitely while wheat continues to fall on the world market,' Connie continued, after a moment. 'It makes no economic sense.'

I wondered which of the local farmers she had got her opinions from, for while she might have been clever, after such a short time in the countryside I was sure she could not yet have formed them herself.

'No, we must look to our own,' Father said decisively. 'Especially when times are hard.'

'That's why I believe there should be a new Agricultural Bank, to help farmers,' Connie replied. 'And it must be run by farmers themselves, not by the – well, not by international financiers.'

It was beginning to grow dark when Connie left that night. She and Father talked on while Mother and I cleared away; Doble and Grandfather lingered, too, but John said he needed Frank's help to clean the horses' feet, and so took him from the room. From the backhouse I caught bits and pieces, but I had long grown used to farming talk and so I let my mind wander, picturing London with Connie: Horse Guards Parade, and shopping emporiums; tea at a Lyons' Corner House, and the British Museum. I sometimes wonder, if the visit had happened, whether it would have been anything like my imaginings. I have still never visited London, and so have had no means to find out.

There was a bedtime trick I had discovered, which involved lying on my stomach with my right leg crooked up, and that night, in bed, I allowed myself the secret pleasure of it. I tried to think of Alf, for surely he was my sweetheart, but my mind refused to picture him. In the end there was just an image of John's strong hand wrapped around the handle of his knife.

VII

The weather seemed to have fallen into a pattern: the days dawned fair and warm, clouded over, and then each afternoon came the sound of thunder somewhere far away. And yet it didn't rain, and the air stayed humid and close.

One morning I came downstairs to find the landrail in the kitchen, peering about inquisitively and making short runs under the table and between the chairs. It had grown since I'd last seen it, its newly dappled back, pale chest and grey head cleaner and more distinct.

Mother was kneeling by the range and jiggling the handle of the ash pan, which often became stuck.

'It was at the back door, Edie, and the cats are about. I had to let it in,' she said. Just then it looked at me, flipped back the lid of its head and uttered its unearthly *crex-crex*.

'It'll drive me round the twist if it keeps doing that. You'll have to take it further out – far enough so it doesn't come back.'

I knelt down by Mother, still half asleep, and it ran to me and pecked at my hands. 'I haven't anything for you,' I murmured. But it flustered its wings suddenly, and even as I flinched and rocked back I found it settling on my thighs like a hen.

'Well,' said Mother, sliding the ash pan out and standing up, 'happen as you have yourself a familiar, Edith June.'

'A familiar?'

She laughed. 'A pet, at any rate.'

I stood up, and reluctantly it allowed itself to be tipped from my lap.

'I'll take it to Far Piece when I've had breakfast.'

'And when you've done that you might give the floor a mop, too.'

'Is there any porridge?'

'Keeping warm on the range.'

I took a bowl and a spoon from the dresser. 'Can I have golden syrup?'

'You may.'

I fetched the tin from the pantry, brought it to the table and levered the sticky lid up with my spoon.

'Can I have a new dress?'

'You don't need a new dress.'

'I do. I've grown.'

'You had two of Mary's not six months ago. You've not grown that much since then.'

'Why can't I have anything new?'

'What's brought this on, Edie? You're not the sort to care about clothes.'

'Well, perhaps I am. I might be. Anyway, it's not fair.'

'Fair doesn't come into it, as well you know. There isn't the money for fripperies.'

Surreptitiously I spooned more syrup onto my cooling porridge and mixed it in. 'Mary always got new clothes.'

'Course she did, Edie, she came along first, and we had to clothe her somehow. And anyway, times were easier back then than they are now.'

Crex-crex, crex-crex, creaked the landrail, and pecked around my bare toes.

Mother came to sit down with me at the kitchen table and sighed.

'Mother did say you were tetchery. Tell me, Edie, what's this about?'

I had stopped eating my porridge and was just playing with it now, pushing it around my bowl, something I knew that she hated.

'Is it that you want to go to a dance after all? Frank did say you were feeling a bit stuck at home. Well, I've been thinking about it, and perhaps your father's right after all. There's a band coming to the village hall at Monks Tye at the end of the month, and Frank's said Alfie'll take you, and he'll ask someone along, too. I know he's sweet on Sally Godbold – you know, from the end cottage on Back Lane?'

'Frank said — ? What's Frank been saying behind my back?'

'Nothing, Edie! Nothing! He just mentioned that you might like to go. It'll be a jazz band, he said. Or there's the village hop in Blaxford? I'll wager your Constance would take you to that if you asked.'

'But I'm not interested! I don't feel stuck at home!'

'Oh! Well, that's good. I'm ever so glad. Why didn't you say?'

I closed my eyes briefly. I loved Mother, but recently I had begun to find her insufferably obtuse at times. All one could do was change the subject.

'She was here until late last night — Connie, I mean.'

'That she was. I offered her Doble to see her home, but she said she's got a lamp on her bicycle now.'

'Do you like her now?'

'Well, she's got her head screwed on more than some, I'll say that. Your father says she talked a lot of sense last night.'

'About farming?'

'And politics.'

I considered this. The two were the same in our house, or nearly; but while in those years there was more and more talk about the country in general, and Europe too, I paid it little mind, for it all seemed so far away and could never affect us. That's what I thought back then — although of course I never read the newspapers, so the world seemed to me for the most part a good place. But although my ignorance made for a pleasant life, growing up has taught me that you can never go back to more innocent times, or behave as though something complicated is as simple as you once thought it. It doesn't work.

'You didn't like Connie at first, though, Mother.'

'That's true enough.'

'So what changed?'

'Well, she came looking to speak to John about the horses and I sat her down and told her a thing or two. She took it on board, to her credit – there's not many as'll do that.'

'So now you're friends?'

'I wouldn't go that far, but someone had to teach her some manners if she's to go around bothering folk. Otherwise she'll get nowhere fast, and we'll have her on our hands forever and always.'

John tapped at the kitchen window, and leaned in at the open casement.

'Morning, Ada; morning, Edith,' he said. 'I've a job for you, unless your mother needs you.'

'Look, John!' I said, pointing at the landrail with my spoon.

'Yes, I saw. Best keep it out the way of the cats.'

'I'm going to take it to Far Piece. What d'you want me to do?'

'Well, to my mind Seven Acres may be fallow, but we'll want the use of it next year, God willing, so I've harrowed it and now I aim to cross-plough. Can you fetch some elder for the horses? I'm going there now.'

I walked to Far Piece through the cornfields, the landrail tucked peaceably under my arm and Mother's pruning-shears in my skirt pocket banging against my thigh. Elder was plentiful in the hedgerows there; when I was as far from the house as I could get I set the bird down in the rustling wheat and cut armfuls of green leaves for John to weave into Moses and Malachi's bridles against flies and clegs. The landrail investigated each of the leaves I dropped, and I knew, as it pecked around my feet, that it would try to follow me back; and so when I had gathered enough leaves I ran, my loose hair streaming: first along the margin of Far Piece, and then I skirted Newlands into Seven Acres, where John, following the horses beneath a hot blue sky, had started the first furrow in the hard task of cross-ploughing, a job that would take him a week.

I can't remember a time before Moses and Malachi, although Mary could just about recall the team that came before. That pair was old enough in 1915 that they were spared the trenches, although the Remount Department requisitioned the pony we had then, and many of the horses from Rose Farm, Hullets and Ixham Hall.

To me, Moses and Malachi represented the very definition of horseflesh, exemplars from which all others deviated in size or colour, temperament or strength. How many times did I ride on their broad backs when they were in harness, going to the fields and back; how many times did I watch John groom their glossy chestnut coats, or just stand with them in the stables, whispering my trivial secrets into their twitching ears and stroking their great necks? They were more than just horsepower, they were our wealth, our pride. And we loved them as animals, too — each of us, no doubt, in different ways. I can still remember how I envied Mother's gentle voice with them, how she'd blow into their nostrils and let them mumble at her neck.

Once, at the table, Frank had asked Mother if she was a true horsewoman — if she really had 'the power', as it was called. We were fascinated by the secret ritual we had heard tell of, something about fern seeds and a toad's bone floating upriver — though Mary said we were confusing it with witches, and the way they were once 'swum' to see if they sank. Granfer, no matter how pressed, would reveal nothing of horse magic, but some of the old wives in the village muttered about it, and Frank had gleaned bits and pieces from other boys at school.

Of course, we knew it was poppycock — that over-willing a horse might be difficult, but there must be a science to it, or at least an art, and that it was something to do with the tiny bottles and bags of herbs we knew John secreted about his person. I suppose we just wanted to know if Mother had been initiated, all the same, and whether she really was as rare a woman as we wanted her to be; or whether she had just attempted to do a man's job for a few years, in the War.

'Oh, give over, Frank,' she'd replied, and changed the subject; but I saw that John was giving her a long, level look.

'You must miss it, though,' Frank continued blithely. 'Being useful, I mean.'

'She doesn't miss it,' said Father. 'She's had you three to keep her out of mischief – isn't that right, Ada?'

Then, as Doble began to hum under his breath, John excused himself, got up and walked from the room.

That afternoon, after I had swept and mopped the floors and seen to the hens and Mother had weeded the vegetable-garden and done some mending, she and I went to the village. We walked up the lane past Hulver Wood and turned right at the four-a-leet, both of us glancing over at Hullets as we passed; smoke was issuing from the end chimney, and I found myself trying to picture what it was like inside. I wondered how many children were living there, and settled on two: a girl my own age, and a younger boy. I allowed myself a daydream in which they became my friends, and we played together. I could show them the farm, and let them meet Moses and Malachi, perhaps lend them my books: there was a nice, useful feeling about that, and I enjoyed imagining how grateful they'd be.

We reached the Stound and crossed it on the packhorse bridge. When we were almost at the draper's, Mother woke me from my reverie.

'I thought we'd stop in here, Edie, and look at the patterns. What do you think? And you can choose some material if you like.'

'Patterns?'

'For a dress. Your father says you're to have a new one for the fete.'

'Did he really? Oh Mother – thank you!'

I took her arm, and smiled up at her, although she didn't return my smile. And then we went in, the shop bell tinkling gaily over our heads.

'Mrs Mather, how lovely, do come in. And young Edith too, what a treat!'

Mrs Eleigh came out from behind the counter and held both our hands, limply. She was a widow, and Mary and I thought her impossibly dried-up, although she can't have been more than fifty years old. Not much taller than a child, she peered up at us both near-sightedly.

'Miss FitzAllen isn't here, though, I'm ever so sorry. Though you're welcome to wait.'

'Oh, but we're not here to see Constance,' said Mother. 'Edie here needs a new dress.'

'Oh, certainly! Certainly! What a pleasure. Something ready-made? We have some rather pretty girls' frocks...'

'We'd like to see your ladies' patterns. And will you measure her, please, while we're here?'

While Mother flicked through a pattern book, Mrs Eleigh ushered me into her little fitting-room, fishing a tape measure from the pocket of a lawn apron finely tucked and shirred to advertise her skills. I didn't want to be measured; I couldn't see why Mother couldn't do it when we got home. Besides, I wanted to look at the patterns with her. It was to be my dress, after all.

I took off my blouse, vest and skirt and waited with my arms crossed over my chest, wondering why it was that Mrs Eleigh would leave me so tactfully to undress alone when she was going to come in and see me in my drawers anyway. 'That's right, dear,' she said, coming in and pulling the curtain back into place. 'Now, both arms out.'

Looking down at her I wondered, as she slipped the tape around my ribs, how many bosoms she had seen, there in the corner of her little shop. All Elmbourne's women must have passed through here, I supposed; her nimble fingers must have taken in and let out thousands of skirts, blouses and dresses and measured for hundreds of liberty bodices, combinations and girdles over the years. She knew all the shameful secrets of our womanly flesh; and yet, like a priest, she would never, ever tell.

'Mrs Mather, your daughter needs a brassière,' she called through the curtain to the shop floor.

Mother came into the little curtained room then, and the two women stood looking at me critically. I hunched my shoulders and tried to keep my arms down by my sides.

'Her bust is quite developed, do you see? How old is she now?'

'She's fourteen. Do you think it's quite necessary yet? Mary was nearly sixteen, I'm sure of it.'

'Oh yes, I would say she needs support. Look –' and she lifted my left breast in her chill hand, and let it drop. 'Besides, a brassière will help give her a neat figure for her new dress. Don't you think?'

I wasn't accustomed to thinking much about my figure. We had no full-length looking-glass at Wych Farm, something Mary had often complained of; but apart from when I was ill or hurt I felt for the most part as though my body didn't really exist. I lived, I suppose, in my head: thinking, imagining or worrying. Yet other people had bodies that were *them*, it seemed to me – that spoke who they were, did their work in the world. Most of the time mine was nothing to do with me; and sometimes – with Alf, for example – I felt as though I became invisible inside it. But why, if my body barely mattered to me, did I now feel so strangely ashamed?

'She can wear an old one of Mary's. There's still a box of her things at home,' Mother said, and folded her arms. It was clear Mrs Eleigh was not going to make the extra sale.

'And how is your Mary? It seems only yesterday that she was in here, discussing her *trousseau*. And you a grandma now! How the time does fly.'

'She's middling. Her confinement – well. It wasn't easy, as I expect you've heard. But it'll come right in time; and in any case, she dotes on that baby, she really does.'

'And that's the main thing. They're such precious angels when they're tiny, aren't they? It makes it all wholly worthwhile.'

'It does.'

'And her Clive, is he...' – her voice dropped several tones – 'is he *understanding*?'

'Are any of them?'

Both women laughed.

'Well. You can get dressed again now, dear,' said Mrs Eleigh, and they left me alone.

I expect they thought I didn't know the first thing about sex, but I did, of course. There had been a boy at school who was notorious for taking his thing out and frightening the girls with it – apart from Hilda Cousens, that is, who was said to let boys see her private parts for sixpence. As for what it felt like, I had asked Mary about it when she was expecting. She told me that usually there were parts that felt nice and parts that felt horrible, but that when it was happening to you, you could tell yourself a romantic story that made it all right – and that, in any case, it was soon over.

'But why do you let Clive do anything that feels horrible?' I'd asked her. 'Why don't you stop it?' – but she had just laughed.

'You mustn't complain, or break the man's concentration, or it won't be a success,' she explained. 'One day you'll understand.'

Mother let me decide between two patterns that day. One had short, puffed sleeves and a sweetheart neckline; the other had a wide collar and ruching just below each shoulder. That was the one I chose. Mrs Eleigh measured out the cloth – a sage-green poplin patterned with sprigs, since I wasn't allowed to have scarlet – and we settled our account and left, the shop bell tinkling again over our heads. But instead of feeling excited about the new frock I was to have, all I felt was unease.

VIII

It isn't easy to conceive, when you are growing up, that the world could be any different than how you find it, for the things you first encounter are what normality comes to consist of, and only the passage of time teaches you that your childhood could have been in any way otherwise.

Even so, it was impossible in those years not to know that there was an army of men missing from the fields and farms. Some were our fathers and uncles; many were farm boys or horsemen. We knew them by the empty pews at St Anne's and the seats untaken at the Bell & Hare; the hay-rakes and scythes leaning unused in the barns; the ricks thatched indifferently for want of skilled men. Although most farmers themselves were excused, the War left gaps in the land and the working of it, and even if you were born in peacetime, as I was, you could feel it everywhere.

Mary, Frank and I would always have had to help in the fields, for the work on a farm is never finished, and can always be done better with extra hands, or finer weather, or more time. But had Tipper and Uncle Harry's names not been written in gold in the Book of Honour in the church, perhaps our hedgerows would have been better managed, for in those years they began to creep out into the fields. In spring the crops might have been better weeded, and the clods harrowed more thoroughly from the winter clay. The ditches might have been cleared more often and thus kept the lowest-lying fields from becoming stoachy, and all these things might have meant that we had better yields.

One morning Father set Frank and me to hoe and hand-pull Crossways, while he and Mother went to work on Far Piece. It was nearing the end of July and the wheat was golden, the barley ash-blonde; but despite all we'd done earlier in the year, amongst it all grew corn poppies and cornflowers, dockweed, thistles, wild onion, mousetail, cleavers, shepherd's needle, charlock, rye brome and corn buttercup, and before we could harvest, as many weeds as possible had to be pulled, for too much green in the sheaves would make them heat and spoil in the rick. It was the kind of work I hated: mindless and monotonous, hard on the back and hands, and it went on for days. But there was no sense in complaining: the task had to be done if we were to farm, and there was only us to do it. And so we went.

Crossways was a big field, and oddly shaped. It had once been two fields, both belonging to Hullets; Father had bought them after the War, when I suppose Hullets' fortunes were first falling – though we none of us knew that yet. He and John had borrowed the Fordson we later bought to grub up a hedge of field maples, making one large field that was easier to work. It proved since then to be some of our best land.

On the third day of weeding Connie joined us, her hair hidden by a red peasant scarf. We laughed at her at first, Frank and I, for not knowing one plant from another, and for her difficulties in keeping her big feet between the narrow rows; yet by the time we stopped work she was keeping pace with us.

'It's just an amusement to her, Ed,' Frank said when at last she left to bicycle home. 'A day in the fields. It's something for her to write down and tell city folk about.'

'I think you're being unfair on her. She worked hard to-day.'

'She won't be back. You mark my words.'

But she was. Connie helped us weed Crossways, and then The Lottens too, and despite her reddening arms and face, despite her height that must have meant she felt each stoop more keenly than I did, she never once complained. She joined in when we sang, too, for we usually sang while working: 'Green Bushes', and 'Come All You Bold Britons', or perhaps something from the music halls, her clear, warm contralto ringing out over our more artless voices in the warm summer air.

'How are you enjoying your time in the country, Constance?' Frank asked her late one afternoon. She had told him time and again to call her Connie, but he wouldn't; still, at least he no longer addressed her as Miss FitzAllen, as though she was a teacher, I thought.

'Very well! I feel I get stronger every day, and healthier. London seems like a different world to me now.'

'Don't you miss anything about it?'

'Not a thing, if I'm honest. Drawing-room conversations? Dressing for dinner? Everyone rushing to see the latest avant-garde play straight from the Continent, or opine on some ridiculous modernist art? None of it seems quite real compared to life here.'

'It's queer, though – most people here would bite off your hand for the chance to live in the city.'

'Well, then, they'd be fools. The rich there are boring, the poor for the most part live intolerably, and the intellectual set are degenerates and inverts, to a fault. Sex! Good Lord, they're obsessed with it – almost as much as they're obsessed with themselves.'

I laughed to see Frank's face, for while I was growing used to Connie's forthrightness, he had turned red as a beet.

'Oh, Connie, you mustn't tease him,' I said. 'He doesn't know you yet.'

'You two are *lambs*. I apologise for my vulgarity. Here, Frank – shake my hand, won't you?' – and a little shyly, but grinning, he did.

'So you're writing a book about us?'

'A series of articles for now. Don't worry, I shan't use your names.'

'Well, you can if you like. I should quite enjoy being famous, I think.'

'Oh, really! Well, then, perhaps I will: "Introducing Frank Mather, flower of rural youth, model of our native breed."'

'You're teasing me again.'

'Perhaps I am – but you're learning to like it, I can tell.'

Father had set one of the village boys to scare pigeons, and from Greenleaze came the sound of a wooden clapper and his faint shout: '*Oy, oy, oy!*'

Frank stooped and cast a big flint underarm to the edge of the field. 'More stones than corn this year, near enough. You'd think we'd sown gravel.'

I laughed. 'You can see why farmers used to think the earth grew them. You can clear a field as many times as you like, but still they come up.'

'What about the ones with the holes through?' asked Connie. 'Aren't they supposed to be good luck?'

'Adder-stones, they're called, or hag-stones. John's the one to tell you all about those.'

'Oh, now look what I've found – !' and she crouched, and before either of us could warn her not to she scooped up a late clutch of baby larks and held them out to us, struggling, in her hands.

By Saturday, John had finished with Seven Acres and Father had trimmed all our hedges that faced the road, so that laden wagons – our own and our neighbours' – could pass comfortably through the narrow lanes. We still had some wheat to weed, but the barley was nearly all clear, and while it would all need to be done once more before harvest it felt as though we had achieved something, that we had, by our toil, helped a little to safeguard the crops on which our future depended. And so Mother made beef with boiled potatoes and cabbage and a jam roly-poly, and invited Connie to eat with us again.

I laid the big table in the dining-room, for Mother said she didn't want Connie casting her beady eye over everything she did in the kitchen, as she had last time. When the family had taken their places Mother and I brought the food through, and then John and Doble filed in and sat down. Father, at the head of the table, began to carve, and when we had all been served I shut my eyes and prepared to say Grace.

'I should like to hear our guest say Grace to-day, Edith,' said Father. 'Constance, would you oblige?'

'Oh – well, I don't – I mean I haven't –'

I glanced up and saw that Connie was actually blushing, unless it was just the effects of four days' sun.

'I'm so sorry, George – but I'm an atheist,' she said. There was a silence in which I could almost feel the air of the room pressing on my eardrums.

'Well, I'll be darned,' said Father, at length. 'Happen as I'll say Grace, then, to-day. But mind you bow your head, Constance FitzAllen. I'll have no disrespect.'

'Tell me, Ada,' said Connie when he'd finished, pouring gravy liberally over her plate, 'do you know much about the people who're living at the empty place – Hullets, it's called, isn't it?'

'Oh! Well. We're – we're not sure,' said Mother. 'Are we, George?'

'It's a family, from what I've heard,' Connie continued. 'They're not from around here.'

'Can't say as we know a great deal about their history, Constance,' John said.

'Oh yes, or so Violet – Mrs Eleigh – told me. Ada, this cabbage is delicious. Did you fry it in the beef dripping after it was boiled?'

'So it's common knowledge, then – about Hullets?' Mother asked. 'We knew there were people there; we saw smoke, so John went over in case someone had fired the thatch. He said they were decent enough – didn't you, John? – just that they'd fallen on hard times.'

From Frank's bland expression I could see that none of this was a surprise to him. I wondered when he'd found out, and why he hadn't told me; when we'd been weeding Crossways, Hullets had been in view nearly the whole time. Yet he'd said nothing at all.

'Oh yes, everyone knows,' Connie said. 'The two Rose boys were the first to mention it, I think. At the Bell & Hare.'

'I might have known,' said Mother. 'Frank, what did I tell you about gossiping?'

'I didn't say anything!' he protested. 'Rose Farm borders Hullets, too; they probably found out about them themselves, just as we did.'

'Well, anyway, I'm going to pay them a visit tomorrow morning,' said Connie.

'Can I come?' I said. I still felt the injustice of their trespass, but my sense of curiosity about them was growing keen; and in any case, I just wanted to spend time with Connie. I didn't really mind what we did.

'You may not, young lady,' said Mother. 'Tomorrow's Sunday. We'll be at church.'

'After church?'

She gave me one of her looks.

'But why didn't you want anyone in the village to know about them, Ada?' asked Connie, helping herself to another potato and passing the dish to John.

'Ada's worried that people will be unchristian and move them on,' said Father. 'She's soft-hearted – that's what it is.'

'I sense you differ in your opinion, George?'

'Well, it's allus been more my view that charity begins at home.'

'I tend to agree with you,' said Connie. 'It's all terribly unfortunate, but the public assistance bill is already far too high.'

'Well, it's out of our hands now,' said Mother. 'But if they're still there tomorrow, do take them over something from the kitchen here, Connie. Whoever they are, I'll not see a family starve.'

'What are your politics, Constance, if you don't mind me asking?' John said, addressing himself to his plate.

'Well, I'm not a supporter of the Labour Party or the Conservatives these days, if that's what you mean. I gave Socialism a chance after the War, but since Labour failed I've rather abandoned the party system. I believe that this country requires a far more ... wholesale change.'

'Do you mean to say that you are neither for the Right nor the Left?'

'They're indivisible, to my mind. Progress is impossible without stability, and stability is impossible without progress. That's what I believe.'

That sounded like good sense, I thought, reaching for a second helping of beef, but Father stopped me with a warning glance. 'That girl will eat us out of house and home before long,' he sometimes grumbled to Mother, so that I would hear.

John continued: 'And what is the great change that our country requires, would you say?'

'Well, we're living through a depression that isn't of our own making,' she said, her voice suddenly practised, rather than spontaneous. 'We need a strong government to free us from our dependence on the international finance system – one which will act in the best interests of the British people, that will favour British manufacturing and farming, and ensure this never happens again. We need a British system of credit that benefits Britain alone, rather than lining the pockets of usurers and profiteers – and that means proper import quotas, and reform of our agricultural system. We must bring down national debt and return to full employment, of course; and we must look to the shires and their ancient traditions, not to the intellectual classes in the cities, for a new sense of national identity and pride. Places like here,' she said, smiling at all of us and sitting back, her little speech over.

'Hear, hear,' Father said.

'A strong government, you say? I'll wager I can guess who it is that you mean,' said John.

'The silly little fencing-master?' she laughed. 'Good Lord, no, you're quite wrong on that account.'

'And where do you see your place in all this?'

It was unlike John to ask so many questions, but Connie seemed to take it in good part. Yet despite her smiles and John's mild tone, something crackled invisibly in the stale air of the dining-room, and I could feel it. I wondered who on earth the fencing-master was.

'Well,' she said modestly, 'for now my aim is simply to be an observer, to set down the life of the countryside as I find it. It is for others to decide what course the country should take.'

'And yet you told me you were a Suffragette,' said Mother, quietly.

'Only in a very minor way – I didn't smash any windows or anything. I was just a little too young, more's the pity.'

John sat back, surprised; I looked at Frank, whose fork hung motionless half-way to his open mouth. I knew all about the brave Suffragettes, of course; Miss Carter had taught us about them at school. And Connie had been one – our very own Connie! I felt my admiration for her grow.

'Did you cast a vote last time, Ada?' Connie asked.

'I – I did.'

'Quite right. Every woman must,' she said, and smiled warmly. 'Don't worry, I shan't ask you which way.'

The air in the dining-room seemed to have become very still, although Connie seemed not to notice it. Doble, too, ate on stolidly, quite his usual self.

'Now, look you here, Constance,' said my father, wiping the last bit of gravy from his plate with some bread; 'I thank you for your help this week, but I must tell you that those views are not welcome here, and I won't have you talking like that again in this house. If Ada votes next time, it will be as I decide.'

IX

The first hymn at Sunday service was 'O God of Earth and Altar', one of my favourites, and that day I sang it with great vigour as though to make up for Connie's apostasy – or perhaps to bolster my own stolid, if rather unimaginative, faith. For I knew at the back of my mind that I was in some way susceptible to her; who could say whether she might already be having an effect?

Mother and Father hadn't seemed altogether shocked by her being an atheist, but I kept worrying away at it. To my mind only heathens didn't believe in God and heaven and the Devil and so forth – and only then because they hadn't yet heard the Good News. But Connie was not only English, she was the daughter of a minister; how could she just decide not to be a Christian any more?

The curious thing, too, was the fact that she had been to church at St Anne's on more than one occasion – I clearly remembered seeing her in a nearby pew in a skirt and sensible hat. Surely her hypocrisy put her at risk of even further damnation, if such a thing were possible.

The sermon that day was on the theme of Empire – the rector had a son in the Colonial Office, something he was very proud of – but try as I might I struggled to prevent my mind from wandering. Connie was nowhere to be seen; was she even at this moment at Hullets, meeting the family Mother said had fallen on hard times? What were they like?

'For just as we administer our colonies for their own benefit, so God, a kind father, lovingly corrects and punishes His flock,' the Reverend Woodgate intoned. 'For as the heathens have flowed unto us, and swelled our Empire, our own people still stream out into all lands. The effects of this are open to the dim guesses of all, while it baffles the most far-seeing calculation to determine what they will be. For our days are cast amidst events of great magnitude and a new import. Never was an Empire so extended as Britain's; never has a race been entrusted with such a mission as ours, the last to which, it may be surmised, the subjugation of the material world and the enlightenment of our subjects is committed; for it is our burden to educate, and our privilege to achieve the final destiny of Christ's kingdom on earth.'

Beside me Frank was fidgeting with his collar, which was too high and too tight. On the other side of him, Mother gazed impassively ahead; there had been hard words between her and Father after Connie had left the previous night. I'd come down in the morning to find that breakfast had not been laid out, and when I asked why Mother was still abed, Father snapped at me to 'leave her be'. At last she'd come down, dressed, when Meg was in harness, but I saw a bright mark on her cheekbone that had not been there before.

I don't think he was a wicked man, my father. Mother must have seen the good in him to have married him, and although he became more and more locked away from us by the secrets he kept through the years of my girlhood, he and I had once been close – and I never stopped believing that if I could only do or say the right thing, that closeness would one day return.

When I was very young – young enough not to be an annoyance – he would sometimes take me with him when he walked the fields on a Sunday afternoon. I've sometimes wondered if it caused Mary or Frank any jealousy to see him setting out with me on his shoulders, his two hands holding my little feet in their Sunday shoes, mine on the rough wool of his cap.

I don't remember much about those walks, excepting the last one he ever took me on. It was spring: the blackthorn hedges were white with blossom, and the air was just beginning to be warm. In the elms by the house the rookery was busy, and clutches of buttery primroses lined the hedge-banks in the lane.

As we crossed from The Lottens into Broad Field he swung me down from his shoulders and made me walk; probably I had been holding his ears, which always provoked him. I ran ahead, laughing to see two hares stop their boxing and race one another for the field's edge.

When I turned to tell him about the hares, I saw him sitting on the ground at the field margin, his arms around his knees. I ran back to him, and he smiled and sat me between his legs and said that we would sit awhile in the sunshine so that he could think. But after a few moments I felt his chest heave, like hiccups, and when I wriggled around in his arms I saw that he was crying, his lips drawn back in a rictus and his cheeks streaked with tears.

'Dadda! Dadda!' I cried in fear, and flung my arms around his neck; but though I begged him not to cry, he didn't stop, and so I wept too, his hand on my hot back no comfort and only the mechanical notes of hedge-sparrows and chiff-chaffs to break the sound of our sobs.

It can't have been more than a minute or two, although it felt – it still feels to me now – as though it went on for a long time. But at last he pushed me away, and took his handkerchief and wiped his face; and then he fished in his waistcoat pocket for his tobacco and began, with shaking hands, to fill his pipe.

'Go on, now, child,' he said gruffly. 'You know the way back to the house.'

'But are you still sad, Dadda?' I asked.

'Sad? What's there to be sad about? Go and tell your mother to make some tea; I'll be there directly. And Edie?'

'Yes, Dadda?'

He looked away from me, his mouth hardening to a line. 'Don't – don't you ever –'

'I won't – cross my heart,' I said; and I felt proud then to have been taken into his confidence, to know something about my father that nobody else in the world knew.

Of course, I was too young to have any real understanding of the secret I was keeping, and could not know how much better it would have been had Mother known of his distress.

After church, Mother and Mrs Godbold drew away from the rest of the people milling around the lych-gate and stood talking in low voices by the yew. Frank had gone off for a walk with Sally Godbold, and Alf and Sidney Rose were showing John the new motor-cycle and sidecar they'd driven over in. Doble had decided to walk back; on days when his rheumatics were bad he said the hard seats of the trap played havoc with what he called his 'natomy'.

At last Mother was ready. John and Father sat at the front and she and I climbed in behind, then John clicked his tongue to Meg and we started back.

'What did Ivy Godbold want with you, Ada?' Father asked over his shoulder. 'I hope you weren't gossiping about family matters.'

'No, George. Just some advice. She found an old bottle when they were taking up the flags in their kitchen to lay some linoleum, and when she lifted it the neck broke.'

'A witch-bottle?' I asked.

'They're just good-luck charms, Edie,' said Mother. 'From a long time ago – back in the olden days.'

'They're women's foolishness,' said Father. 'What did you tell her to do with it?'

'I thought I might walk over there this afternoon,' Mother said. 'That is, unless you've any objection, George.'

No farm work was done on Sundays, of course, but after dinner Father liked to spend the afternoon walking the fields with John and Doble, checking the field drains and snares and discussing the progress of the crops. Not long after they'd set out that day, Mother left to walk over to Back Lane, leaving me and Frank in the parlour, where we were supposed to sit reading improving books. Frank had wanted to go with her to the Godbolds', but we were told in no uncertain terms that we were to remain behind.

'Shall we walk over to Hullets?' I asked the moment Mother had disappeared up the lane.

'Ed!' said Frank. 'You know we can't. We'd get in a world of trouble if anyone found out.'

'Just to see if she's there – Connie, I mean. Or if we see her leaving we could see if she wants to come here for – for some tea.'

'I'm sure we'll see her in the week, Ed. We can ask her about everything then.'

We read in silence for a while. I had a large, illustrated copy of *Christie's Old Organ* in my lap with *The Jungle Book* concealed inside. We had four O. F. Walton books, all given to me as school prizes, and they were without exception insufferably dull. I scanned the pages for a line of seven words, and, finding one, shut the book with a snap.

'Did you know Connie was an atheist, Frank?'

'No, but it doesn't wholly surprise me. She's contrary to a fault, or so I hear.'

'But how can you not believe in God, if you used to?'

'I don't know, Ed. Perhaps something terrible happened to her in the War, and she lost her faith. I wouldn't let it concern you, though; a person's religion is their own affair.'

I sighed.

'Sally told me about the bottle earlier,' Frank said after a while. 'She said her mother was taken bad about it.'

'Why, what happened?'

'Well, you're not supposed to break them in case you let the witchcraft out. Now she doesn't know what to do.'

'Who put it there in the first place?'

'No way of knowing. It was probably there ever since the place was built; lots of the old houses have them. People find all manner of things, you know: dried-up cats, horse skulls, shoes hundreds of years old.'

'Do we have anything magical, do you think?'

'Most likely. There's those circle patterns by the hearth, look – and that one on the big beam above your bed.'

This was true, for every night without fail I traced the daisy-shaped mark on the old wood above me to keep me safe while I slept, a silly ritual I knew I should break myself of but which I continued nevertheless to perform. But some of the pews at church had the same marks, too, so while their meaning was mysterious, they still felt rather everyday. But witch-bottles were fascinating: some were said to contain hair or nail parings, or sheep's urine, or even blood.

'If we did have a witch-bottle, where do you think it would be? Under the hearth, or in one of the walls, perhaps?'

'Don't you dare go picking off the plaster, Ed. Mother'll have a blue fit.'

'Why's she gone over to the Godbolds', anyway? Can't they decide what to do with it themselves?'

'Why d'you think, dimwit? Because she's a witch, and Granny is too, that's why – and it's about time you knew it.'

Dumbly I stared at him, but he just folded his arms. I couldn't tell if he was pulling my leg.

'She is not,' I said uncertainly.

'Is too. And you would be, if you weren't quite so slow-witted. They do say it runs in the blood.'

'Frank!'

'All right, I'm joking, I'm *joking*!' he said, laughing. 'Blimey, Ed, don't lose your rag.'

From outside the window then came a sudden and unmistakeable *crex-crex, crex-crex.*

'Oh Lord,' I said. 'The landrail's back.'

We both got up and went outside to find it pecking around boldly near the pigs. Frank was still laughing.

'You should name it, Ed,' he said.

'Don't be daft. It's not a pet.'

'Oh, come on – there's no getting rid of it now, unless the cats get it. You might as well get used to it.'

Hearing my voice, it had run to me and was inspecting my feet in their Sunday sandals. 'Well … is it a boy or a girl, would you say?'

'It's singing, after a fashion, so I suppose it must be male.'

'I name it Frank, then.'

'Oh no you don't. I'm not having it flapping around my ankles every time someone says my name.'

He had a point. 'All right, then. Edmund.'

'That's decided, then. It'll come to your call in no time, I'll wager – which will be helpful, seeing as you'll have to teach it to fly.'

'What do you mean?' I asked. The truth was I had never, to my knowledge, actually seen a landrail fly; they always ran along the ground.

'It'll want to be off on its travels when the weather turns. And anyway, it might need to escape the cats.'

'I can't teach a bird to fly, Frank!'

But again, he was ribbing me, and I saw it by his sudden grin.

'Oh, give over, will you. It'll work it out itself.'

I knelt down, and immediately it hopped up onto my lap. 'Hello, Edmund,' I said.

Frank, who had been disappointed not to be asked to inspect the fields with the men, wandered off to the barn to discover how many sulphur cartridges Doble had laid in to deal with the rabbits. Snaring or ferreting them was preferable, of course, for that way the meat wasn't spoiled, but when numbers were high we gassed them in their burrows, as all our neighbours did. It was a task Frank always helped with since, for reasons connected with the War, John refused to take part.

I wandered along the boundary of Great Ley and Middle Ley, roughly in the direction of Hullets – though I didn't plan to cross the road. If I happened to see Connie pass by on her bicycle, so be it; but Frank was right, we'd find out more soon enough. Edmund followed after me, and I let him, slowing every so often if I saw that he had stopped to peck at something, or fallen behind.

At the circle of oaks I ducked into their dappled shade and greeted them all individually with a pat of my hand; it was much cooler there than in the sunlit fields around. I sat cross-legged, my back against one of the trunks, and as Edmund settled contentedly in my lap I looked out through half-closed eyes at Crossways' rippling acres of gold.

I wondered if I should tell Connie the stories of the six oaks for her book, or whether bringing her here might be wrong in some way, as Mary kissing Clive here had surely been. Above me, lost in foliage, a robin was singing quietly to itself under its breath; not in full-throated song, but as though practising, working out the notes as a man might hum a tune he aims to learn. In a few months, I reflected, it would be the only bird singing in the valley; the throstle would call out a few phrases in midwinter, but for the most part there'd be little music between harvest-time and spring. But spring would come, and the ground would warm again, as it always did, and all the summer birds, including Edmund, would one by one return to mate and build their nests. The bluebells would come out in Hulver Wood and our bees would wake and begin to forage; the grass would grow tall in the hay meadows and be mown, the peas would blossom once more and smell sweet. And the cornfields would be green, then grow tall and turn golden; and so would pass the next year, and the next.

I closed my eyes and let myself sink into sleep, and I dreamed about the horse-pond. Not the one near the house, which had once been part of a moat – so Grandfather said – and was now colonised by garrulous ducks; the other one in the middle of Greenleaze, which we used on hot days now and then if the team was too far from the house. From the margin of the field it just looked like a clump of alders, but the trees hid a pond whose water was shaded and brackish and black.

I dreamed I was inside the pool, deep down under the water – but I wasn't drowning; in fact I felt calm and safe. There with me was Grandma's gold-rimmed tea service, which I knew I must somehow bring up or it would spoil. But I didn't want to leave the water for the loud, hot world above, and then it was not teacups I was holding but dead frogs, pale and bloated and rotten, and I fought my way up through the lassitude of sleep to surface, gasping, among the roots of the oaks.

We had a cold collation for supper on Sundays, then we generally sat in the parlour, where Mother and I would read or do some mending, Father would smoke a pipe or play cards with Frank, and Grandfather would sit and listen to the four of us talk. John and Doble, meanwhile, withdrew to their separate quarters, or on summer evenings they sometimes had a game of quoits in the yard. Mother couldn't abide the sound of iron horseshoes repeatedly striking the cobbles, but 'For God's sake, woman, let the men have their fun,' Father said.

As I hoped she might, that evening Mother brought my dress down and turned up the wick of the lamp. The collar was hand-work, but she'd used her Singer to do the seams, darts and hems. I had darning to do; Frank's socks were holed at the heel again, testament to my poor skills as a seamstress. Mother's darning, I knew, would without any doubt have held.

'Is that Edie's dress you're making, Ada?' Father asked.

'It is.'

'Good. I expect you to make sure she's nicely turned out for the fete.'

I looked up at him and smiled; it was kind of him to bother about me having a new dress, especially with money being so tight. I loved him ever so much just then.

'Where's that bird of yours, then, girl?'

'I don't know; I could have sworn he came back with me earlier, but I looked around and he wasn't there.'

'Just as well, if you ask me,' said Frank. 'Though I do wonder where it sleeps. Off the ground, if it has any sense.'

'Mother,' I said.

'Yes, Edie?'

'What happened at the Godbolds' to-day?'

'We drank tea and gossiped like two old crones. Did you know, Mrs Prettyman – you remember, she used to have the sweet shop – well, she took ill from drinking bad water and nearly died? Poor old dear; she couldn't manage the pump with her arthritics, and rather than bother her neighbours she was fetching water from the stream. We shan't see her come out of the workhouse infirmary, I expect.'

'But the witch-bottle...'

'Oh, *that*. Ivy just threw it out.'

Grandfather rapped his stick upon the floor. 'A very bad business,' he said.

I went out before bed to see that the hens were safely locked up. Moses, Meg and Malachi had been turned out into Horse Leasow, and although I could not see them I could sense their breathing presence somewhere out there in the dark. To the north-west blazed the Plough, and there was a quarter-moon rising, very low and bright.

I thought about the picture Miss Carter once showed our class of a cornfield by moonlight, by a painter from a neighbouring county whose name I could no longer recall. The moon-shadow, or perhaps just the artful way he had painted it, made the stooks seem mysterious rather than ordinary; or perhaps it was just that anything you made into a picture would seem significant, because you'd chosen it and not something else.

I suppose, now, that Miss Carter had shown us the painting of the cornfield because she thought it would be familiar to us country children, and might interest us more than, say, a classical sculpture, or a Toulouse-Lautrec. But either of those would have been better: they would have let us look out at the world, rather than in. I had liked the picture well enough, but now, reminded of it by the moon over Home Field, all I could think about was the old-fashioned way in which the stooks in it were tied.

I used the privy, then stood by the barn for a few moments before going back in, moths thronging my lamp and a midsummer dor – Doble called them 'old witches' – flying mazily around my head. There were crickets calling, some very near me in the farmyard, others in the orchard or the meadows or the lane, and from above me came the wet-glass squeaks of hunting bats. From the fields carried the buzz of landrails, and drifting down from over the stable came the comfortable sound of John whistling quietly through his teeth as he readied himself for sleep.

For a moment I thought of going to find the horses, just to hear their soft breathing and see their black eyes glint under long lashes in the dark. But I knew they must have their rest, just as we did, and so I turned and went in and left the farm to the night.

X

The barometer fell, and I felt the weather change as I slept. A wind got up and made the house creak, and it sighed and blustered in the fireplaces all night. In the morning the sky was overcast, and the late-July air felt cooler than it had in weeks.

I dreaded Mondays, because Monday meant wash-day. It hadn't been so bad when Mary was at home to help; now, though, it was just Mother and me, and even in summer it took us all day. In winter the lane and yard became wet and slubby; John would wear his old army puttees, and Doble would go about swathed in sacks, but still mud caked our clothes and all the clean linen had to be hung inside to dry, making wash-day even worse.

'I don't know how I'll manage the wash when you're gone, Edie,' Mother would sometimes sigh. 'I just don't know how I'll get through it all myself.'

First we lit the fire under the copper; Mother would usually put some porridge on the stove while it got going, and I'd make a pot of tea. Then we'd strip the beds and put the top sheets on the bottom until next week, and bring everything to the scullery and sort it into piles. John and Doble brought their working clothes to Mother to wash on Mondays, of course, but we were fortunate in that they did their underthings themselves.

Once we'd eaten some breakfast and the water in the copper was hot, we'd bale some out into a tub for the coloured linen, then put the sheets and shirts and tablecloths in the copper to boil. We'd spend the morning with our sleeves rolled up, working the wet cloth in the tubs with the wooden dolly or rubbing it against the washboard, our hair stringy from steam and our hands red and sore from carbolic soap. We didn't talk a great deal on wash-days, but 'Give it some gumption, girl. It won't wash itself,' Mother often said.

At noon we had bread and dripping left over from Sunday's roast, and the men had to do for themselves. Then, after we'd eaten, we rinsed the washing in cold water, with Reckitt's Blue for the whites, then put it all through the mangle, piece by piece, and rinsed it again. We didn't commonly use starch, as Mother thought it a waste of time and effort except on her good lawn tablecloths, and those we hardly used; in fact I don't think we starched anything at all after Mary left.

At last, after a final mangle, we would peg it all to the lines in the orchard and pray that the weather stayed fine; or if it was raining there was a ceiling airer and the fireguard. We'd aim to fold it all up when it was still ever so slightly damp, because between us it would all need to be ironed, and that would help.

'I don't suppose your Constance has ever washed her own smalls,' said Mother, wringing out a pair of Father's drawers and dropping them in a tub ready for the mangle. 'Let alone anyone else's, come to that.'

'I expect not.'

We scrubbed in silence for a while.

'She'll be paying Violet Eleigh to do her laundry for her, no doubt.'

'Do you want me to ask?'

'Don't be daft, I couldn't care less. But I'll wager she won't be writing an article for her magazine about how we do the washing.'

'I doubt it. Who'd want to read about that?'

'Well, she was agog when your grandfather told her how to use a scythe; I saw her write it all down as though it were Gospel. I don't see why that should be any more interesting than women's work.'

'Have you taken against Connie again, Mother?'

'Course not. Why would I do that?'

'I don't know. You seem ... vexed, that's all.'

'I just hate wash-day, Edie. You know that.'

It didn't rain, and the blustery weather was as good as sunshine for drying the clothes. After supper we were in the orchard bringing the last of it inside when Connie appeared, waving a piece of paper triumphantly above her head.

'It's in! They ran it! Ada, Connie, come and see!'

We brought the corners of the sheet we were holding together, Mother taking it from me, folding again, then rolling it tightly up. She laid it in a basket with the others, then began unpegging a pillowcase from the line.

'What do you mean – what's in?' I asked.

'My piece for the *Pioneer*, the first I've written about Elmbourne! Gosh, I have to say, I'm quite pleased with how it's come out.'

'What's it all about, then?' asked Mother through a mouthful of pegs.

'Well, it's only an introduction to the series, really; they wanted me to set the scene.'

Connie thrust the paper at me, grinning, and I stood by the clean washing and read out loud:

~ Sketches from English Rural Life ~

Earth has not anything to shew more fair than an English village under summer skies. The meadows have been harvested, the hay piled into ricks; the cornfields are ripe and golden, awaiting the day of harvest, and the winding lanes around the village are loud with the song of birds. Well may the hiker, cycle-tourer or day-tripper venture forth from the city in search of a rural idyll he knows is his; for we all hailed from such villages but lately, and rightly do they remain the repository of our national pride.

Here is the little church, and village pump; here is the inn where the thirsty traveller may refresh himself with a mug of 'old and mild'. Here beats the heart of our nation, hale and lusty: Englishmen and Englishwomen, living in harmony with the land. They may sweat, and they may toil, but there is a purity of purpose to their labours; for it is not enrichment they seek, nor government assistance, but the simple perpetuation of their own kind.

In the village, bread is still baked the old-fashioned way: in a proper brick oven, in round 'cottage loaves'. The village housewives take pride in it: 'I don't hold with shop-bought bread,' they'll tell you – and quite right! Some of the old folk still recall the days when everything was cooked so cleverly together in an iron pot hung over the fire; but none decry the labour-saving invention of the modern range!

Neither are the menfolk strangers to invention: the tractor-drawn reaper-binder is used here as well as the horse. They know, though, that the old ways are valuable, and they will not allow them to be lost; for in the English village can be found much wisdom, as well as the curious traditions of a bygone age.

Here the most pallid, enervated urban youth will discover a sense of pride in the outdoor life: in strength, health, and husbandry, and love of the natural world. 'Why, one has no time to be bored!' the farm girl will tell you, her complexion clear, her eyes bright. Nor do they – and nor has this writer since arriving in the village, for here one may truly find everything essential to a happy, healthy, and productive life.

The English Pioneer *will feature a 'Rural Sketch' in every edition until further notice. Your countryside correspondent is*

Miss C. N. J. FitzAllen.

'What do you think?' Connie asked, snatching it back from me. 'Say you like it, oh *do*.'

'It's very nice, Connie,' said Mother, handing me a pile of clothes. 'Very clever. You're very good with words.'

'Oh, I'm so glad you like it. I thought you would. What do you think, Edie – did you recognise yourself?'

'That was me, the farm girl? Saying there's no time to be bored?'

'It was! Don't you remember? I made an especial note.'

'I – I didn't realise you were writing down everything I said.'

'Well – I always feel a few quotes, judiciously used, bring an article to life. Don't you think?'

Of course she was right, and I was silly to even think of minding; what did I know about such things, after all? As Mother and I carried in the washing and set it on the rack in the scullery, Connie following us, chattering, behind, I thought how intoxicating it must be to see your name in print and know that strangers were reading your words. Who had first told Connie that her opinions mattered, I wondered; how had she come to believe that the world would listen to what she had to say?

'The next one is already written – all about wholesome rural food – and I thought I might do one on poultry-keeping and brewing, too. And then I absolutely *must* write about our soil and how to keep it pure and productive – these new artificial manures are a terrible worry, don't you think?'

'What about witchcraft?' I said; I suppose I just wanted to be involved in her project in some way. 'I mean, all the old superstitions and traditions – you mentioned them in your piece. One of our neighbours found a witch-bottle in her house the other day – didn't she, Mother? Mrs Godbold, on Back Lane. You should write about that.'

'Oh, is that right, Ada? How completely wonderful. Has she kept it, do you know? I'd *so* love to see.'

'People find all sorts of things hidden in houses, don't they?' I went on. 'Shoes, and dried-up cats, and poppets...'

'What's a poppet?'

'Just a child's toy – a doll,' Mother said. 'Edie, will you go and see if your grandfather wants anything? I thought I heard him call.'

'Which reminds me – folk songs!' I heard Connie saying as I reluctantly left the room. 'Ada, you simply *must* get Albert to sing for me one of these days.'

We had two days of light rain, which topped up the horse-pond a little and came as a relief. My monthlies arrived and I spent a day in bed with cramps, but I took some of the 'composition' powder that mother got from the carrier, stirred into hot water, and was able to get up the following day. Doble gassed the warrens and when he was done he built a pyre of rabbits, poured kerosene over them and set them alight. 'I've stopped up all the buries,' he told Father over supper that evening; 'the dead 'uns underground'll stink otherwise.' The following day John, Frank and Father set out with their guns, and with Mr Rose and his two sons they shot a good number of pigeons, and Mother and I plucked our share and jugged them with port wine.

On the Thursday, Connie and I bicycled to Blaxford so she could visit the tiny flint church with its thatched nave and chancel and round Anglo-Saxon tower. I remember how we gingerly climbed a rickety wooden ladder to the belfry and found change-ringing sequences scratched on the walls by bell-ringers who knows how many decades ago.

While we were up there the church door banged; it made us both jump, and we looked at one another, eyes wide. A woman had come in, and after some footsteps, then silence, we realised that she had taken a pew and begun to pray. As the minutes passed it became increasingly impossible somehow to reveal our presence above her, and so we waited, breath held, a kind of hilarity gathering all the while. When the woman stood at last, and broke wind so that we could hear it, we doubled up in helpless, silent giggles, and when the church door banged again we lay on the dusty boards and laughed until we cried.

By the end of that week, and if he was in earshot, the landrail would come when I called 'Edmund!' – although whether it was because he had learned his name, or that he simply came to the sound of my voice, I cannot say. Like Connie, he didn't spend all his time with us, but we saw him nearly every day; none of us, however, knew where he went at dusk, or whether he was safe.

Saturday dawned clear and dry with the promise of heat to come. Frank polished all our shoes ready for the fete, including Father's boots, and combed his hair flat with water and Brylcreem. Mother had her good bag and a natty new trim made of feathers for her hat. My dress was finished, and when I came downstairs with it on Father told me I looked pretty – and I felt it, too, for the very first time in my life.

We set out mid-morning, all of us together – even Doble and John, who were lending a hand behind the scenes, for which they were promised three pints of mild each, not to be taken at once. Mary had sent word that Terence had colic and so she wasn't coming; I was disappointed not to have her to go about with, but I resolved to enjoy myself anyway.

The road to the village was busy with people on foot and in traps, and as a motor-car passed us at some speed Mother and I pressed ourselves into the hedge.

'We'll stop here and wait for the Roses,' said Father at the four-a-leet.

'I'm sure we'll see them there, George,' Mother said, taking my arm.

'We'll stop here nevertheless.'

'Morning, all. New dress, Edie?' Alf asked when they arrived. He shook hands with Father; 'Mr Mather,' he said, and grinned.

'Yes, Mother made it.'

'She wanted it in scarlet, would you believe,' Mother replied.

'Plenty of time for all that,' said Alf, and gave me a wink that brought the blood to my cheeks. 'Anyway, green suits you very well.'

We set off. When the lane curved towards the village the sun was directly ahead of us, and very bright. I lowered my head and watched the road dust take the shine from the toes of my brown Sunday shoes.

'Your pa and ma not with you?' asked Frank. 'Surely they won't want to miss out?'

'They're coming after dinner,' said Sid, his head jerking with palsy. 'My – mm – my old man won't eat anything Ma hasn't cooked.'

'He's a crackpot, our dad,' Alf said. 'He runs Ma ragged. I keep saying we should get someone in to do for us – they're not getting any younger, either of them. But he won't hear of it. Well, what can you do?'

Beside me, Mother made a quiet tutting sound under her breath.

'Suits us, though' – and he elbowed Frank in the ribs; 'means we're free for the morning! What about you, can you be spared?'

'Oh, I think so,' said Frank, turning to Mother and walking backwards with his thumbs in his waistcoat pockets and a grin lighting up his face. He looked as Father must have looked once: young and strong and happy as a lark.

'Oh, go on with you, boys,' Mother replied, and with that the three of them whooped and broke into a run.

'See you at the Hall, slow-pokes!' called Frank as, their six boots clattering, they raced one another across the packhorse bridge over the Stound.

The grounds of the Hall had been tidied up a little for the fete, the weeds cleared from the centre of the carriage ride and the grass cut. Sir Cecil didn't allow the Hall itself to be used, not even the kitchens, but it was nice to see the shutters off the windows all the same.

We found Connie in the refreshments tent help-ing to make fish-paste sandwiches with Elisabeth Allingham and Miss Eleigh. The whole village knew that those two didn't like one another, but with Connie joshing them along they had been coaxed into good humour, the sandwiches mounting up in neat piles under net covers and four huge baskets of strawberries waiting to be cut next.

Father tipped his hat to Connie before saying he was going to find Sir Cecil, and Connie joined Mother and me for a stroll around the fete. It was astonishing how many people she knew – everybody in the district, it seemed – yet she had been in Elmbourne for only two months.

When Connie had first arrived, alone, in her man's clothes, I had thought the village would talk – and while they had, it hadn't been disapprovingly: in fact they seemed rather to have taken her to their hearts. What a thing charm was, I thought; probably you were born with it. At school my efforts to be liked had always seemed to have the opposite effect.

We took a turn at the coconut shy, and Connie had her fortune told in a gaily painted booth and came out shrieking with laughter at the things the woman had foretold. 'Six children? I don't think so. And another thing: she's no more a gipsy than I'm Mae West,' she said, which made Mother laugh.

'We used to have a proper gipsy fair, you know, Connie,' she said. 'There were swing-boats, and a travelling menagerie, and a fat lady you paid a penny to see. Whatever's happened to the gipsies?

You never see them any more. It's a crying shame, it is, the way all the old things are lost.' It was a curious speech for her, which is why I remember it: Mother so rarely spoke of the past, being generally of the opinion that even ill years turned rosy in the mind's eye, and that nostalgia was not something one should trust.

After a while Connie excused herself, saying that she had promised to help serve the sandwiches in the refreshment tent. Mother stood talking with some women; she told me to go and enjoy myself, and to join her in half an hour for something to eat.

The great lawn before the house was thronged with people now, many of the women in light summer frocks and hats. I walked rather quickly, hoping it looked as though I was on my way to meet a friend somewhere, for I recognised several of the girls and boys I had gone to school with and a couple of farm-hands from neighbouring farms. Some of Mary and Frank's pals were there, too, and Mr Blum who bought our eggs strolling arm-in-arm with his pretty wife, and the wheelwright's apprentice, a barrel-chested boy a little older than Frank whose name I didn't know. Children ran about between the grown-ups' legs, shrieking; a knot of them had gathered by a stall selling penny ices and peppermint rock, their faces sticky, one or two already fractious in the heat. They were like little animals, I thought, turning away as the band struck up; and there, not ten yards away, stood Alf, very still and looking directly at me through the crowd.

Dinner was a shilling each, or sixpence for children, for which we were given sandwiches, cold cuts, potato salad, pink blancmange or strawberries, and as much tea as we could drink. Afterwards, Mother and John went home, Mother to make a start on the marrow jam, as following the rainy spell we had a glut, and John because it was only a half-holiday for him.

A dozen or so deck-chairs had been set out in the shade of a huge cedar of Lebanon and I went to sit there for a while, watching and listening to the hubbub of the fete; I crossed my feet at the ankle, which I felt looked elegant, and then stuck them straight out and leaned back nonchalantly, as I imagined Connie would. Slowly the chairs around me were occupied as the older people grew tired, and mothers brought their babies to settle them for a while. I must have dozed, for the next thing I recall was Father kicking the leg of the deck-chair where I sat.

'By yourself again, girl?'

I sat up and shaded my eyes with my hand, for the sun was behind him, turning him into a silhouette. It must have been close to four o'clock.

'Hello, Father. Are you having a nice time?'

He stared down at me. 'Oh, a smile at last, is it? First one this year. Why d'you never smile, girl, eh?'

'What's the matter?'

'Six month. A six-month remission. While he ... he gallivants around in that damned Rolls Royce.'

'What's happened? What do you mean?'

'*What's happened? What d'you mean?*' he mimicked, cruelly. I could see now that he was unsteady on his feet.

'Father, *please*,' I hissed. People were looking.

'Don't you hush me. I'm head of this house.'

I looked around for Mother before remembering, with a sinking heart, that she had gone home. It wasn't the first time I had seen Father in his cups, by any means, but it was the first time I'd had charge of him myself, and although he was my father and I knew that he loved me, it was frightening, for he seemed different in a way that was more than just about unsteadiness or the slurring of his words. Seeing him stripped of self-control, his anger naked, gave me a feeling inside that was a kind of stifled horror, as though he had been replaced entirely and was no longer my father, George Mather, at all.

I got up and tried to take his arm, but he shook me off.

'You'n Ada! No bloody idea, the pair of you,' he said.

The cursing was quite shameful. I glanced around; one or two people were staring, but most were turned studiously away. An old lady in worsted began to get up, her jaw jutting; but her husband muttered something and she subsided again. Father regarded me for a few moments, swaying, and then he spat, and wandered off.

I found Frank strolling arm-in-arm with Sally Godbold. Her straw-coloured hair had been cut into a bob, and she was wearing it in finger-waves.

'Hello, Edie. Look what Frank won for me at the hoopla!' she said, holding out a gilt brooch in the shape of a flower set with little chips of red glass. I felt shy of her; she was only a couple of years older than me, and had been held back a year at school so that she was but one class ahead, but all dressed up she seemed like a woman: not, perhaps, as Connie was, or Mother, but certainly she was no longer a child. It was nice to have her speak kindly to me, though; she had always ignored me at school.

'Oh, that's ever so pretty, Sally. Frank, can I speak to you a moment? It's Father; I think he might be a little – tired.'

I found that I was trembling, and my voice came out high and unsteady; it made me realise that I was more upset than I had thought. I tried to remind myself that Sally's family had their own shameful secret: her sister had gone away to have a baby when she was twelve, and had never come back. It was whispered in the village that she had been locked up in the county asylum ever since.

'Don't fret, Ed, John will keep an eye on him,' Frank said.

'But John's gone home.'

'Oh – of course. Is he causing bother?'

'I'm not sure. Perhaps.'

'Right. Let's go and see what's what. Sally' – and he gave a little bow – 'will you excuse us for a few moments? A family matter to attend to.'

'Of course,' she said, and smiled.

We found Father asleep behind the refreshments tent. He was on his side, one arm flung up above his head and his hat upturned on the grass. He looked like an infant, but the queer sense of horror I felt concerning him still lingered. I just wanted everything to go back to normal again.

'We'll let him sleep it off, Ed. It's for the best.'

'But why is he like this?'

'He's – it's the harvest.'

'Isn't it always?'

'It's worse this year, Ed. I think –'

Just then there came the sound of a gong, for it was time for Sir Cecil to make his annual speech to the village. We assembled respectfully around him where he stood on a slightly unsteady-looking wooden chair that was being grasped firmly by a crouching manservant who was trying hard to make himself as unobtrusive as he could. Connie found us, and drew her arm through mine. 'There you are, darling,' she whispered, and squeezed. I leaned my head on her shoulder for a moment, and thought how utterly reassuring it was to have her there.

Sir Cecil was as old as the century, which is to say, thirty-four. He was high-boned and handsome in the way only the gentry can be; you could never have mistaken him for a working man, even if he'd been got up in working clothes. He made almost the very same speech every year, and this was no exception. When he had finished, and had climbed down from his chair to polite applause, the Reverend Woodgate led the village in a chorus of three cheers. I nudged Connie, expecting her to roll her eyes, but she was cheering Sir Cecil even more loudly than the rest of us, her face eager and open. Her Socialist days were behind her, it seemed.

It was the last day of my childhood, and somehow I knew it even as each moment flowed through me and fell behind. The grounds of the Hall looked briefly beautiful again, like an old aquatint, and the weather was fine; everyone said afterwards that it had been a splendid day. I wonder if the Elmbourne fetes are still held there nowadays; perhaps the world has changed, and such simple pleasures have fallen out of favour, I don't know.

But through it all for me ran the dark undertow of Father, and the bright, taut thread of Alf's gaze. I knew he would find a way to be alone with me before the day was out, and it set me on edge and gave everything around me an oddly vivid cast. When I recall that day now I think of the young deer we'd nursed to health a few years before: the way it would hold itself so very still in the Pightle when any of us approached. It's strange — stupid, really — but I sometimes feel I could weep to think of that poor creature now.

In the end, it was easy: when at last the stallholders began to pack away, Frank was required to take Father home — much to his chagrin, for Doble was nowhere to be found. And then, when they had gone, it was just me and Alf, my heart beating high and fast in my chest.

'Would you like some rock?' he said, taking a stick of it, wrapped in pink paper, from his trouser pocket. The smell of crushed grass filled the air around us, trampled by feet.

'Oh — no, I won't, thank you,' I said.

'Are you sure? Your old man told me I should buy it; he said you had a sweet tooth.'

'Honestly, I'm all right.'

'Shall we go for a stroll, then, Edie?'

I nodded, feeling the inevitability of it, the way these things happened as though following the script of a play. Was this 'walking out'?

At the gates of the Hall we turned not right towards the village, but left, leaving the shouts and the singing and revelry behind. It wasn't late, and the sky was light over the cornfields, though in the distance the copses were starting to look shadowy and dim. The sun was low behind us as we walked, and after a while Alf took my hand in his and gently scratched at my damp palm with one fingernail in the particular way that he had. I tried to keep my arm and hand relaxed, so that he wouldn't think me prissy or tense.

'Yes, it's very fetching, your dress,' he said, as though carrying on a conversation from before. 'You look very grown up. I said as much to Frank, I said, "Your sister looks a rare treat to-day!" There, how does that feel?'

'Thank you, Alf,' I said.

'Quite the grown-up, I'd say.'

I tried to squeeze his hand, but his grip was so strange and I didn't really know what else to say, and then a motor-car came and we both stood to the side to let it pass. I hoped my hair was still tidy, for soon, I knew, he'd turn to look at me, and then he'd kiss me. Not yet, though; perhaps when we were a little further along the lane.

'Did you enjoy the fete, Alf?'

'Oh yes, it was capital. Even better than last year, don't you think?'

'Yes, I suppose so. Only − I wish Father hadn't enjoyed it quite so much, that's all.'

'Why, can a man not enjoy a drink now and again, Edie? Half the men in the village were tipsy to-day − there's no shame in it.'

'I suppose you're right. It's just – well, Mother will have a rare time of it this evening, that's all.'

'Let's not think of your mother just now, shall we?' And he stopped, just as I had known that he would, and turned me to face him there in the shadowy lane. I raised my eyes to his and he looked long at me in a way that made my breath come fast, and then he leaned down and kissed me, stale beer and peppermint on his breath, his hands gripping the tops of my arms and pressing the little buttons that trimmed the sleeves of my new dress into my skin. He began to push his tongue inside my mouth, as he always did, and I pictured how my face would look if anyone could see it, my nose squashed to one side and my mouth open; I always tried to make my tongue respond to his, but I was never quite sure what it was that he wanted me to do. I couldn't breathe properly, but breathing was less important than him thinking well of me, so I didn't pull away. And then his hands were on the front of my dress, pushing and kneading; I realised my eyes were still open and I closed them tight and concentrated instead on the sound of a dorhawk churring from somewhere not too far away.

'So pretty,' he breathed into my mouth, his fingers pinching and bruising at my breasts. 'So pretty.'

I raised my hands from where they rested limply on each side of his waist and began to unbutton the front of my dress; last time it had made him more gentle to see the bare skin, and he had hurt me less.

'Yes, that's right,' he muttered, pulling away to watch as I fumbled at my buttons. 'Oh, Edie, you're so...'

I reached behind me to unhook the unfamiliar brassière and immediately he pushed it up and out of the way. The evening air brought my nipples out and he put a big palm on each breast for a moment and just stood. I dared a look up at his face and it was strange, transfigured, as though he wasn't there. Perhaps I looked the same.

He took my left hand then and pulled it to the front of his trousers, where his thing was, and pressed it there so I could feel it twitch. I wondered how much he wanted from me, and how long it might take; I wondered when we could turn and walk back to the village again.

'Edie,' he said, his voice thick, and then he leaned down to kiss me again. 'Please, Edie,' he breathed into my mouth, and I moved my hand a little, trying to discern what it was that he wanted me to do. It didn't feel romantic, and I moved my hand away; but he just put it back and pressed it there, hard.

'See what you do to me?' he said. 'I just can't help myself.'

It was very flattering, of course, and I did feel powerful in an odd way. It was as though Alf Rose was all of a sudden helpless, as though I could make him do anything I liked. He leaned down then and began to suck on one of my breasts, and I cradled the back of his head in both hands and looked down at him there, his eyes closed, his mouth working away. I wondered if I should say 'I love you, Alfred' – whether that was what was happening. I thought perhaps it might sound right.

After a few moments he stepped back and looked at me as though from very far away. 'Come on,' he said, taking my hand decisively; but instead of turning back towards the village he marched me further up the lane and scrambled through a gap in the hedge. I ducked and pushed my way through after him, holding my dress closed with one hand, my heart banging. I wasn't really thinking of anything any more, only that we weren't going back to the village yet.

What happened next was nothing – the work of a few moments in the corner of a dim field. He told me to lie down, and I did, briefly picturing my bed at home and the ancient witch-mark that watched over me from the beam above. Weeds prickled my arms and the back of my neck as he stood over me and unbuttoned his trousers so that his pale thing poked out; it was the first time I had encountered the strange look they have when stiff: a mixture of defencelessness and horrible vigour. He worked it in his fist for a moment, staring down at me with his mouth open where I lay with the bodice of my dress undone, my arms rigid by my sides. I tried to think of a romantic story to explain what was happening, but my mind was a desperate blank; then he was kneeling and pushing my legs apart, and muttering 'Edie, Edie' to himself while I stared unblinking past him at the sky.

XI

The climax of the year was nearly upon us. In the days following the fete, John and Father inspected the corn twice daily; the wheat would be cut and stooked first, and we would then start straight in on the barley, which did not need to be left to dry but could be carted in sheaves the same day. Father said that even if the first few acres of barley had a little green in them it was better than the last being over-ripe and the grain shaling out of the ears.

We would need to weed and hoe one last time. Even then, the harvest would not be as tidy as it should have been, but Father said that any remaining weeds — for we would only have time to pull the worst — would mostly be threshed out. Too much green could cause the rick to heat, while weed seeds in the threshed grain risked it fetching a lower price.

John had already cleaned and oiled the reaper-binder and made sure our wagon was in good repair, and now he took first Malachi, and then Moses, to the smith to be shod. A feeling had come over the farm of anticipation, and when any of us came into the house from the fields we'd find Grandfather standing by his parlour chair, leaning upon his stick.

'Well?' he'd ask, his shuttered old face hungry for news.

The first morning after the fete I remained in bed until I heard the sound of the trap's wheels receding up the lane and the church bells slow and stop. Mother had tried to rouse me, but I'd turned away and pulled the sheet over my head; she'd sighed and laid a hand upon my hair, but at last she'd let me be.

My little casement window was open to the summer morning; a turtle dove purred, and from somewhere drifted in the *zip-zip-zip* of a scythe being sharpened with a whetstone. Hopefully it was Doble, and Father hadn't remained behind indisposed, for after his drunkenness at the fete he seemed changed to me in some way, and I didn't want to see him yet.

I had barely slept all night, my mind fixated for some reason on Sir Cecil's speech. Through all the dark hours I'd been strangely gripped by the need to recall his exact words – despite the fact that I had barely listened at the time. What if there had been a message there, a message for the village, something everyone else but me had heard? Or perhaps we'd all missed something important, something concerning our future that it was imperative we should know.

That final hour of the fete: I kept going back there in my imagination, compulsively assembling and re-assembling all the details – the footman holding the wobbling chair, Connie squeezing my arm, Father's hat on the grass – as though they mattered in some way. And yet the events that followed seemed almost to have been obliterated from my mind.

I knew that I must force myself to get out of bed, for if I did not do so something in me would fail. At least growing up on a farm had given me enough backbone to overcome laziness and self-indulgence, for the hens would not let themselves out of the coop nor feed themselves, and there were always a thousand other tasks that would not wait. I got up and let yesterday's drawers drop without looking at them, for I knew that they were foul, splashed my face with water and went gingerly down the stairs.

Mother had left me scrambled eggs but I found that I could not eat them, so I slid them into the pig-bucket, stepped into my boots and walked out of the house in my nightdress, leaving my plate and the frying-pan unwashed. I used the privy, and found Edmund waiting for me when I came out; then after I had seen to the hens I walked up the lane with him towards Hullets, the sun hot on my arms and the back of my neck. My hip joints felt stiff, and the muscles on the inside of my thighs were painful, but it felt important to ignore the soreness and try to walk in my usual way. Beyond that I did not think for one single second about the night before. It was a perfect blank, like the high, unstable whine of a tuning fork that one simply tunes out and doesn't hear.

I kept to the edge of Hulver Wood and followed the margin of Crossways. The barley was tall and made the field impossible to cut across; it would have been easier to have gone by the road, but I wasn't sure whether everyone at Rose Farm would be at church. Crows called hoarsely from the tall trees of the wood, and I shuddered a little to think of their beady black eyes watching me pass.

When I was nearing Hullets, I pushed through the hedge to the road and crossed it to the farm buildings. I put Edmund down, and as he roused his brown-dappled feathers and began to preen I shaded my eyes and looked about. A stone roller and a mangle were rusting gently into the nettles by the house's front wall; the north gable was almost entirely claimed by ivy, which was fingering its way into the upper windows and making its way across the roof. An ash sapling issued from one of the chimneys and had split it, sending several of the old bricks down into the thicket of elder and nettles that had sprung up where what looked like a hen-house had once been.

Peering into one of the front windows, I called out a faint 'Hello?', but it seemed clear that the house was unoccupied. I felt a stab of disappointment; I'd been so curious about the family there, and now they were gone.

The farmhouse's oak front door was much like our own, with iron studs and a thumb-latch, warm from the sun, that felt familiar to my hand. Inside I found that the parlour and kitchen had been neatly swept and were clear of the dead leaves, rubbish and jack-daw nests that filled the other downstairs rooms. The walls were discoloured, the parlour's paper peeling and buckled, but there was little smell of damp.

In the parlour the hearth looked to have been recently lit, and there were some twisted paper spills beside it such as Father used to light the fire at home. Crouching, I unrolled one; it was a page from the *Gazette* dating back to 1929. 'GRUESOME DEATH', it announced. 'William Vhrym (44) of Corwelby did away with himself on Tuesday last by cutting his throat with a corn sickle. The Coroner was of the opinion that he would have taken about half an hour to die.' And then an advertisement for bile beans.

I suppose I was still hoping for a trace of the family, some kind of clue or sign, but the two rooms told me very little, for they had left nothing mean-ingful of themselves behind. Still, though, something lingered, if only in my imagination; the people felt more real to me now, instead of just a tale. I tried to imagine what it must be like to have nothing and to travel from place to place, always being moved on and never welcomed, but it was like trying to im-agine the lives of animals: it just wasn't something I could do. Whose fault was it that they had lost their home – were they simply idle, or was the father a dipsomaniac? Or perhaps they were of bad character, or Irish, or all of these things, I thought. For while there were in those years many indigent men tramping the roads in search of work, that was just the way of things, and I could not conceive that an ordinary family – a family like ours, for example – would ever let themselves be reduced to living in that way.

There was a fluster at the backhouse window and I saw that Edmund had flown up onto the sill and was regarding me inquisitively. Beyond him must lie the garden and orchard, or whatever was left of it, and I decided to have a look.

The back door, which was cheap and of a much more modern type than the front, had swollen and jammed in the frame, but with a heave it opened, dragging a half-circle across the old, dipped stone of the step. Just beyond were five rows of seedlings, neatly hoed and weeded and edged with the coppery buttons of marigolds. The young plants had been recently watered and picked clean of caterpillars, and the climbing beans were coiling more strongly up the bean-sticks even than our own. For some reason I couldn't make sense of, the sight nearly took the heart from my chest.

That's when I saw them, sitting in the shade of an overgrown apple tree heavy with hard green fruit: a woman Mother's age in a dark dress and headscarf, and a little girl no more than four years old, lying on a rush mattress with her head turned towards me and gazing at me with deep-shadowed and strangely fervent eyes. I froze in the doorway, but then I saw that the woman was sleeping, her head resting on the tree's gnarled trunk. Letting out my breath, I looked back at the child, and although she smiled a little – I'm sure she did, I'm sure to this day that she smiled at me – she did not blink or look away.

Back on our land the corn was a golden sea divided by the dark summer green of its hedges and spinneys. I walked quickly along the field margins, my breath coming fast and Edmund hurrying behind; again the crows in Hulver Wood watched me carefully, and this time I glared defiantly up at them as I passed.

In the shade of the ring of oaks the fine hairs on my arms and legs stood up and shivers chased each other over my bare skin. My nipples became pinched and felt sore, and I was overtaken for a moment by a shame so strong it could not be withstood. I crouched and closed my eyes, whispering a jumble of phrases under my breath to drown out what I was remembering; then, on a strange impulse, I stood and traced the circular pattern that was on our hearth and the beam over my bed onto each of the six twisted trunks.

Have you ever cast a coin into a fountain and made a wish, or touched wood to ward off ill luck? You know very well that it's foolish, but a compulsion comes over you to do it anyway – for where's the harm? Just as I always stopped reading only on a sentence of seven words, for seven was a good number and would keep my family safe, now I discovered that making the sign of the circle with its secret inner petals felt steadying, and I saw no reason to prevent myself from performing this harmless act.

Then I looked anew at the flints the trees held, one of them a great holed hag-stone, and it came to me that all along they had been a secret sign meant for me, and that very soon I would understand what it meant. That was the moment, I suppose, that I began to suspect that everything had changed, and that my life might yet have a new purpose and direction – and God forgive me, I pushed the child at Hullets far from my mind.

I squeezed my eyes shut against the traitorous tears that were rising, tipped my head back, and tried to slow my breath. Yes, we would bring in the harvest: the six of us and Connie, making seven, a good number, and Grandfather in the house to sing us in each night – for surely this year, of all years, he would sing. We would bring each golden field home in the wagon and I would ride atop the last one bearing a green bough like Demeter, in triumph, Moses and Malachi ringing their harness bells proudly as they hauled the final load home. Then the rick-yard would be full of wheat and barley, Father would be himself again and we would sit down all together for a harvest meal. In autumn we would plough and harrow and drill once more, and when the steam tackle came we would thresh, and afterwards sell the piles of bright grain. No more harm would ever come to us, and so it would go on forever, world without end: the elms always sheltering our old farmhouse, the church looking out over the fields. For the fields were eternal, our life the only way of things, and I would do whatever was required of me to protect it. How could it be otherwise?

Back at the house I found that everyone was back from morning service, Connie with them, and preparations for dinner were underway. Father and John had gone out to look over the fields and check for leatherjackets, and had taken Frank with them; Doble sat on a stool in the yard mending a pair of boots. He had a wooden last to which he had attached the broken handle of an old hay-rake and this he gripped between his knees, topped with a boot, so that he could hammer the hobnails, pelts and Blakeys in.

While he worked he sang in a cracked and reedy voice, and Connie, in skirt, patterned blouse and Sunday hat, leaned on the wall and gave me a wink as she wrote the words down in her notebook:

You will see the poor tradesmen a-walking the street
From morning to night their employment to seek.
And scarcely they have any shoes to their feet,
And it's O, the hard times of old England,
In old England very hard times.

In the kitchen I found Mother in a bate about the pots I'd left unwashed. 'And your hands are filthy, and you're not even dressed, girl! For goodness' sakes, what's the matter with you? Get upstairs, now. And shut that dratted bird in your bedroom while we eat.'

I flinched a little from her curtness. 'Is there any water in the copper?' I managed to ask.

'You had a bath yesterday, Edith. And now is hardly the time, not when I need to get all these potatoes peeled. Now *go*.'

Up in my room I pulled my nightdress over my head and at the basin I washed my armpits, with their new downy hair. Then I washed my private parts, the soap stinging, and put on clean underwear. I left Mary's frayed brassière on the chair with my new green dress and put on a very old blouse that was far too young for me, really; the cuffs didn't even reach all the way to my wrists. Then, on an impulse, I went through to Frank's room and rifled through the shirts and long johns and corduroy trousers in his chest of drawers until I found an old pair of his school shorts, and I put them on.

Back in my room I kicked my discarded drawers under the valance of my wash-stand and sat for a moment, stroking Edmund, who had settled on the counterpane. 'You're my best boy,' I crooned to him softly, tracing a circular pattern seven times on the lovely feathers of his back. 'Yes, you are. You're here to protect me, aren't you? I understand it now.'

After dinner I left Edmund foraging in the orchard and went out for a walk with Connie, for I didn't feel able to ride my bicycle that day. Mother had made me take off Frank's shorts the moment I appeared downstairs, under threat of a thrashing from Father, so I'd gone back up to change into a skirt. On the stairs I heard Connie, who was helping with the potatoes, say mildly, 'But Ada, why should the girl not wear short trousers if she's a mind to?'

'I'll not have a child of mine made a laughing-stock – begging your pardon, Connie, for I know you favour men's attire. And that may be all very well in London, and on you, but she has to fit in here.'

'Does she?'

'Course. You know that.'

We walked along Newlands to Far Piece, past Copdock Farm and out along the field paths towards Stenham Park through seas of rustling yellow corn. It was oppressively hot and there were clouds of butter-flies everywhere: orange-tips and skippers, fritillaries, meadow browns and others whose names I did not know, dancing their patterns and secret ciphers upon the innocent summer air. It was all so familiar, yet at the same time nothing around me felt quite real; for minutes at a time things would feel almost ordinary, but then an image, or a sensation, would rise up from somewhere unspeakable and assail me, and although I would reply to Connie and hear my voice talking, inside I was terribly far away.

'Wasn't the fete wonderful!' she exclaimed. 'I did so enjoy myself. Didn't you? And isn't Cecil Lyttleton handsome! Honestly, I had no idea.'

'Yes, I suppose.'

'And Frank, arm-in-arm with Sally Godbold! I must say, they were a picture, although I don't believe she's terribly bright.'

I felt myself almost smile. 'She's a waistcoat short of a button, Mary used to say.'

Connie hooted with laughter. 'What a wonderful expression! Do remind me to write it down later. But she'll make Frank a good wife, don't you think?'

I stopped walking, for it felt like falling very fast: of course, Frank would one day be master at Wych Farm, with Sally his wife and the mother of his children; and then what would I be?

'Are you all right, Edie?'

'Oh – yes. Sorry, Connie,' I managed, with some effort. 'It's just –'

'You don't like Sally, do you? Sisters always think their brothers can do better. You'll come to love her in time, I'm sure.'

'No, it's not that. I just – I must ask Frank about his plans, that's all.'

'I'd say your father won't be ready to give up the reins for some years yet. Perhaps in a year or two Frank will take a council farm somewhere nearby. I'm assuming he'll farm, of course?'

'Yes, of course.'

'And you, Edie?' She turned to me as we walked and peered at me closely. 'I like to think we know each other a little better now than when we first met, back when you were haymaking. It was only a couple of months ago, but it feels like years.'

'What about me?'

'What do you want from life?'

'I – I don't know, Connie. I really don't. I wish people would stop asking me that.'

'Well, what if I were to ask you to come to London with me?'

'Yes, I'd like that, of course –'

'I don't mean a visit; I mean for good. You're too clever to stay in Elmbourne, Edie, everyone can see that.'

'Connie, I –'

'And you don't want to marry some … some wretched farm boy and push out a baby a year, do you? You'd be bored to death. Go on, tell me I'm wrong.'

I shivered at the picture she drew of my future, which felt closer now than it ever had. Whitethroats and wrens sang loudly to me from the hedges, their reedy voices full of clues that I would soon learn to understand. Connie and I crossed a stile, heading north now through sweet-smelling fields of flowering beans.

'But Connie, what about "Englishmen and Englishwomen living in harmony with the land"? What about "the perpetuation of our native kind", and all that?'

'Oh, rot.'

'Connie!'

'I know, I know. And I meant it! And town life can be dreadfully enervating, it's true. But do you really want to spend your whole life in the same place, among the same people, doing the same things year in year out, until you die?'

'I don't know. Mother and Father want me here, and I've – I have things I need to do.'

'Do they?'

'Want me here? Why, yes, of course.'

'How do you know?'

I turned. 'Has Mother said something to you, Connie? Something about me?'

'Good golly, child, of course not. Only – I have a feeling Ada would like to spare you marriage if she could. She just can't see how, except by keeping you at home.'

There it was again: the idea that Mother was somehow holding me back from the world. Frank had said the same thing. I felt confused and unsettled, as though perhaps Mother might be against me, something I couldn't have borne. More than anything I just wanted the conversation to end, for us to talk of other matters – village superstitions, perhaps, or the best way to brew beer. I began to trace a circle on my hip through the cotton of my skirt. I did it seven times.

'Actually, Mother asked if I wanted to go to the hop in Blaxford,' I said. 'So I just – I don't understand all this talk. And I don't know why you're so interested, anyway.'

'Because ... because you're like me, Edie. And I want to help.'

'Am I?'

She linked her arm through mine and squeezed, and I could feel the hot flank of her body through the silk blouse she wore.

'*Yes*, darling. You are.'

We came at last to the Stound where it flowed through rich water meadows, slower and broader than further upstream where Frank and I had swum. Crack willows grew along it, and in places the banks were thick with angelica and comfrey; where the river cast itself in wide loops the grass that grew there was unnaturally green. A dipper with a white bib like evening attire sang to me like a wind-up musical box from some exposed tree roots.

We turned and began to follow the river slowly back to the village. When we got there, I decided, I would say yes to a lemonade in the Bell & Hare. For I wanted to stay with Connie for as long as possible; I didn't want to go home. But something nagged at me, and I had to speak.

'I went over to Hullets this morning,' I said, gazing at the sparkling water, where azure damselflies darted and flashed.

'So that's what you were up to! Why on earth does that old ruin fascinate you so?'

'I wanted to see the pauper family.'

'And did you?'

'Yes. Well, I saw a lady and a little girl.'

'And did you introduce yourself?'

'No, I –'

She laughed. 'You spied on them! How perfectly thrilling.'

'I didn't mean to. They were asleep. Well, the lady was – outside, under a tree.'

'Ah yes, indolent to a fault. I wonder where the menfolk were. I've a good mind to write to Cecil Lyttleton, you know. It's no way to be bringing up a child.'

I thought about the neat little garden; I thought of the glittering eyes of the girl staring at me from the bed. At some point, my feelings about the family's trespass had undergone a queer kind of reversal.

'But they aren't doing any harm, are they?'

'Edie, they simply don't fit in here – quite apart from the fact that they're living scot-free on Lyttleton land, while your father and everyone else pays rent. They're undesirables. You'll have to take my word on that.'

'Do you mean Irish? Because in the olden days there used to be Irish harvest gangs in summer and they were very hard workers – that's what Granfer and Grandma always say.'

'They're *Jews*, Edie. And we don't need any more of them in Elmbourne – the egg merchant Blum and his wife are bad enough.'

I hadn't realised; I had assumed they were just people. I could still be so terribly naïve sometimes.

'Oh. But – why don't you like them?'

'Well, I'm no anti-Semite, of course. But they're not *from* here, and if we're not careful they'll mar the character of England forever – not to mention the way they undercut wages and take work away from ordinary people, just as the Irish did.'

Perhaps she was right – but it gave me an unsettled feeling, this kind of talk. I didn't want to think about difficult things, or imagine the world changing. I just wanted to grow up and live an ordinary life among familiar people: people I knew and understood.

'But Connie, if they're not allowed to stay on at Hullets, will they be found somewhere else to live?'

'Of course, darling! No need to worry on that account. Now, what's that twittering I hear?'

She took my arm and we fell to talking about the hedgerow birds and their songs, and I began to tell her the names the older people still used for them – but something else about what she had said was niggling at the back of my mind.

'So … Hullets belongs to Lord Lyttleton too?'

'That's right.'

'He must hate to see it untenanted for so long. It reflects badly on a landlord to have land lying idle. Land is like a woman, you know: it must produce.'

Connie gave me an old-fashioned look. 'Is that right? Well, I doubt it's troubled Cecil much, all in all.'

'What do you mean?'

'Oh, just that perhaps if he put on the odd shoot, as they do at Stenham Park, he'd take more notice of the condition of his land, but he doesn't – it's a crying shame, really. Anyway, it seems the farmer had got himself into arrears. Cecil remitted the debt for two years and then he had him evicted; there was a bit of a stink about it at the time, or so I'm told. Gosh, Edie, nobody tells you a thing, do they? Poor lamb.'

The word 'remitted' caught like a burr in my mind and stuck there, itching.

'And why hasn't he re-let it – you know, to a better farmer? Or sold the land off?'

'I suppose because nobody's been able to come up with the readies. It's a national disgrace, really, but farmland is being let down to grass all over the country nowadays. Unless you've got a lot of capital behind you, there's just no money in cereal at the moment; no money at all.'

We came to a place where a cluster of willows formed a shady bower at the water's edge, the river a deep, slow pool. The opposite bank was churned up where cattle had come to drink, and on our side the rich grass was strewn with a few white feathers from the ducks that must have roosted under the willows each night.

Connie stood for a moment, her hands clasped behind her back, gazing at the cool water slipping by. I felt so strange; it was as though I was floating, or in some other way unmoored.

'England, my God!' she said. 'Now, *this* is what it's all about. It really does nourish the spirit, I find. Mr Williamson believes that "Only from nature could the truth arise" – and I think he's absolutely right.' Impulsively then she began to unbutton her blouse. 'Damn it, Edie, there's nobody about. I'm going to have a dip.'

I flushed and turned away as she kicked off her shoes and stepped out of her skirt; I didn't know where to look. What if someone should come along – little boys fishing, or the water-bailiff, or someone from Elmbourne out for a stroll, as we were? But Connie, in an eau-de-nil slip slightly torn at one seam, didn't seem abashed at all.

'Oh, darling, don't be a prude. I don't mind if you don't.'

But I did mind, I *did*. I didn't want to see her naked, it was wrong, it was too much; I felt as though I might be overwhelmed, as though with the sudden removal of her clothes Connie might reveal herself to be monstrous, or at the very least somebody else. It was my fault, of course, for I *was* a prude, a silly little girl who knew nothing of the world. But I couldn't stop it happening, and I was frightened, and I suddenly felt as though I might panic; and more than that, I hated myself.

She let her slip fall, unrolled her stockings and added them to the pile of her clothes and under-things on the grass. Her body was long and very white, like a church lily, with small, high breasts and generous hips. Her knees, a little dropped and wrin-kled, were somehow troubling. They seemed very exposed.

'Won't you join me?' she asked, turning to me and grinning, her hands on her hips.

'I – I can't.'

'Is it your time of the month – is that why you weren't at church this morning? I must say, you do look terribly pale.'

'No – I –'

'Oh, *darling*. *Please* don't be embarrassed. There's no need, I promise you. Haven't you heard of the Sun Ray Club? Well – never mind.'

The shadow of a bird passed over the water, and I was gripped by helpless fear: Connie must not go into the river, she *mustn't*. She would drown, I was sure of it; she'd sink like a stone, and I'd be helpless to stop it happening. It would be like my dream of the horse-pond, but it would be she who'd be under-water: trapped down there, thrashing, dying.

'Don't go in, Connie – please don't. You mustn't. It's not safe here. The current –'

'Don't be silly, it's shallow!'

I grasped her arm then, and she turned from the water's edge, bewildered.

'Edie! Whatever's the matter?'

And I burst into ragged, helpless tears, and she held me, her arms wrapped strongly around me, my hands on the warm, bare skin of her back and her chin on the top of my head.

We walked the rest of the way back to the village arm-in-arm and in silence. Once I'd stopped crying, Connie had fetched me her hankie and put her clothes back on, and then we'd sat for a moment on the bank while I composed myself. A swan drifted past, spotless and serene, and I wondered whether it was swan's down that we were sitting among – if this was in fact their nightly roost.

'Come on, then, duckie. A brandy's what you need,' Connie had said at last, nudging me gently, and I'd smiled weakly and got up.

It wasn't my first time inside the Bell & Hare – I'd been sent to fetch Father back on a few occasions, and with Frank I'd fetched mugs of ale out to passing motor-cars for a ha'penny tip once or twice. But it was the first time I had walked in as a customer, to sit and have a drink, and it felt different. I wondered if Connie knew that, and whether, if I told her, my hesitation would even be something she could understand.

The inn was low-ceilinged and cool, with a stone flagged floor and wooden benches and tables. On the right was an L-shaped bar-room, at the back of which was a little raised snug; on the left was the tap-room, with stairs at the back that led up to the inn's rooms; this was where the dartboard was, and where Father usually sat. On the walls hung faded lithographs of hunting scenes, framed photographs of meets at the gates of the Hall, and here and there old fox masks, the eyes replaced with glass and the lips forced up into a snarl.

I could hear the murmur of voices from the tap-room, while in the public bar near the snug the foreman and carter from Holstead Farm were sitting at a table with a man I didn't know whose empty sleeve was pinned up to the shoulder. The landlord was nowhere to be seen; the inn was supposed to close for three hours on Sunday afternoons, although in summer this was rarely enforced.

Connie led me through to the snug and sat me down on a bench, then went to the bar and loudly cleared her throat. At one time the little enclosed area would have been entirely private, but at some point in the Bell & Hare's long history the wattle and daub of its studwork partition had been knocked out, leaving only six vertical timbers between it and the bar-room beyond. Still, it felt a little better than being out there under the curious gazes of the Holstead men, and I leant back against the rough, cool whitewash of the wall and briefly closed my eyes.

What could I say to her? What was there to say? The harvest was only days away – that was the main thing. Nothing else mattered, *could* matter now. It would do no good at all – might only make things worse – to tell her what I suspected about Father and Lord Cecil; and I had no wish ever to reveal to anyone what had happened after the fete. If we could only get the harvest in, and without any help from the Rose boys, all would surely be well.

'No, no,' I muttered aloud. It was best not to think about Alf, and I tried to suppress the image of him standing over me. '*Stupid*,' I whispered, and clenching my fists under the table I dug my fingernails into my palms as though to punish my hands for having undone my buttons so brazenly. Then I opened my hands and traced the circular witch-mark on one palm with my finger: again, again, again.

At last Connie brought over two brandies and I drank mine off like horse drench and coughed until I retched.

'I let Alf Rose kiss me last night after the fete,' I gasped, when I could. I had to tell her something, and while a pure invention might have been preferable, the truth was filling my mouth like bile.

'And that's what all the tears were about?'

I nodded. 'I know I shouldn't have. I know it's wrong.'

'*Dearest* child,' Connie said, laughing and sitting back, 'there is absolutely no need to get so upset. Anyone would think you had committed a mortal sin. Do you like him, that's the main thing? He seems rather sweet.'

'I don't want to marry him, if that's what you mean. I don't even want to walk out with him, or – anyone.'

'Do you want him to kiss you again?'

I found that my legs under the table were trembling, as though with pent-up energy, and I concentrated on keeping them still.

'No.'

'Old thing, did you not like it?'

'I –'

'For that matter, I didn't enjoy my first kiss much either – I wonder if any woman really does. Perhaps it's something you just need to endure until you're used to it, like cigarettes. Give it time.'

'I don't want to be kissed again. Or – anything. I don't want him to kiss me; I don't want *anyone* to kiss me.' Despite myself the trembling was becoming more general, and I stared down into my empty brandy glass and realised I was holding my breath. It was like floating away, or wanting to; I tried to tether myself to the bench where I sat with my hands. I felt very pale.

'Oh, Edie, you'll feel differently in a year or two, I guarantee it.'

'I won't. I won't!'

'Darling, you're *vibrating*,' she said then, laying a cool hand on my thigh. 'Let me fetch you another brandy. You sit there and take a few deep breaths.'

'May I just have a lemonade, Connie? Please.'

'A brandy is what you need, Miss Mather, I promise you. But sip it slowly this time. I don't want you being sick.'

I don't know what time it was when I left the Bell & Hare; the drink had fuddled me, and I was exhausted, too, by everything that had happened, by my lack of sleep, the effort of talk and the difficulty of keeping in everything I knew I mustn't say. We walked to the draper's, where Connie embraced me firmly before letting herself in the shop door with a latch-key; then I continued past the pump on the green and turned left to cross the river and follow the cut that came out on Back Lane. There, I slipped between two cottages and climbed the bank until I came out onto our own land, and I took the field path home.

I have always thought that there is something holy about dusk, when the light begins to fade and the fields lie empty, the lamps are lit indoors and the birds are seen winging to their roosts before darkness falls. The evening sun was low and warm, my shadow running over the soft heads of wheat, and somewhere nearby a turtle dove was making a low, contented sound. Alone, I felt all my confusion ebb and my soul expand – yes, that was it exactly, as though I was part of everything, and everything loved me and reached out to me somehow: our quiet cornfields, the evening sky, the trees. And then a dorhawk began to churr, the feeling faded, and I shook my head and picked up my pace.

XII

~ Sketches from English Rural Life ~

There is surely no better repast than country dishes,
innocent of the fashions of the modern age. They may not
be refined, but here there is good, wholesome food such
as may be found on every English farm where butter is
churned by hand, cheese is made, and bread is daily baked.

In the village everyone, from blacksmith to publican,
farm-hand to agèd cottager, has his vegetable-garden
from which he may take freshly dug potatoes, runner
beans, radishes, carrots, marrows and salads in their
season, the seed saved parsimoniously in a twist of
paper for the following year, or to be exchanged with
friends and neighbours for their own. He may tend
raspberry-canes, or a damson-tree; he may keep a skep
of bees, and a pig or goat if he has room; thus, rarely
does the country-dweller want, for by his own labours
he feeds himself and his family, instead of subsisting
on devitalised factory foodstuffs and tawdry foreign
goods.

And there is yet more to recommend this system: for
work performed in nature purifies the spirit, and keeps

the Englishman in contact with his native soil. 'Only from Nature could the truth arise,' said a wise man; and in such health-giving labour may be found the oft-occluded well-spring of the nation.

A recipe for harvest cake: Mix 8oz. good, white flour and two of corn-flour, a little baking powder and bicarbonate of soda, and some spices. Add a pinch of yeast, then stir in 8oz. sugar. Rub in 4oz. lard. Beat together a pint of fresh milk and an egg and stir into the mixture; then add 8oz dried fruit and some candied peel, if you have it, and combine well together. Turn into a cake tin, cover and leave to rise. Then bake for two hours, and at last glaze with a little milk, while still hot.

A recipe for marrow jam: Peel, seed and dice your marrows, say 6lb, and add the same quantity of jam sugar. Leave in a cool pantry or refrigerator overnight. Then take your largest preserving pan and fill it with the mixture, adding the juice and zest of four lemons. Take 3oz. fresh ginger root and bash with a rolling pin, then place this in a muslin bag and add to the pan. Bring to the boil and then simmer until, on a cold plate, it can be seen to set. Strain and jar as usual.

This is the second instalment in our new 'Rural Sketch' series, which will appear weekly until further notice. Your countryside correspondent is

Miss C. N. J. FitzAllen.

I put the cutting down and picked up my teacup. Mother, Mary and I were at Grandma and Granfer's once again; it was the last chance to visit before harvest began. I had havered over coming; I had no wish for Grandma to look into me or ask me questions, but the air at home was tense, Father checking the barometer almost hourly and John and Doble doing their best to stay out of his way. It made me jittery, for I have always been unable to prevent myself from absorbing the moods of everyone around me; and it was worse just then than ever, for since the fete I'd felt so queer and nervy. Lack of sleep must have been the culprit; once again I had lain awake nearly all night, my thoughts seething strangely and becoming dark.

'That's my recipe, you know,' said Mother now, 'the one for harvest cake. I don't know where she got the other. Fresh ginger!' and she shook her head.

'Ah, but it was my recipe afore you, Ada,' said Grandma. 'You've got no cause to take on.'

'I don't know. I just don't feel comfortable,' Mother said.

'You must bring her over to meet us,' said Granfer, who was leaning in the doorway of the railway carriage and chewing his unlit briar. 'Happen I'll never get another chance to meet a famous author 'fore I die.'

'Oh, don't say that, Granfer,' said Mary, baby Terence clamped to her blue-veined breast. 'You'll be years with us yet.'

'I'll bring her next time, Granfer. You'll like her – everyone does.'

'Even you now, Ada?' he asked.

'I've grown used to her, I'll say that. She can be helpful – did I mention that she arranged a new buyer for our eggs?'

'Is that so?'

'Yes, we don't sell them to Blum's any longer; they go all the way to London in a van, and we make an extra twopence per load.'

'George must be pleased with that,' said Grandma.

'He says he's more pleased not to have to deal with a Sheeny any more. Connie's going to speak to some of the other women in the village, too.'

'What's a Sheeny?' I asked.

'A Jew, Edie,' Mother said. 'Not that I've got anything against them, of course.'

'Why doesn't Father want us to deal with one, then?' I asked. 'Nobody ever minded before.'

'They're not like us, that's all.'

'Some do say they shirked the call-up in '14,' Mary interjected, 'though Clive says that's nothing but a slander.'

'Will you ladies excuse me while I see to the pig?' Granfer said; he never liked to hear talk of the War. Fishing a screw of tobacco from his waist-coat pocket, he descended the little steps, out of sight.

Mother and Mary began talking about the baby, and I reached for the cocoa tin on the table to see if there might be another piece of fudge.

'Edie,' Grandma said.

'Oh – sorry. I was being greedy,' I said, and put the tin back.

She shook her head and regarded me for a long moment. 'The bird is alive, and it's not the woman troubling you – although perhaps she should. You and your brother are friends –'

It wasn't a question or a statement, but a conclusion she had come to from looking at me. I nodded and picked up my empty teacup and began to turn it in my hands, looking down at its familiar pattern of pink roses.

'Yes, Frank's well. We all are.'

She said nothing, but continued to regard me closely.

'Nothing's the matter, Grandma, for goodness' sakes!' I snapped.

The talk went on but I did not take part in it, thinking instead of Connie, and whether she had really meant that I could go and live with her in London, and what that might be like. So it came as a sickening shock when Mary, the baby asleep at last, asked if it was true that I was walking out with Alfie Rose.

'No! Of course not – who said that?' I replied.

'Oh, she's colouring up!' Mary laughed.

'Walking out? You never are!' said Mother, turning to me where she sat, her face hurt.

'It's rubbish, Mother, I'm not walking out with him. Honestly,' I said.

'That's not what I've heard,' said Mary, smirking. 'I've heard you went for a twilight stroll together after the fete. Oh, Ed, it's high time you found yourself a sweetheart. Don't look so upset.'

'You didn't say anything about a walk, Edie,' said Mother. 'I thought you stayed on to help clear up!'

'I didn't actually say that – I didn't say anything!' I said, and felt myself beginning to flush red. It was anger, of course, though I was slow to recognise it, for only Father, in our house, was permitted such a thing.

'Oh, and why did you not speak out, then? Keeping secrets from your mother?'

'Ada,' Grandma said.

Something rose in me then, something taut like a bowstring. I stood up, and it snapped.

'Secrets! *Secrets!* I didn't tell you why I was late because Father was blind drunk when I got home, if you remember – he'd kicked over John's garden and he was being sick all over the boot scraper, and the yellow vase had been smashed and was in bits on the kitchen floor, and actually it was shameful, *shameful*, the way he carried on at the fete, so if we must talk about secrets, let's talk about *that*, shall we?'

Looking down at the three women's shocked faces and the still-sleeping child, I felt powerful and elated: my blood had surged and slowed again, and its receding tide had left me feeling as clear and unambiguous as a glass bell. I lifted my right arm then, and with one trembling finger traced a witch-mark in the still air that hung between us. Mary gasped and put her hand to her mouth.

As I turned to leave, I saw Granfer standing quietly in the railway carriage door.

'Come on, child,' he said, his voice steady, and held out his crabbed hand. 'Let's you and me see to Meg, now, shall us? That's right.'

Whatever motor-cars may offer in terms of speed and convenience they surely lack in tranquillity. For a good pony knows what she is about, and can for the most part be left to her own devices; her head bobs in front of you, ears up and alert, leaving you free to look at the passing hedges, and over them to the fields on either side; to gaze down into gardens, and into cottage windows, too – all of it at a pace gentle enough to cry 'Good evening!' if one is in good humour, and exchange a little news with anyone you pass. The birds and wild creatures are not frightened away by your passage, for the only sounds you make are the steady *clop, clop* of the pony's hooves and the crunch of the trap's wheels on the road. And should darkness fall you can light the carriage lamps and watch the moths crowd around them, or you can trust your pony, who sees and hears far better than you, to steer you past any motor-cars or foot travellers in the dark. Then the steady motion rocks you into a trusting dream – not quite asleep, but not awake – in which you know yourself to be but one in an unending chain of people through the centuries who have worked in partnership with horses in war and in peacetime, and always will.

That afternoon we drove home for the most part in silence, Mother, Mary and the baby in the front of the trap, me in the back with Mary's perambulator lashed securely beside me; we were going to take her as far as the village, where she planned to call on some old friends and then walk the last few miles home. I said nothing, merely watched as the road unfurled behind me, the dust raised by Meg's hooves hanging in the air. In the front, Mother and Mary exchanged a remark now and then, but very little was said; from the hedges, though, blackbirds sang, low and melodious, and sparrows chided and fought.

I felt tired now, and somehow dull, like a blunt knife or dirty pewter. In place of the recent, strange intensity of my thoughts there was only a blankness, for something inside me had shifted and I had surrendered almost gratefully, in the way that you sometimes surrender to sleep. I knew that there would be questions later, and I did not know what I would say, but for now there was only the journey; the homely railway carriages and the smallholding receding behind me like a lost world.

Granfer had led me to the little paddock where he tethered the goat and called Meg over, and then he had taken my hand and rested it on her warm flank. I leaned my cheek against her neck and closed my eyes while he held her head and spoke to us both quietly, telling us about the bees in the clover, and where the throstle was nesting, and the hare he had watched at sunrise suckling two leverets. Heaven only knows what the three women were saying about me indoors, but I listened to Meg's breathing and felt her gently toss her head, and after a while they came out and I heard the murmur of their voices, and I opened my eyes again.

Granfer had gone over to talk to them, and presently Grandma came over to me in the paddock and held both of my hands in hers. Tears sprang to my eyes in case she hated me; but she looked keenly at me with her good eye, studied each of my hot palms and nodded. Then she pressed an old silver florin and a sprig of marjoram into my hand.

'Thank you for the news of your father, Edith,' she said. 'Though Ada should by rights have come to me herself. As for the Rose boy —'

'But Grandma, I —'

'Hush, child. Hush. Don't you give him another thought.'

We stopped by the pump in the village for Mary to get out. She climbed carefully down with the baby while Mother untied the cord holding the perambulator to the back of the trap and eased it down gently to the road; then I jumped down and led Meg to the horse trough so she could drink. Terence woke and began to scream and wave his red fists; Mary pulled up the hood for shade and rocked the perambulator on its big wheels.

'He's hungry, poor mite,' Mother said.

'I know,' said Mary, one arm awkwardly across her chest.

'Oh, Mary, love,' said Mother, and they embraced. I set my jaw and looked away.

Mother climbed back up to the front of the trap and took the reins, and Meg raised her head and shook the clegs from her ears, bright drops of water flying from her velvet lips. I looked over to my sister where she stood with the perambulator, and she looked back at me.

'You should come and visit, Edie,' she said. 'We'll — go for a nice walk, or something. Come soon.'

'I will,' I managed, in a whisper. 'I'm sorry. I'll come when the harvest's in.'

'Good. After all, you must get to know baby Terence. You've hardly spent any time with him at all.'

I remember every detail of that day, even all these years later, for when we turned the trap into the lane we saw a figure clinging onto the farm gate and waving to us as though in alarm. Mother shook the reins and Meg broke into a trot, and I saw that it was Grandfather, bare-headed, his stick lying on the ground beside him, his old black suit pale with dust and chaff.

'What is it? Is it John?' Mother shouted as he fumbled open the gate and swung it back to let us in.

'It's Doble, Doble,' he called out in reply. 'They've carried him to his own housen. You'll find them there.'

I jumped down and picked up Grandfather's stick and gave it to him, and held open the gate. 'I'll follow you there,' I called to Mother.

'You look after your grandfather,' she replied, turning the trap in the farmyard and driving Meg hard back up the lane.

I shut the gate and took Grandfather's arm and we began to cross the yard, everything else, including the visit to Grandma and Granfer's, driven entirely from my mind.

'Whatever's happened, Grandfather? Are you all right?'

'I heard him fall, Edie – oh, it were terrible! Crashing down, he came. Acourse, your father and John were away in the fields, and Frank – I couldn't find him; I shouted, but he don't seem to be nowhere about. Oh dear, Edie – '

I settled him into his chair in the parlour and crouched beside it, holding his free hand.

'Was Doble in the barn? Is that where he fell?'

'He were making it ready – your father and John'd gone over all they machinery, oiling it and what-have-you, banging away, and you know how Doble can't abide things being a mess. So he tidied it and plugged up the holes where rats lived, and readied the thatch-rope and the barley forks ... I don't know, he must've got up on the crossbeam to fetch the sacks as was hanging there to keep, and next thing I know, down he's came!'

'Oh, poor Doble. Let me make you some tea, and then I'll go over. I'm sure he'll be all right.'

Grandfather's voice began to quaver then, and he seemed for the first time to me small, and very frail.

'Nobody came for nigh on an hour, though – nobody came! I couldn't do a thing for the poor soul in his agony – what could I do? His eyes were open, for I touched his face with my hand, but I don't think he were seeing anything through 'em no more'n I.'

Doble's cottage was on the far side of Long Piece, where it met the road, and I hurried over there as soon as I was satisfied that Grandfather was all right.

'Take him his cap, child – it's in the barn,' he said as I set out. 'He'll not want to be bare-headed, if he – if –'

I entered the barn with trepidation; and sure enough, there was Doble's ancient, greasy cap on the floor near the Fordson. There was blood on the floor there too, dark like port wine, and filmed with dust.

It was past six o'clock when I set out. I wondered whether I should have put together a basket of food to take over, but while I could picture Mother telling me that I was thoughtful to think of it I could also picture her saying that I should have come over without such delay. The truth was, I didn't know what I should prepare for, or how, and I was frightened. I just couldn't imagine Doble dead.

It had been humid all day but now the air was moving, and from the hedgerows spinks sang, though not of coming rain. An evening breeze rippled the sun-bleached barley and soughed in the leafy castles of the elms, and there were banks of cloud on the horizon, low and barred. It wasn't enough for wet weather, I thought; but I didn't have the knack for reading the skies that my grandparents, or Father and John for that matter, seemed to possess. But if Doble was all right — and he must be, I thought, he must — if Doble was all right I would remember to ask John before bedtime if the weather would change.

At the cottage's back door my legs suddenly weakened, and I nearly turned as though not of my own volition to walk away. I am a coward, that much is true — but looking back now, I can see that I was also worn out by everything that had happened, and by the effort of making sense of a world which had begun to seem strange. In that moment I would have given anything to have remained outside in Doble's garden with its well-hoed rows of vegetables, and not have had to go in.

It was only a moment, though, and from indoors I could hear voices, so I made myself lift the latch and push open the door.

There were only two rooms, the first with a grate and an old wooden chair beside it, some cooking pots and kindling by the hearth. I ducked under the low lintel to the other room, where I found Father and John standing, bare-headed, and Mother sitting on a stool.

They had laid Doble on his cot and loosened his collar, and there was an old feed-sack folded behind his head. His eyes were closed now, his mouth slightly open to show his brown peg teeth and the gap in them where his pipe usually sat. Without his cap I saw that his forehead and scalp under his thin hair were as white as the flesh of a mushroom, whereas the lower part of his face was brown from the sun. All his skin was underlaid with greenish-grey.

'Is he dead?' I asked.

Mother sighed. 'No, Edie, but he's in a bad way.'

'I can't manage without him, not at this time of year,' Father said. 'Damn the man! What was he thinking, monkeying about up there?'

'George, we will *manage*,' said Mother levelly. 'Edie, come and sit with him a moment. Sing out if he moves, all right?'

So I laid Doble's cap on the threadbare coverlet and took her place, and she took Father out to the little

garden with its canes of fragrant sweet peas among
the potatoes and cabbages. I could hear them talking
in urgent voices, not quite loud enough to catch the
sense.

John cleared his throat after a few moments. 'Edie,'
he said. 'Edie – we need the doctor.'

'Well, can you go for him?'

'No, I can't.'

'Why not?'

'George – your father won't allow it.'

'But –'

'He says it's too expensive, Edie, do you see? To call
the doctor out.'

I clutched the antique coin Grandma had given
me where it lay in my pocket. 'What does Mother
say? Surely –'

'It's – it's hard for her; you know that. He said she
should make him better with – with herbs, or something. Told her to use her knack.'

'And did she?'

'Well, acourse not, Edie. She can't work magic, and
your father should know that. It could be that the
man's back is broke.'

'What do *you* think, John – can Doble pull
through?'

'I can't say for sure, only – only that he should
have a chance. All his life that man's worked for your
family, and worked well; and I served with his boy
in France and I saw him – I saw him killed. I won't

stand by and see Tipper's father left to die like a dog. It in't right.'

'But what —'

'Edie, I can't go agen your father. You know that. I'm asking you to go over to Rose Farm and get one o' them boys to ride over on that motor-cycle and fetch the doctor back.'

XIII

On a cornland farm, such as ours, the pause between haysel and harvest is like a held breath. The summer lanes are edged with dog-roses and wild clematis, the hedges thronged with young birds. At last the cuckoos leave, and you are glad of it, having heard their note for weeks; but the landrails creak on interminably, invisible among the corn. The nights are brief and warm, the Dog Star dazzles overhead; the moon draws a shadow from every blade of wheat. All day, dust rises from unmade roads and hangs in the air long after a cart or a motor-car passes. Everything waits.

In midwinter the farm is one thing, you see. Then it is a world. There are the hay-ricks and root clamps, the huge piles of logs and coal, the flitches of bacon, jars of lard and preserves. The animals are all close by, and all the long labour of summer is gathered to hand. Should snow fall, or the road to the village thicken impassably with mud, the farm, entire unto itself, must be able to go on.

But in high summer it is another thing. The farm-house windows are left open for any breeze, its occupants far distant, labouring in the fields. The beasts are largely working or grazing, so the yard is quiet; the ricks are long gone, and perhaps only some oats and oilcake, and a little chaff, is left for feed. The land lies open to the weather and undefended, exposed to the ripening sun.

God forgive me, but the main thing occupying my mind as I hurried to Rose Farm was not poor Doble but Alf Rose, for the thought of him made me want to turn and run the other way, as silly as that might seem. I wondered whether Doble's accident meant that we would now need help with our harvest, the closest help to hand being either Alf or Sid. '*Please no, please no,*' I muttered to myself as I approached the farmyard, and on the silver florin in my pocket I traced a witch-mark with my right fingertip.

I found Sid in the farmyard, where a brand-new Massey-Harris stood, bright red, its modern contours gilded by the low light of the setting sun. There was no sign of Alf, and I felt almost light-headed with relief. Sid was a good person; I could trust him. I felt sure of that.

'Hullo, Edie!' he called, grimacing only slightly. 'C-come to see? We've had a regular stream of visitors to-day. What d'you think, will John want to borrow it to get your corn in, or is he still w-wedded to horsepower?'

'Sid, is my brother here?'

'No, I haven't seen him all day – why, is he not with you? P-p-perhaps he's over with Sally,' he said, taking a short pipe from his waistcoat pocket and beginning to fill it. 'W-what's wrong?'

'Doble's had an accident, and we need the doctor. Could you go on your motor-cycle?'

'Oh dear. M-must be serious for your father to get old sawbones out. What happened?'

'He fell, in the barn. It's – it's John who wants the doctor. Look, I've got this –' and I held out the florin, damp bits of marjoram dropping from it to the ground.

Sid laughed. 'Put that away. Yes, I'll r-r-ride over. I'll bring him back with me if he's at home, and if he's not I'll leave a message. Where's Doble – at your place?'

'No, he's in his cottage. He's not moving, Sid. It's bad.'

When I got back to the cottage John and Father were gone, and Frank had arrived. It was beginning to get dark.

'Did you send for the doctor, Ed?' he asked me straight away. Mother was sitting with Doble; he and I were in the other room, where Frank had made a fire to heat water for tea and lit Doble's ancient lamp. I saw that he'd brought a basket of food over for Mother; it was Grandfather's doing, no doubt, for he would never have thought of it himself.

'John told me to. Is it all right?' I asked. 'Sid's riding over on his motor-cycle.'

'Yes. Blast him! It's not right.'

'Blast who – Father?'

'Yes. He said – he said that even if Doble survived the night he'd be useless now, and so it were better that he died so we could get a new man into the cottage, quick.'

'Frank! He didn't!'

'He did, Ed. And Mother – she didn't take it well.'

'Did John hear?'

'No, thank heavens. Things are bad enough. And don't you go telling him, either.'

I felt cold and still inside. 'Frank, there's something wrong with Father.'

For once he didn't chaff me, or tell me I was being silly.

'I know there is,' he said.

'He isn't himself any more,' I said, dropping my voice to a whisper. 'He hasn't been since the fete, as a matter of fact. I think he's ... somebody else.'

It may seem strange, but it felt true to me as I said it, and not a figure of speech. Father wasn't Father; an imposter had somehow taken his place, and I was the only one in the family who wasn't fooled.

Just then Mother appeared in the doorway from the other room and looked very levelly at us both. My heart banged, for I thought she was going to tell us that Doble had died.

'Edith, Frank: I never want to hear you speaking ill of your father again. Either of you.'

'But Mother, he —'

'That's enough, boy; you're not master yet. Edie, go home. You're ready to drop, I can see.'

'I want to be here.'

'And I'm telling you to go. I'll stay here with Doble, and Frank will wait with me for the doctor to come. He's had a far easier day than you – he's been gallivanting around with Sally all afternoon.'

'But —'

'*Enough!* Go and rest. Come back in the morning, if I haven't sent Frank with word; and bring breakfast over – enough for Doble too, in case he wakes. And find out from your father if he still wants to start tomorrow. The wheat's ready, and the weather won't wait.'

Her expression softened then, and she held out her arms to me.

'Come here, girl. There's things we need to talk about, you and I. But not now. Tomorrow, when you've slept. All right?'

Wrapped in my mother's arms and held against her broad, familiar body, so different from Connie's, I nodded; and under Doble's low, mould-spotted cottage ceiling I realised that I was growing taller than her. I wanted to weep, I wanted to tell her everything; but I knew that I must keep all my feelings within me, and make sure only that we got the harvest in.

'Everything will be all right, Edith June, I promise,' she said, releasing me with a pat.

Again that night I did not sleep. I lay fretting – not about Doble, or Father, or Sir Cecil's speech at the fete, but about Edmund, for some reason; I kept picturing him being taken by one of the cats, or by a fox if – as was likely – he was roosting on the ground in one of the dark fields. It was such a silly thing to worry about, given everything, but lying in the dark with my eyes wide open I didn't feel in control of my thoughts.

Perhaps I should keep him with me always, I told myself, turning over yet again; perhaps he would be safer in a pen at night; for although he was here to protect me, I had rescued him from Moses' hooves and so was responsible for him for the rest of his life. Yes, he was mine, and I decided that he must not fly south in autumn, as all the other landrails did; he must always stay at Wych Farm, with me, where we were safe. Yet no sooner had I resolved this to my own satisfaction than the thought somehow began again and I had to pursue it until it had run full circle, and this seemed to go on for hours. Perhaps, I thought, as a gibbous moon outlined the edge of the wooden window shutters, sleep didn't really matter any more.

I suppose I must have dozed at last, for Frank came to wake me at six. He brought a cup of tea up, and by this I knew that Mother had said something to him – most likely that I had women's troubles, for that would embarrass him and keep him from asking what was wrong.

'Frank – come back,' I said, sitting up in bed. 'Is Doble – how is Doble?'

'Awake and talking, after a fashion. Looks likely he'll survive.'

'Oh, that's wonderful! What did the doctor say?'

'He came, but Doble'd already woken up by then. It was a miracle, Ed. I was in the chair by the fire – I was asleep, I suppose – and the first thing I knew Mother was shaking me and telling me to warm up some milk. I thought it must be for her, but she said he was stirring, and when I went in to see, his eyes were open and looking straight at me. It fair gave me a shock, I'll admit.'

So the doctor hadn't saved Doble; this was interesting news.

'How did he seem?'

'Befuddled at first. You know, his speech was strange. I think his head hurt – he kept touching it and closing his eyes, though he didn't actually complain of it. Mother sat and held his hands and talked to him, and after a few minutes he – he began to cry.'

'Doble? Cry?'

'Yes. Oh, Ed, I hated to see it. I went and sat by the fire again.'

'So ... his back isn't broken?'

'Doesn't look like it. But I don't think he'll be back on his feet straight away. Did you know he'll be seventy years old come September?'

'What did the doctor say?'

'Well, he couldn't credit it, really – not when Mother told him how far he'd fallen, and how long he'd been out cold. He checked him over and dressed the wound on the back of his head; he said the fact he fell on the threshing floor had probably saved him, it being beaten earth and not brick.'

I sipped my tea. It wasn't the floor of the barn that had miraculously saved Doble; that much was clear to me, if not to Frank.

'Does Father know? About the doctor, I mean.'

'No. He'll want paying by the end of the month, though.'

'We'll manage something – perhaps Doble has some money put away.'

'Let's hope so. God knows we've none here.'

'Is Mother still over there?'

'Yes – she said to send you over when you woke. I was thinking: what about your Constance – could she help nurse Doble for a few days? Father wants to start on the harvest this morning, and we need you and Mother in the fields.'

'I could ask, but we'll still be short-handed. For one thing, Mother'll need to sleep now, if she's been up all night.'

'We'll manage,' he said. 'I'll get Alfie to come over and lend us a hand to-day.'

Father and John were out in the fields testing the wheat for ripeness one last time; Frank had gone to the barn to see what was left to do to make it ready, and to sharpen his and Father's scythes. Another night with very little sleep had left my eyes feeling slow and catchy in their sockets, and yet strangely I wasn't tired at all that first day of harvest-tide. In fact the farmhouse, the yard, even the black crows in the trees had begun to seem unnaturally vivid, like a painting, and I searched in everything I saw for the secret clues that would help me know what to do when the time came.

I ate a few spoonfuls of porridge from the pot on the range, and then took some tea through to Grandfather; I found him up and dressed already, and anxious, although glad to have news of Doble.

'I don't say as all will quite be well yet, but we've a fair chance. A death at harvest-tide – no, it'd bode very ill, and that's a fact. It's when we come to build the ricks we'll miss him, though. No-one can match Doble for thatching a rick.'

'I'm going to take some breakfast over to Mother now, but – they won't start without me, will they?'

'There was a drench o' dew at first light, girl, can't you smell it? They'll wait for the sun to burn it off. Go on, now. I'll be all right.'

I had always been there at the start of the harvest: every year. Father would cut two stalks of wheat for each of us and twist them together, 'like a man and a maid', the saying went. The men would wear them in their waistcoat buttonholes until the very last load was in, while Mother, Mary and I would pin them to our hats, or tuck them into our headscarves. It was bad luck to lose yours while there was still corn to cut, though

I suppose it must have happened to one of us at some time, and been quietly replaced. I was religious about keeping hold of mine, each year adding another to the jar on my bedroom windowsill, where they remained, desiccated and dusty and never to be thrown away. I don't know what the others did with theirs.

Hurrying along the lane on my way to Doble's cottage I saw Mother coming the other way, carrying a basket. She raised it a little to show that she'd seen me, but I could tell from the way she walked that she was bone-tired, and that bringing Doble back from death's door had used up everything she had. For a moment I saw her completely anew, saw how powerful a woman she really was beneath the toil and how little it mattered that she didn't read poetry, or know the first thing about politics, as Connie did. I felt proud to be her daughter then.

'Frank told me everything,' I said, kissing her cheek and taking the basket from her. 'What's this? And who's with him now?'

'The man needs clean clothes and bed-sheets, so I'll have to wash to-day, if only this. Mrs Rose arrived a little while ago – Sid told her what had happened. She'll stay with him a while.'

'We're going to start to-day – this morning. Father says he won't risk the bran thickening up any more.'

'Which field?'

'I don't know – they're out now to check.'

'Well, I won't be needed straight away; there's dew, for one thing. I'll give these a quick slop-wash, and then I'll rest for an hour. Edie, you must make sure to be really useful this year, though, do you understand me? No wandering off with a book – your father needs your help.'

'I understand perfectly, Mother,' I said. 'Frank says he's going to get – to get Alf Rose to help, but I wondered, could I ask Connie to come instead?'

'Alfie's abed, according to his mother.'

'In bed?' I asked. 'Why, what's the matter with him?'

'Oh, it's probably nothing. But he'll be no use to us this week.'

At the house Mother went to light the copper. I followed her into the backhouse and put down the bundle of clothes and sheets, a mixture of relief and something darker coursing through me at the thought of Alf Rose ill.

'Edie, I want to talk to you.'

'About yesterday?'

'Yes. I know you were tired, and upset with your sister, and the fact is she shouldn't tease you. But what did you mean by drawing that shape in the air?'

'But you know what it was, Mother.'

'Edie, tell me. I want to understand.'

'You *know*, though. You and Grandma. I know you do!' I said, my voice a little uncertain despite the conviction I'd felt growing since Frank had brought me tea at first light.

'Know what, girl? Look, I'm the tired one now. Perhaps I'm missing your meaning.'

I looked past her, out of the little backhouse window. It was time for secrets to be said out loud, for after all, wasn't I a woman now?

'I understand why Mrs Godbold asked you to help her with the witch-bottle,' I said. 'And I know how Grandma perceives things we haven't told her. And – and I know what Edmund really is.'

'Edmund – your bird, you mean? Edie, that's –'

There were voices in the yard: Father and John had returned from the fields and Frank had gone out to meet them. I heard Grandfather, too.

'Mother,' I whispered, taking both her hands in mine to reassure her, 'it's all right: *I know everything*. I know it was you who saved Doble from dying last night, with your powers. And I know who's cursed Alf Rose and made him ill.'

It was nearly nine o'clock when we made a start on Home Field. Father and Frank went in first to scythe the margins up by hand for the reaper-binder; I took a light rake and walked into the corn, standing up any patches that had been laid by wind or animals so that the long blades would not miss them when the machine came around.

Mother had left the washing to steep and came out with Grandfather to see the first cut made, taking her two stalks from Father and putting them into her apron pocket with a brief smile before walking back with Grandfather and John, who had gone to harness the team. I missed her in the field with me, but it gave me time to think.

I wasn't yet clear about everything, and I'd expected that she might not explain it all straight away, but at the same time it had been hard, the way she'd stared at me in the backhouse; I felt lost and adrift, and I wanted her to admit me to the wonderful secret we shared. But the men were nearby, I reflected, and I wasn't yet sure how much they might know, so perhaps it was as well that we spoke about it properly another time. All I knew for certain was that Mother had healed Doble with her powers, and Grandma had overlooked Alf with her errant eye and made him ill – she'd as good as told me she'd sicken him, I realised now. And as for me, the daughter and granddaughter of these women: when Mother said to me that I must help Father with the harvest, there was clearly a secret meaning in it, because it wasn't something, at four-teen, that I needed to be told.

I stood for a moment with my rake in the middle of the golden field and gazed about me at the thigh-high corn rippling out in all directions until it met the massy hedgerows with their dark August leaves. Above me the sun blazed in a blue bowl, but before long the sky would be grey and stitched with wavering skeins of geese; then the stubble would be ploughed to rich brown furrows, the tall ricks would huddle close about the farmhouse, and with the first frosts the Hunt would ride out again over the autumn land.

But not yet. For everything there is a season, and now was the time to ensure we reaped our hard-earned reward from the fields. I wonder, looking back, that it didn't feel overwhelming to have so much resting on me – the future of the farm, and of my whole family, in fact – but it didn't, somehow. It was as though the entire valley was charged and shining, and I with it, blessed among women; and I felt a growing sureness that as long as I played my part in events properly, all would yet be well.

Father and Frank had finished the scything and I helped gather the cut corn from the field's margin into loose sheaves, tying each roughly with a couple of stalks. Then, at last, the reaper-binder appeared at the corner of the field. I could see as I walked over that Moses and Malachi were impatient, for Moses was tossing his head and Malachi's ears were tipped forward, the muscles of his great chestnut neck twitching and shivering away the flies. They knew that this was their great and bounden duty, and they were keen to set about it; John, who whispered to them of everything, had made sure of that.

'Frank, Edie, you'll stook,' called Father. 'I'll see you off, but then I shall go to open up Greenleaze. John, do you send Frank over to fetch me if the string fouls or breaks.'

'I can manage the string, Father.'

'That he can,' said John as he climbed into the high iron seat of the Albion. 'I taught him myself last year.'

'Well, perhaps. Let's see how she begins – she's not the steadiest of contraptions, God knows.'

And so the harvest began. John clicked his tongue and the team leaned forward into the weight of the machine, pulling it at last into reluctant motion; and as its bull-wheel crept forward, the cogs and gears meshed and the great wooden paddles began to turn. The horses could see where they should start into the crop, and all John had to do was encourage them and remind them once of the machine's width; then, as the first of the rustling wheat began to fall to the long, saw-toothed blade, he twisted around in his seat to see it move up the canvas elevator to be tied and ejected from the side in a neat sheaf.

I laughed then, and saw Frank grin too, for it was always a miracle: not just the clanking great contraption – although it was a strange beast, and far too modern, really, for the timeless fields – but the way the corn changed from a plant to a crop in a moment, first one thing and then another entirely. Every year it was the same, and every year it was new.

Frank and I began to stook. If you have ever done field-work of any kind you will know that it never leaves you; your body writes it into your muscles and bones, like riding a bicycle, I suppose, or perhaps sowing by hand, as Grandfather had done. I had helped stook since I could toddle, Mother and Father knowing that however ineffective I was then, their patience in letting me learn early would repay them in years to come. And I liked it, particularly wheat; for although wheat-sheaves were heavier than barley, the barley-awns would work their way into your clothes and scratch at your skin. Wheat was cleaner to stook, unless the field was thistly, as parts of Greenleaze and The Lottens were; then I'd untie the scarf from my hair and use it to swathe my bare arms. And when the time came to stook the barley, I would wear sleeves.

Stooking was quiet, steady work: we didn't sing, for we had to be ready to shout 'Loose!' if the knotter failed and the machine began to send out unbound corn, and we had to listen, too, in case it cast a bolt or screw, causing its note to change. Then one of us would cry 'Stop!' straight away, for fear that it would shake itself to pieces, and we would search the cut and uncut corn for whatever had come off.

At Wych Farm we always made stooks of eight for wheat. We'd swing the sheaves with the knots to the outside, dropping them down over the previous pair in the stook so the heads would join them together; Father and John would be displeased if any needed standing up again in the following days, while we waited for the wheat to dry so that we might cart it back.

We had dinner at noon. Mother brought a basket from the house, Father following with two buckets of water for the horses; John jumped down from the Albion and took the buckets from Father and then set them down before the team. They took both food and water from John, so that they would always know who they worked for – though he would allow Mother to help groom them, of course, and she gave them an apple or a bit of carrot sometimes.

It was only a short break, so we remained in the field. There was beer in a stone jug for John and Father, and for Frank too, I saw, this year. Mother and I had cold tea.

John hunkered down by the machine and took a piece of bread and dripping and a peeled onion from the basket; then he began to slice the onion carefully with his old bone-handled knife. Finally he folded the bread around it and began to eat.

Frank was cramming bread and cheese into his mouth at his usual rate. 'Aren't you eating anything, Father?' he asked.

Father shook his head. 'No, I'm not of a mind to eat just now.'

'Not even an apple?' I asked, crunching into mine.

'No, girl. Where's that bird of yours, anyhow?'

'Edmund? I don't know; shall I –'

'Don't call the pesky thing to us. Sit back down.'

'Why do you ask?'

'I put up a landrail on Greenleaze, near the horse-pond – very bold, it was. Might've been yours – you don't commonly see see the noisy buggers, after all.'

'George,' Mother said.

I gave Frank my apple core to eat. Mother's hand rested lightly on my hair, smoothing it. It felt nice.

'Edmund's all right, wherever he is just now. I'd know otherwise.'

John swallowed his beer in one draught, wiped his mouth and addressed Father. 'What d'you think to Greenleaze?'

'Middling,' Father replied. 'Thinner than it should be, but not as bad as last year. We've a good crop of nettles and thistles around the pond; I might take Doble's sickle to 'em.'

'That old pond makes the job half as long again, don't it?'

'Well. I shall have it done this afternoon.'

I pictured the black pond on Greenleaze. Grandfather said that once upon a time there had been an old cob house next to it, but it had long sunk away and 'gone home'. When he was a little boy, he told Frank, you could still make out where it had stood when the crop was low. There was nothing at all to mark the place now.

'Do we need more hands?' John asked.

'We'll get by for now; come time to cart we'll feel the lack.'

John nodded. 'Best in the county for building a rick, some say.'

'Doble's not dead,' Frank said.

'Might as well be, boy, for all the use he is.'

'I'll go over this afternoon,' Mother said. 'See how the poor man is.'

'No you won't, Ada. You're needed here. Fact is, he'd be better off in the workhouse, as well you know.'

Mother's hand came to rest very still on my head, but she didn't speak.

'Better for you, you mean,' Frank muttered under his breath.

Just then there came a familiar 'Halloo!' and we turned to see Connie striding over, followed by a small man in a dark suit carrying a leather case.

'How are you all? Wonderful harvesting weather, isn't it? So sorry I missed you cutting the first ears this morning; I went to meet Charles at the railway station. Oh – this is Charles Chalcott, everyone: he's a photographer. He's come to capture some rural scenes – isn't it the most perfect English Arcadia, Charles? What did I tell you! Glorious. Well, is the wheat "addling" well, as they say here, George? What have I missed?'

Mr Chalcott shook Father's hand, and then John's and Frank's, and tipped his hat to Mother and me.

'How d'you do. Very pleased to meet you all,' he said.

Connie put her hands in her pockets and grinned. 'Oh! Doble's sitting up and taking some broth, Ada – I stopped in on the way here. Isn't it a miracle? Mrs Rose says you're not needed this afternoon – she'll stay with him until supper.'

Mother smiled. 'Thank you for that, Connie. It's kind of you to let me know.'

'You look peaky, Edie. Were you up all night with Doble too?'

'No, I just – I didn't sleep well,' I said.

'Well, you'll be sure to tonight, after bringing in the harvest all day,' she said. 'Now, Charles, are you ready? Can I do anything to help?'

Mother was packing the remains of the meal back into the basket; John was rubbing the horses' noses and speaking softly to them and Father was lighting his pipe. Mr Chalcott, meanwhile, had taken the black camera from its case and was peering into the top. I hurriedly moved out of the way.

'Oh, don't worry, miss,' he said with a smile. 'I'm just making some adjustments for the light. I'm not taking a picture of you.'

I was relieved: there was something horrible about the thought of a man peering at me through his apparatus and taking an image of me away. Mary would have jumped at the chance to be photographed, no doubt, but for some reason it felt unbearable to me. And perhaps a photograph would reveal what had changed in me, something that for now I needed not to be seen.

'Mr Mather, may I have your permission to take photographs on your land?' Mr Chalcott asked formally.

Father gazed out at the ripe wheat, at the red reaper-binder and at Moses and Malachi, glossy and well groomed, and for a moment I saw what he saw, and what he wanted the farm in that moment to be.

'Work away, Mr Chalcott. You photograph anything you like.'

'Not quite,' John called over as he climbed back up onto the Albion's metal seat. 'I'll thank you not to make any images of me.'

I had been sure that I would sleep that night, as Connie had said, but again I lay awake, hot beneath my sheet despite the open window. I was tired, but it was as though I had somehow lost the knack of letting go; instead I kept seeing sheaves, and stooks, and hearing in my head Connie saying 'an English Arcadia', over and over again.

At last I turned onto my front with one knee up and put my hand to myself, and I thought this time of Connie, her long white body and its frankness, the triangle of damp hair I had seen between her legs. I let my hand move slowly, and imagined lying down with her by the water and kissing her lips and her breasts; I pictured touching her between her legs as I was touching myself, and her letting me, liking it, smiling and telling me she loved me. I put off the spasm of pleasure by stilling my hand, and whispered 'I love you, Edie, oh I love you' into my pillow so that I might hear it, and it feel real. At last, though, I let sensation overtake me, and afterwards I did at last drop from the world into sleep.

It was sometime near midnight when I awoke with the sense of something vast and obscure having fallen into place. I had slept enough, I knew straight away; and I also knew that I must go to the horse-pond in Greenleaze. Connie had not gone into the water – I had stopped her – but now I must, for the sake of the farm. It seemed in that moment very simple, and I felt relieved, for I had not known what to do; but now I understood that each thing would become clear when I came to it, and that all I had to do was trust. I got up and pulled a cardigan that had once been Frank's over my nightdress, crept down the creaking stairs and put on my boots.

The yard was quiet, its cobbles, the barn and dung-heap lit by a bright, full moon. The parish lantern, Grandfather sometimes called her, while Granfer and Grandma said her name was Phoebe. I was glad of her now.

On each stable door hung a holed stone on a loop of wire and a rusty iron nail, and now I took one down and gently eased the nail from the wood, hoping that the horses wouldn't startle and wake John. Then I took the nail, raised my nightdress and traced a witch-mark gently with the point of it on my belly's pale, fine skin. I drew no blood, for I didn't need it to last more than an hour or two.

One of the horses blew and stamped as I eased the old nail back into the wood, making my heart thump and sweat prickle under my arms. But above the stable, John did not stir. Only a couple of the farm cats saw me cross the moonlit yard and walk into the darkness under the elms.

Father had scythed the margins of Greenleaze, and late in the afternoon, before she went to sit with Doble, Mother had sheaved and stooked the corn he had cut. In the moonlight it looked a little like the painting Miss Carter had shown us at school, and I wondered if perhaps she had meant it as a sign for me, one I was only now beginning to understand. There was a deep significance to everything I saw around me now – the black trees, the moon, the fields – and it was almost overwhelming. I knew I must learn to decipher its messages or everything might be lost.

I knew that Father would have had to walk through standing wheat to cut around the horse-pond, so I looked for his line and followed it. The crop around me was full of little movements, and I imagined all the harvest mice and hares that were doubtless watching me walk through its tall stalks and wondering why I had come. Ahead lay the black clump of alders that huddled around the water, the inky night sky, strewn with bright stars, beyond it and above.

At the edge of the trees I called softly for Edmund, and he came immediately, appearing quietly at my feet. I picked him up and cradled him against my chest for a moment, and I couldn't help the tears from starting to my eyes, because I knew by his attendance on me there that everything I had suspected was all true – all true. I felt like a child all of a sudden, I felt so small and desolate – which was strange, as surely I should have felt at my most powerful then. I pressed my wet face into the bird's soft feathers and felt his heart beating in my palm and I made myself think of the farm, and of Mother and Grandma; of all that I loved, and that might yet be lost.

'I'm ready now, Edmund,' I whispered at last, and set him down in the stubble, where he roused his feathers briefly and began to preen. And then I took off Frank's cardigan, folded it up neatly, and ducked under the alders to the weeds and flag irises at the margin of the pond.

The water was chill at first, but by the time it was around my thighs it felt blood-warm; the pond might have been shady, but the weather had been hot for weeks. With each step my unlaced boots sank into the depthless mud beneath me and at last I flung out my arms for balance, water arcing from them, so that I wouldn't fall. I had expected ducks or moorhens to explode from the margins, as they would have had I gone into the pond by the house, but it seemed that no wildfowl made this pond their home.

When the dark water was at my shoulders I stopped and pushed my palely billowing nightdress down into the water, and waited for the ripples to subside. I felt so clean all of a sudden; cleaner than I had since the fete. And it was worth it just for that.

I felt my breathing slow with the fading ripples and let my awareness of the cornfield around me, and the night sky, return. At last, I breathed out all the air I could from my lungs, took two tip-toeing steps forward, closed my eyes – and let go.

I don't know how far down I sank, or whether I truly reached the bottom, though I felt roots and other black, invisible things touching my hands and grazing my buttocks and knees. I felt as though I descended a long, long way, the water growing colder and more silent as I fell until it was as though the world above winked out – and was lost. It seemed like hours I was under the water, but I know that can't have been the case.

At last I bobbed back up to the surface as I had known that I would, gasping for air and with the taste of iron in my mouth. I trod water, then struck out for the place where I had got in, clutching at the flag irises and streaming pond-water, my body casting a moon-shadow across the sucking black mud at the bank.

'Edie – Edie – oh, my Edie,' I heard Mother cry.

XIV

It must have been mid-morning when I woke, for the sun was high and I could hear no sounds of break-fasting from below. I lay naked, my much-darned sheet kicked away and tangled at my feet, listening to the distant whirr of the Albion and a wood-pigeon cooing contentedly on the roof. The skin of my belly was pale and unmarked, and my limbs were full of a luxurious torpor. Everything felt right.

Despite the brackish water streaming from me, Mother and I had embraced fiercely by the black pond and I had comforted her, rubbing her back until her sobs died down. I was euphoric, utterly transported – but it was private and inward, not something yet that anyone else could see.

'Sit down with me a moment, Edie,' she'd said at last.

I was shivering a little, although the night was warm, and I found Frank's cardigan among the this-tles and willow-herb and put it on. We sat side by side and I used Mother's shawl to rub some of the water from my hair and my legs. My feet were cold in my wet boots, and I couldn't help smiling, but the starry sky seemed unchanged from when I had stood on the bank alone, as though indifferent to everything I had done. I looked for Edmund, but he was nowhere to be seen.

'Edie –'

'How did you know where to find me?'

'Your grandfather heard you leave the house – you know how sharp his ears are. He called up the stairs and woke me up.'

'Does Father know?'

'No, he was snoring; he drank to the harvest after supper last night. I didn't think there was anything in the house, but by his breath it seems he's been hiding a bottle of whisky away somewhere. You're lucky, child.'

I didn't reply, and after a while I felt her gather herself.

'Talk to me, Edie.'

'What do you want me to say?'

'Tell me – tell me what's happening. Why did you go into the horse-pond?'

'Because I had to.'

Her voice was pleading. 'But why? Were you trying to – to do away with yourself?'

'Mother, of course not! You should know that. It was – a swim.'

'You went for a swim in the middle of the night? Edie, I don't understand. And everything's so – I mean there's Doble, your father –' Her voice was rising in pitch and sounding almost panicked now.

'Doble will be all right. You'll make him well again.'

'And the harvest – there's too much barley – I told him – you know what a risk it is – oh Edie, I don't pretend to understand what's wrong, I just want you to be well, I *need* you to be well now.'

'But I *am* well! And the harvest will be good this year, I swear it. And all manner of thing shall be well.'

She looked at me strangely. 'Edie –'

'Don't you ever get angry, Mother?'

'Angry? With who? With you?'

'No, with – with all of it.'

She sighed. 'There's no sense in women getting angry, child. It changes nothing, or it changes everything. And neither's any good.'

I felt her hand find and grasp mine in the dark. 'Edie, the sign you made when we visited your grandparents. We must – we must talk properly about that.'

'You recognised it, Mother. I know you did.'

'Course I did. I know what the sign is –'

So she admitted it. I smiled in relief, and stood up, but she remained sitting, the yellow moon low on the horizon now behind.

'Tell me why you made it,' she said again. '*Tell* me!'

There was no reason for her to fret about me, of course, but I could see how much she wanted me to reassure her that I knew what I was doing, and that I would make everything right. And I didn't want her to think I wished ill on her or Mary or Grandma and Granfer, for nothing could be further from the truth.

'It was a silly mistake, I know that now,' I said soothingly. 'I'm sorry – honestly, Mother. It won't happen again.'

I helped her up, and in single file we began to walk away from the shrouded pond through the tall corn.

'And you're sure you're all right?' she asked from behind me. 'You'd tell me if there was … anything else? Anything worrying you?'

'Of course I would,' I lied.

I had lingered in bed far too long, I knew. At last I got up, put on a dress and brushed my tangled and still-damp hair, looking out of my little window at the familiar view. There was a clarity and a calmness to my thoughts now, the confusion and fear of the last few days held in abeyance. I felt as though I had been chosen, as though I understood everything – the whole of creation, perhaps – although I couldn't have put any of it into words.

Grandfather was in the kitchen when I went down. The breakfast things had been cleared away, but he remained sitting at his usual place.

'Well, child?'

'Good morning, Grandfather.'

'*Edith.*' And he thumped his stick hard on the brick floor.

I sat down. He turned his face towards me, his eye sockets sunken and blank.

'I was hot. I went to the pond to cool off.'

'That's a lie, girl.'

'It isn't.'

'It is a damned lie, and you and me both know it! Now, be you going to tell us what went on?'

I stared out of the window. I could see Meg grazing in Horse Leasow; she had an easy time of it at harvest, while the draught horses were out in the fields.

'Are we in debt, Grandfather?'

He seemed almost to recoil. 'Now, whatever d'you want to know a thing like that for, girl?'

'Is it a lot – do you even know how much? Does Father tell you?'

'Never you mind.'

'Well, never *you* mind, then, either!'

And with that I got up and walked from the room.

Out in the yard I called for Edmund, but he didn't come. The weather had changed, I realised; the sky was white and the air felt dabbly and close, as though threatening rain. I saw that John had salvaged what he could of his flower-garden after Father's drunken rampage: the rose bushes had had their broken stems bound and were carefully staked, and the little plot was once again neatly edged with stones, but the orange wallflowers were gone and there were gaps among the sweet williams that hadn't been there before.

I walked to Great Ley, where the hen-huts were, but someone had already fed them and let them out of their coops. Where was everyone? John would be on the reaper-binder, of course, but who was stooking – Frank and Mother? Perhaps she was over at Doble's cottage, in which case Father would be doing it, something I knew he did not like.

It went without saying that I would go and help in the fields as soon as I got up during harvest, but now that I had done my part I felt sure that our corn would come in well; in fact I even knew that it wouldn't rain. Instead I decided to visit Mary, to find out whether she was truly with me or against me, for I knew that I would perceive it immediately if I could only speak to her properly, alone. It was a couple of hours' walk to Monks Tye, but I didn't mind.

I cut under the trees by the rick-yard, as I had the night before, passed the Pightle, then took the field path that ran north between Great Ley and Home Field, humming a little to myself under my breath. The path brought me out by the steep bank between the houses at Back Lane, and then I crossed the Stound to The Street and turned right towards the church. Sparrows chattered from the village roofs and gutters, and around the chimneys of the Bell & Hare jackdaws jinked and quacked.

I hadn't been to church since the Sunday before the fete, and as I passed St Anne's I paused and looked up at the squat flint tower with its brick parapet and the homely tiled roof of the nave. It was so familiar, so comforting somehow, but I felt sure in that moment that I would never go back inside. That was all right, I thought; I didn't mind it. Yet a little further along the lane I found that for the third time in recent days my cheeks were wet with tears.

Connie and I had come this way on our bicycles a couple of weeks before, and I found myself thinking about the conversation we'd had. I'd questioned her about why she went to church when she had told us that she didn't believe in God. Wasn't it hypocritical, or, worse, a sin?

'Darling, it's about fitting in,' she'd replied.

'But I thought you didn't care about that!'

'I don't – in a way. I don't mind if people think I'm eccentric or different, because compared to village folk, Edie, I am. But it wouldn't do to scorn the things that people believe in. And in any case, I have a lot of respect for the church's work when it comes to out-of-the-way places like this.'

I'd pondered what she said about not minding being different, and it had occurred to me that for all my conception of myself as a bookworm I had always really wanted to be like everyone else; in fact at school I would have traded my cleverness in a heart-beat for the chance to have made even one proper friend.

'How do you do it, Connie – how do you make people like you so much?'

I'd blushed as I said it, for it might have sounded rude; but not to her, for she wasn't in the habit of seeking out slights.

'I suppose ... I suppose it's because I don't need anything from people, and so they can relax.'

'Yet you do nothing but ask people questions!' I protested.

'Well, that's very true, darling,' she laughed; and then we spoke of other things. But I knew I hadn't understood her, and I wondered now if I ever would.

After I had been walking for an hour or so I began to tire, and I realised that I hadn't eaten or drunk anything since supper the previous night. Where were the crows that had yesterday been sent to watch me? I hadn't seen a single one, although there should have been several about.

The road to Monks Tye was quiet, for most people were harvesting; I only saw a baker's van and a couple of farm wagons on the road. But around me in every direction the golden acres were busy with tractors and horses, and here and there a field lay razed to raw stubble and dotted with stooks.

At last a smart blue motor-car drew up beside me, its side-window lowered.

'Hullo, miss; would you like a lift?'

I peered in; it was a young man of about Sid Rose's age, or perhaps a little older. His hair was neatly combed and he was wearing drill shorts and a shirt with the sleeves turned up. He picked up a canvas pack from the seat beside him and slung it into the back, and then leant over and released the door catch. Clearly he had been sent to help me.

'Hop in. How far are you going?' he said.

I got in, smoothed my skirt over my knees and smiled at him. 'Monks Tye. Do you know it? I'm Edith, by the way.'

He grinned back. 'I'm Neil. I don't, but you can tell me where to stop. Is it far?'

'Only a couple more miles. Where are you going?'

'Well, I'm trying to get to Blaxford; I'm meeting some friends there for lunch. I say, I should probably call it dinner in these parts, shouldn't I?'

I laughed. The car began to bounce along at quite a pace, the sound of its engine cheering, somehow. 'You're not from around here, then.'

'Well spotted! Whereas I can tell from your voice that you're a native — am I right?'

I nodded. Did I have an accent? I hadn't thought so — certainly not like the threshing team, or my grandparents, if it came to that. Connie had never mentioned it.

'Well, lucky you! It's a beautiful part of the world.'

'So everyone says.'

'Don't you think so?'

'Oh – I'm just used to it, I suppose. Are you here for a holiday?'

'You're a regular sleuth, Edith. Yes, we're going hiking; we plan to follow the course of the Stound all the way to the sea. Tom and Gladys and I – we're students, you see, and it's the Long Vac. Tom's always reading out bits from *In Search of England* – you know, that Morton chap from the *Express*. It's been driving us potty. Do you know it?'

I shook my head. 'Are you at Cambridge?'

'We are. Tom and I are doing Greats; Gladys is a mathematician. She's the brainiest girl I've ever met.'

'*And is there honey still for tea?*'

'Pardon?'

I felt myself flush red; why had I tried to impress him? Now he would realise how unlikeable I was.

'I think I should like to go to the seaside, if I had a holiday,' I said hurriedly. 'Or London, perhaps. I'm not sure I see the point of traipsing all over the countryside and wearing out perfectly good boots. Is it just the three of you?'

'It is.'

'Will you be camping? In tents?'

'That's right. But – there's nothing, you know, improper. Gladys is great fun, but she's not that kind of girl, do you see? Anyway, we're all far too frightened of her for that.'

'You should be frightened of me,' I said.

He laughed. 'Why, are you terribly brainy?'

'Yes, I am. I can do all sorts of things.'

'How old are you, if you don't mind? No — let me guess. Sixteen?'

'Nearly seventeen,' I lied, and felt myself blush again. He was very nice.

'So shall we see you at Girton soon? Or Newnham, perhaps?'

'Probably. I haven't decided. Oh — we're nearly at Monks Tye. It's just up ahead.'

'Righto. Well, it's been a pleasure talking to you, Edith. And good luck with your studies. Shall I let you out here?'

He brought the motor-car to a stop outside the Waggon & Horses, a pheasant exploding from the hedge-top as we pulled up. Two elderly farm-hands in smocks sat outside with their mugs, and one touched his cap

'Neil, I —'

He was smiling at me, his hand out. I didn't take it.

'Can I come? With you, I mean. On your hike. With Gladys and — and Tom?'

His face clouded, and he put his hand back on the steering-wheel.

'Oh, I — I don't — I'm sorry, Edith. It's been lovely to meet you, but — don't you have somewhere to be?'

'My sister's — but she won't mind, honestly. She doesn't even know I'm coming. Wouldn't two girls be better than one? I can show you the way, I know all the paths and roads —'

'All the way to the sea? Look, it's terribly kind of you to offer, but I can't very well take a sixteen-year-old girl along with me, just like that. It would be kidnap, don't you see?'

'No, it wouldn't, not if I wanted to go with you.'

'Edith, this is — I —'

Suddenly I saw that he just didn't like me — that was the reason; and why should he, when I was so stupid and so young? I knew from his face that he wanted me to get out of his motor-car so he could drive away and go on his holiday with his clever friends. For a moment I wondered what would happen if I refused to get out; but it was no good.

The engine was still idling, and I released the latch and pushed open the car door. I felt angry and humiliated, and for the very first time I let myself notice it while it was happening, instead of belatedly. I thought that I was angry with Neil.

'You can *piss off*,' I said, and I slammed the door as hard as I could, enjoying the sound it made. 'Piss off, and all of the rest of you, too!'

My voice had risen to a shout, my fists were clenched and my face flushed. Neil stared at me, stunned. One of the old men on the bench stood up.

'Go on, then! *Go!*'

And with a roar of the engine, he did.

The old man followed me almost to Mary's door, and as I waited for her to answer I turned and glared at him. He was pretending to be concerned about me, but I knew that really he wished me ill; he hated me and wanted me to be small and weak, as they all did. Although he asked me questions, I barely heard them, and refused to speak. There was a feeling in my chest – something high and tight and somehow familiar. My jaw ached, and I realised I'd been clenching my teeth. I was about to trace a witch-mark in the air between us, but just then Mary came to the door.

I pushed in past her and shut it behind me, and then embraced her tightly. I wanted the feeling back, the one I'd had when we'd shared a bed and she'd made me feel happy and safe and loved.

'Ed! Did you walk over? What's the matter?' she asked when at last I let her pull away. But I just shook my head. Perhaps I shouldn't explain anything to her, for after all, she was excluded from the secret; it was me, Mother and Grandma, and nobody else. All those years I had been envious of her prettiness and her bond with Mother, when in fact it was I who was special all along! But I loved her – of course I did – and looking at how tired and worn-out she seemed now, I knew I should be kind.

In the sitting-room I said that I didn't want to hold the baby, thank you, and she looked at me open-mouthed as though she had not just asked me a question but rather given me an instruction of some kind. I simply smiled, and sat down.

'So why are you here, then, Ed?' she asked, and settled the baby back on her hip. There was a trace of resentment in her voice.

'To see you! You invited me to come, remember?'

'Aren't you harvesting?'

'It's all in hand.'

'Without Doble? Are the Rose boys helping?'

'No, but it's all going perfectly well.'

'Do Mother and Father even know you're here?'

'Mary, have you got anything to eat? I missed breakfast.'

'You missed breakfast? What do you mean?'

I sighed impatiently. 'I slept in. And then I came straight here. Honestly, you don't seem very happy to see me.'

Her face flushed. 'And you don't seem very happy to see baby Terence, either!'

I held my tongue.

'Look. Can I have a cup of tea, at least? I'm parched.'

She glared at me for a moment and then, defeated, went to the little kitchen at the back, the infant drooling and complaining at her hip. I sat back on the settee and let out a long breath.

While the tea was steeping she put the baby in its basket, talking to it in the daft way that she had. I wondered whether Mother had once cooed over us like that when we were children; certainly neither she nor Grandma resorted to it when they held Terence now. Perhaps it was just her.

She had put six bourbon biscuits on a plate, and I ate three while she was bent over the basket. Their sweetness left a film on my teeth.

'Shall I be mother?' I asked. I was so thirsty, and I had the beginnings of a headache.

'If you like.'

She took her cup and went to sit in one of the armchairs. There was something prim in her movements, as though she was on show, or being judged. Why couldn't she belch, or throw one leg over the arm of the chair, I wondered; was she feeling nervous for some reason, or was this what being a married woman meant?

'Why was Buller Blythe following you, Ed?'

'The old man outside? I don't know.'

'Yes, you do.'

'Oh, it was nothing. He wished me ill, and I won't stand for it any more.'

She frowned at this.

'How's Father?'

'I *hate* him, Mary!' I hadn't meant to say it; it just came out.

'Ed, you can't hate him!'

'I do, though! You didn't see him at the fete, it was awful.'

'I've seen him drunk enough times; I know he can be a handful. Why do you think I don't come back to visit more?'

'It's got worse, though. Even Frank agrees with me.'

'Frank? Really?'

I nodded. 'There's something ... *wrong* with him.'

She sighed. 'You know, Grandma blames Mother for it – she said Mother allows it.'

'*Allows* it?'

'By covering up for him, keeping it a secret. She said we've as good as made a rod for our own backs.'

'I sometimes think' – I dropped my voice to a whisper – 'I sometimes think he isn't actually our father at all, but somebody else.'

'Whatever do you mean?'

'I can't explain it. But you should watch him very carefully next time you see him. Do you mind if I finish the biscuits?'

She shook her head. 'Ed, I'm – I'm worried about you.'

'Me? Why?'

'You seem very ... you don't seem yourself.'

I sat back and laughed. 'Not myself! Like Father, you mean? Oh, I can promise you I really am very myself. More so than ever, in fact.'

'But – you seem so different.'

'I *am* different. Everything's changed.'

'What's changed, Ed? You can tell me, you know; I'm your sister. You really can. It's Alfie Rose, isn't it?'

I felt like a rubber balloon at the instant all the air goes out of it, or like the wireless when the battery fails. It must have shown in my face, for she put down her cup and came to the settee, and put her arms around me.

'Oh, Ed, you're my sister, and I love you, do you know that? Tell me – just tell me what's happened!' she said.

The sobs that heaved out of me then were frightening, and I clutched at Mary and cried and cried. Snot ran out of my nose, and my mouth was pulled back in a grimace; I heard myself making sounds that were almost screams, but I let it happen, I let it move through me, a juggernaut of fear and pain and shock. I pushed into Mary and clung on for dear life as she rocked me and spoke to me quietly and stroked my head.

At last the sobs began to subside, and I sat back a little and rummaged for my hankie. She pressed a clean one of her own into my hand.

'Ed – Ed. I need to ask you. Did he make you ... did he make you *do it?*'

'He didn't make me,' I managed. 'I let him. It was my fault.'

My crying had woken the baby up and it was starting to whine, and I knew that any moment she would go and see to it. Inside, I made myself ready for the blow of her getting up and moving away.

'Oh, let him cry,' she said, putting an arm around me and squeezing. 'He drives me mad, anyway. I wish I'd never had him sometimes.'

Heavens, the relief of it, to feel her there again: my sister. I couldn't help but laugh, and she laughed too, through her own tears.

'Now, tell me what happened exactly. All of it – don't leave anything out.'

And so, haltingly at first, and then in a rush, I did.

Mary was making us sandwiches when there was a firm rap at the door. She appeared at the kitchen doorway and looked at me; after everything we'd talked about we were neither of us ready to see anyone – particularly anyone from Wych Farm.

But the rap came again. 'I suppose you'd better answer it,' I said miserably, drawing my knees up onto the settee.

'Mary, I'm so pleased to meet you at last,' rang out Connie's familiar voice from the hall. 'I'm Constance. I'm ever so sorry to trouble you, but I don't suppose your sister Edith happens to be here?'

'Ed? Oh – she's –'

'It's all right,' I called out. 'Hello, Connie. Come in.'

With Connie in it, Mary's front room suddenly seemed smaller and cheaper. 'No, don't get up, darling,' she said. 'I gather you're unwell.'

Mary, who had raised her eyebrows at Connie's 'darling', spoke up: 'She's just a little ... overwrought.'

'Overwrought – that's it exactly. May I sit?'

'Please do. Would you like a cup of tea, Constance? I'm just making a pot.'

'Yes please, that would be kind. Did you know it's starting to spit?'

She sat down next to me on the settee. 'I bicycled over – your mother sent me. I'm glad to find you here, I thought you might have run away.'

'Am I in a lot of trouble?'

'No – your Father thinks you're languishing in bed with whatever Alfie Rose has got. He doesn't suspect a thing.'

'But Grandfather –'

'I know, you were vile to poor Albert, apparently,' she said, and grinned. 'But he'll forgive you.'

Mary came through with a plate of sandwiches and a pot of tea. 'She always was his favourite,' she said, but her voice was kind.

'I'll fetch another cup, shall I?' said Connie 'No, you sit down, Mary, I'll find it. I always know where to look for things in other people's kitchens – it's a knack. See, what did I tell you?' – and she reappeared after a moment with a cup and saucer and teaspoon.

'Now, let's the three of us ladies have a proper chin-wag. It's about time, don't you think?'

Before Connie arrived I'd told Mary everything about Alf, going all the way back to when he first kissed me behind the privy at Rose Farm, and including everything I'd been letting him do. She said that in her view we weren't sweethearts at all, and furthermore that on the night of the fete he'd behaved like a cad.

'It's my fault, though – I should have told you what men are really like,' she'd continued. 'I thought there'd be lots of time, and I suppose I didn't think you were interested, always with your head stuck in a book. And – and I suppose I was so taken up with Clive, and then the wedding, and now Terence. I'm ever so sorry, Ed.'

'Oh, that's all right. You won't tell anyone, though, will you? Not Mother, or anyone?'

'Course not – and neither must you, or you'll get a reputation.'

'What if *he* tells – what if he brags?'

'I don't think he will. I'll wager he knows he's behaved badly; I shouldn't be surprised if he isn't ill at all, but feigning.'

I took a deep breath and held it for a moment, and as I released it I tried to let my shoulders drop. 'Mary, I don't ever want him to kiss me again. Or – anything. It was so horrible – *horrible!*' I shuddered, and briefly felt as though I might cry again.

'You'll just have to avoid him, then, or carry a hatpin. They can't help themselves – not once they're, you know, inflamed, or it damages them down there. Men are all the same that way; that's what Mother told me. So it's best not to let them get too near, unless you're really in love.'

'All of them? Even' – I searched my imagination – 'even Frank? Even John?'

'Probably.'

'Was Clive like that when you were courting?'

'Course he was, but – I liked him back, you see.'

'But I – I like Alf. Everyone likes him; I think Father wants me to marry him. And you know Frank sets a store by him, too.'

'Not with your heart, or your body, you can't have liked him. Oh, it's hard to explain.'

'So tell me what on earth is the matter, Edie,' said Connie now. 'You know you've got Ada ever so worried, poor thing?'

'Connie knows that I – that I kissed Alf Rose,' I said to Mary, making sure with a look that she understood.

'Surely it's not all about a boy, though,' Connie said confidingly, taking my hand. 'I mean, dunking yourself in the horse-pond, and drawing magical shapes. Darling, we all just want to understand.'

'Yes, the device you drew in the air the other day,' said Mary. 'I was coming on to that.'

I looked out of the window. On the other side of the road I could see part of the village hall, where the dances were held. Parked next to it was a grocer's van marked 'G & E Evans', and a woman hurrying past in a headscarf carrying a basket of eggs. It was all veiled in light drizzle; the lustre and detail that the past few days had been loaded with, that had given the workaday world such an overwhelming luminosity and significance, seemed somehow to be draining away.

'It was just for good luck, Mary; you know, like touching wood. Don't you ever do that?'

'Ed, it was a daisy-mark, like in the house. And you know it.'

'What's a daisy-mark?' said Connie.

'A witch-mark, some call them. They're all over this part of the world.'

'Gosh. Made by witches?'

'Oh no,' Mary said. 'For protection against them. Ordinary people drew them in their houses a long time ago.'

How could I not have understood that? Why had I so stupidly assumed that the marks were some kind of spell? There was so much I didn't know, or had got muddled about – which was so unlike me, usually. What a silly little fool I was.

'Mary, I need to ask you something. It's about Grandma Clarity.'

'Grandma? What about her?'

'How does she – how does she know things?'

'Know what things?'

'You *know* what things. We used to talk about it when we were children: how she'd always know what was wrong, even before you spoke. She knew you were expecting Terence –'

'Ed, that's just something women can tell.'

'– and she knew about my landrail –'

'Mother had mentioned it!'

'– and there's the way she can make people better, or overlook them and cause them ill –'

'Ed, you know perfectly well she can't overlook anyone.'

'She can make them better, though, and animals. You know she can!'

'She's good with herbs, that's all! Lots of the old women are. What do you think people did for medicine before doctors came along?'

'Is that all, then?'

'What do you mean?'

'It's just that Frank said … Frank said she was a witch.'

Mary burst out laughing then, but Connie's face was grave and still. It was unlike her to remain silent for so long; I had almost forgotten that she was there.

'But Ed,' Mary said at last, 'you didn't believe him, did you? You know what an idiot he can be.'

I shrugged. 'I – I don't know.'

'You'd better not say anything of this to Mother, you know. She'll be terribly hurt.'

'Hurt? Why?'

'Think about it, you ass: she grew up with people saying cruel things about her mother, and now you're doing the same!'

'I'm not! And anyway, why should it be a bad thing?'

'Look, Ed. You have to stop all this, right now. I know you've been – tired, and I understand it, honestly; and I know Father's been under a fair strain of late, which makes everyone's life hard. But nobody's a witch, and you know that very well.'

I nodded and looked down at my hands. 'Excuse me,' I said. 'I must just use the W.C., if you don't mind.'

'Oh – Edie,' Connie said, as I got up to leave the room. 'I think – gosh, I'm so sorry, but I think your monthlies have arrived.'

Connie and I made our way back to Wych Farm on Connie's bicycle, me balanced gingerly on the front handlebars. The sun had come out again, and everything steamed; the rain had laid the road dust, too, and washed its pale bloom from the blowsy hedgerows on either side.

Mary had given me one of her dresses to change into; mine, with a crimson flag on the seat that was probably visible when I stepped out of the motorcar, was bundled up in Connie's bag. Upstairs, in her bedroom, Mary had found me a sanitary belt and towel, and in a whisper pointed out how relieved I should be. The settee would be fine with a little carbolic soap. 'Honestly, Terence has done far worse to it than that,' she laughed.

'I'll wash your dress and bring it back next week, with Mother,' I promised at the front door, hugging her hard.

'No – you keep it,' she said, smiling. 'I won't be able to fit into it soon.' She laid a hand on her stomach. 'But don't you dare tell Mother I'm expecting – and that includes you, Constance! She'll wholly take on if she thinks I told anyone else first.'

Back in the village Connie and I dismounted by the old mill and carried the bicycle across the stepping-stones, then wheeled it along the narrow path to Back Lane. My cramps were starting, and I was glad not to have to balance on the front of the bicycle any more.

'I'll go and let Ada know I found you; you nip straight indoors and go to bed,' Connie said. 'I've left a copy of my latest article for you to read – all about the blacksmith and the wheelwright and the wonderful old farm wagons you see in this part of the world. You must tell me what you think.'

'Thank you, Connie, I'm sure it's marvellous. But – I've been meaning to ask: what happened to the family at Hullets? I've been so caught up in everything at home –'

'Oh, they're being well looked after in Market Stoundham – they're quite, quite safe. Now, I must find out how my Mr Chalcott's getting on!'

'He's still taking pictures?'

'He was when I left him, but the rain probably sent him scurrying indoors. I say, will it have ruined the harvest?'

'Oh no, not just a little bit of drizzle like that. I'm sure it'll be absolutely fine.'

'And how long do you think until you're finished?'

'I expect all the wheat will be stooked in a few days,' I replied. 'Then, while it's drying, we'll cut the barley and build the rick. And some time after that, when the wheat's dry, we'll cart it in and do the same.'

'But there'll be no Harvest Home?'

'No – sorry, Connie. Mother might make something nice to eat, but that's all.'

'It just seems a shame. I've been reading about the old traditions, and it was a chance for the whole village to come together.'

'But we're not peasants now, Connie, harvesting all the fields at the same time for the local squire. The farmers all finish at different times these days; it wouldn't work.'

'Well, I mean to organise something, in any case – at the Bell & Hare.'

'What do you mean?'

'Let's say – once your wheat's stooked, at least, and the barley's in, shall we? I don't want to leave it too long. I've a mind to get the local farmers and farmhands together. I may even be able to bribe them with beer.'

I laughed. 'Well, that should do the trick. Just don't go expecting all the old ballads and harvest traditions; the olden days are long gone.'

'That wasn't what I had in mind at all, darling,' she said, but although I pressed her, she wouldn't tell me any more.

XV

With the first of the cornfields cut to stubble came a presage of winter. At once the hedges stood out more starkly, the land revealing half-remembered contours long hidden by the corn, and it was not so hard to imagine the fields ploughed to rich brown furrows ready for the frost to break up the clods. After all, the cerulean sky of August was not so very different from the skies of a bright and chill November day, when all our acres would lie empty and silent.

Winter, though, would bring with it its own pleasures: the fires lit in the two hearths downstairs, filling the old house with the smell of wood; skating on the horse-pond with Frank, if it froze hard enough to take our weight; trips to Market Stoundham to visit the cattle market and the corn exchange. I suppose these last were less of a pleasure for Father, who had the worry of fetching a good price for his grain; sometimes we would make many trips before he sold it, the barley particularly, his little leather sample bag carefully emptied and filled anew for each trip lest its contents had somehow spoiled in the intervening week.

But for now all that was to come. We cut and stooked Greenleaze and Newlands in dull, over-cast weather, then had another day of drizzling rain in which to rest. But the sun came out again, and shone strongly, and after a further day of watching the barometer anxiously, we began on the barley in Crossways. John let Frank take a turn driving the reaper-binder, and Connie spent a day with us, learning how to toss the sheaves up to the wagon on Tipper's old two-tined barley fork. Meanwhile, Mother visited Doble daily, taking turns with Mrs Rose to bring him his meals. But whether he was still abed or busy harvesting we saw nothing of Alf at Wych Farm, and I did not ask how he was.

I was sleeping better, and as a consequence, I suppose, each day I felt a little less queer. I told Mother so, saying only that I had been foolishly sitting up late and reading lurid books – something she accepted readily, for it bore out what she herself thought of me; after all, less than a year had passed since my obsession with *The Midnight Folk*, when I had pretended for weeks to be a boy who could speak to magical cats. I remained a little shy of Father, but not in the same way as when I'd failed to recognise him as my father, an episode that was almost impossible now to recall. As for witchcraft, at church

I prayed to God to forgive my confusion and childish games. But every now and again I found my thoughts returning to the possibility that my life was secretly significant, and still I traced the witch-mark on my palm from time to time. After all, it wasn't as though it could do any harm.

It was only now, in the slow ebbing away of those strange convictions, that I began to question what had happened to me in the period following the village fete. Had I perhaps been in some way touched, or mad, like the grandmother I'd never met? The idea of it was terrifying – yet something in me missed the elation of those days, and the great power I'd so briefly known myself to have. I shared none of these thoughts with anyone, though, for I knew that no one would understand.

We built the barley-ricks next to the hay-rick, making sure to leave enough space for the wheat to come in when it was dry. Father had been talking for years about putting up a modern Dutch barn with a corrugated iron roof between Crossways and Greenleaze, but somehow he had never quite got round to it, so we carted all our corn back to the rick-yard still.

It is a ticklish business to build a rick so it is weather-proof, safe from heating and – to the greatest extent possible – unwelcoming to rats. A rick must be bedded well with straw, then the sheaves forked from the cart and at first set on end, where the centre of the round rick will be; only gradually, towards the edges, are they laid on their sides with the butts outward. This is to keep the heart full, so that the roof will be conical when it is thatched, and the rain run off. Stack props keep it upright as it is raised, and the man most skilled stands atop it to receive the sheaves that are pitched up to him, laying them in place, treading them down, and at last heading the rick. Then it must be thatched with clean wheat-straw secured with stakes and springles, lashed with rope and trimmed on all sides so that it is neat. And of course, there are as many ways of trimming it as there are farms, with forms and fashions that vary between districts, and even between particular men.

As Grandfather had predicted, we missed Doble when it came to making our ricks, for while Father and John could do it, neither had his keen eye, and so the work was slow. At first the heart didn't hold, but fell flat, which meant that when the rick settled there would be a hollow at its centre and the barley would rot; we had to unstack it, half-built, and start again. Then it wasn't quite circular, which would make it difficult to thatch; but for want of time we pressed on regardless, John pitching the sheaves up to Father, and Father growing ever more irate. Meanwhile Frank led Moses and Malachi to the field and back, Mother and I filling the huge wagon as best we could; after a break for 'fours', as we called it, and then supper, we worked on in the darkening field until sunset, singing

'John Barleycorn' and 'Waiting for the Leaves to Fall' in the style of Jessie Matthews, and a jazz tune popular that year called 'Honeysuckle Rose'.

Connie arrived at Wych Farm late one morning as we were getting ready to head the second barley-rick. Mother had gone indoors to make dinner; Frank and Father were both up on the rick, Father demonstrating how to catch the sheaves from John, who stood on the fast-emptying wagon.

'Gosh, they make it look easy, don't they,' she said admiringly; and there was a deftness to the grown men's movements that was, I suppose, something like grace; as John pitched the sheaf up, Father took it on his fork in one easy movement and swung it neatly into place. Frank could do it, but it was as though he was putting too much energy into it, and I could see from his face that it would soon tire him, whereas the more experienced men still looked fresh.

'Don't think about it so much, son,' said Father. 'Just take it on the swing and let the rhythm do the work.'

'May I have a try, George?' called Connie.

'No, Constance; we're nearly done now, and then we shall thatch. Pity you didn't come yesterday, when you might've been of some use.'

She grinned, and stuck her hands in her pockets. 'I had business in town, George. Anyway, I'm here now, so I can help thatch.'

John snorted.

'I don't think you will, for all that,' Father said.

'Oh! That reminds me, Edie,' she said, turning to me. 'I passed the postman on my way here.' And she drew a crumpled letter from the pocket of her trousers and held it out. It was postmarked Corwelby. 'Don't tell me – a secret admirer?'

But I had recognised the handwriting on the envelope, and drew away from her with a frown.

Dear Edith,

How are you keeping? I do hope that you are well.

I trust you will forgive me writing with news of another opportunity, but I could not in all conscience fail to put it before you, despite what you set out regarding your disaffinity for children in answer to my last idea.

A woman of my acquaintance, a widow, but at only 29 years, is seeking a girl to act as her companion and to assist with the duties surrounding her daughter, a girl of three years old, so that she may pursue her hobby of painting with watercolours. No housekeeping duties are required.

My acquaintance lives at Market Stoundham, in comfortable circumstances. The position is live-in. Upon learning of her requirements I immediately thought of you; but of course, there are likely to be many applicants, so do let me know by return of post whether you would like me to arrange an interview.

Edith, I must be frank with you, and trust that the regard we had for one another when I was your teacher still affords me the privilege of telling the truth. You are only fourteen, and at fourteen girls do not yet know their own minds — although of course one rather feels as though one does! But I know you very well, for I was just like you when I was your age, and now have the added benefit of the perspective of years.

My advice is that you take up this position, and avail yourself of all the advantages of living in town. True, Market Stoundham is not London, but there is the lending library, and a small theatrical society, and the company of many more young people than you will ever meet in Elmbourne. You will be free to cast off the lassitude that I observe to have afflicted you in recent years, and truly begin your life. And I have no doubt that in time you will discover in yourself that which is is most natural to Woman: the instinct to care for children, whether one's own, or those of others.

I look forward to your reply —

Ever affectionately,
Geraldine Carter

'Is everything all right?' asked Connie, as I refolded the letter and put it back in its envelope. I felt rattled, as though a trap was closing, but I pushed the feeling from my mind. I was far too much needed at home, for one thing.

'Just a letter from my old teacher, Miss Carter. We write to one another sometimes. Now, if you'll excuse me, I must go and give Mother a hand.'

In my bedroom I slipped the letter inside a book and ran back downstairs. I had a headache building somewhere behind my eyes.

'Ah, there you are, child. Fetch the pork pie from the pantry – it's under a cloth. And then cut it up into eight, will you? And slice some bread.'

'Mother, are you happy?'

'What do you mean, am I happy, girl?'

'Are you happy? You know, with how your life's turned out.'

'What's got into you now, Edie? Course I'm happy. Why wouldn't I be?'

'Don't you ever wish you'd – done something with your life?'

She frowned at me. 'You think I've done naught, is that it?'

'I mean – well, do you ever miss being a horse-woman, for example? You must have been sad when John came back from the War.'

'Sad? Don't be ridiculous, Edith. I was glad the man survived. We all were.'

I felt as though she wasn't truly answering my question, although her reply was so definite; but perhaps it was just that I didn't believe her, which wasn't entirely fair.

'Is it that Connie putting ideas in your head again? I shall be glad in some ways when she's gone, you know.'

'Why, has she said she's leaving?'

'No, not that I've heard,' Mother replied, picking the shells from a bowl of hard-boiled eggs. 'But she'll want to be back in London come the colder weather, I'll wager. And then we shall have some peace.'

'Mother...'

'Yes, child?'

'Miss Carter's written to me about a position. In Market Stoundham.'

'In service?'

'No. Well, in a way. A lady's companion – a widow. She has a three year-old daughter. She paints.'

Mother finished the eggs and wiped her hands on her apron.

'Well, that's rare news, Edie! Have you replied?'

'Not yet – the letter only came just now.'

'But you'll take it? You'll say yes?'

I felt stung that she seemed so happy; it wasn't what I'd expected. 'But – who'd help with wash-day? And wouldn't you miss me?'

'Edie, you listen to me: it's a good opportunity, and you must take it. You *must*.'

I gathered up the eggshells and put them into the pail for the pigs. Far from keeping me at home, it was as though she wanted me gone now. Perhaps my recent behaviour had exhausted her love for me, I reflected. I felt my headache tighten into a band around my skull.

'Mother,' I said.

'Yes, Edie?'

'What happened to Grandmother?'

'What do you mean, what happened to her? She took ill and died.'

'Was she – mad?'

She sighed. 'Well. I don't rightly know; it was before I married your father, and Albert won't speak of her at all. Some say she was stricken with delusions; but if you ask Lizzie Allingham, she'll tell you the poor woman was just tired.'

Connie didn't eat with us that day, but remained outside, sketching the ricks.

'How long until you bring in the wheat, George?' I heard her ask when I went to tell them to come in and eat.

'A week,' Father replied, but John shook his head.

'Nine or ten days from now, if the weather holds.'

'We'll cart in a week, man – and sooner if I give the word.'

Back in the kitchen, Mother switched off the wireless as the three men followed me in and sat down.

'I'll just fetch Albert,' she said. 'You all start; I know you don't want to be long.'

The talk as we ate was mostly of rick-building. John asked Mother if Doble might be well enough to be brought to see our work, but she didn't think he could manage the distance yet, although he was sitting up now and fretting for news. Grandfather told us about the time when he was a boy and one of the ricks began to smoke; how it had smouldered for weeks without fully catching fire, and how his father had been too afraid to open it up in case letting air into it caused it to burst into flames.

'And acourse, there were some who were firing ricks on purpose in those years,' he added darkly.

'Why?' asked Frank.

'Blasted unions driving a wedge between man and master, lad.'

John cleared his throat. He was a member of our local agricultural union, and went to meetings in Market Stoundham.

'Those days are long gone now,' he said. 'And anyway, isn't your own son here a member of the Farmers' Union?'

'Tain't the same, John,' said Grandfather, 'as well you know.'

'Will you be going to Connie's meeting, John?' said Frank.

'What meeting's that?' Mother asked.

'Connie's arranging a meeting on Saturday at the Bell & Hare – everyone's invited. She says there'll be free beer.'

'Free beer? Whatever for?'

'She said she's been given ten bob to spend however she likes, and she wants as many people as possible there. Ed, do you know what it's all about?'

I shook my head slightly, wincing at the throb my temples gave. 'Only that she was planning it. I thought it was a sort of Harvest Home, though.'

'It can't be, we've still got the wheat to cart yet,' said Mother.

'I don't think I will go, Frank, in answer to your question,' John said, helping himself to a second slice of pork pie.

'Why not?'

'I say you should come with us, John,' said Father. 'Hear what she has to say. Uncommon for a woman to stand a man a drink, for one thing.'

'It's not her money, by all accounts. Anyway, I've heard her speak.'

'At the table, you mean?'

John nodded, and ate on, stolidly.

'You still don't like her, do you?' said Mother. Her voice was soft, and she sounded genuinely curious.

'I don't like or dislike her, Ada.'

'But you're always so scornful of her,' I said. I hadn't meant to speak out, but now that I had I realised that it was true, and that it bothered me.

'I'm sure I don't mean to be, Edith.'

'Well you *are*. It's embarrassing. She's only ever been nice to you, and all she wants is for you to tell her about horses, and — and how you look after them. Where's the harm in that?'

'John forgets his manners sometimes, not being used to female company,' Father said. 'I'm sure Connie doesn't mind.'

Mother got up abruptly and went to the pantry.

'I'm female company,' I said.

'You're family, lass, and so's your mother. You don't count.'

At that moment, Connie put her head around the kitchen door. 'George, there's somebody here for you — a Mr Turner.'

'Turner?' replied Father, furrowing his brow. 'I don't think I know a Turner. What's his business with me?'

'He didn't say — I can ask, if you like, but I don't expect he'll confide in one of the fairer sex. Anyway, I let him know you were eating, and he said to tell you not to rush. He's in the barn.'

But Father had already pushed his chair back.

'I'll be there directly,' he said. 'Why don't you come in? Ada'll be making tea before long.'

Mother reappeared from the pantry with a baking tray, which she slid into the oven. 'Yes, come in and sit, Connie. I'm making coconut shapes. They won't take long.'

By the time Father came back in, John and Frank had gone out to finish the rick. Connie was telling Mother about unpasteurised milk, which, she said, was far more wholesome than the devitalised stuff from the 'centralised milk factory' – wherever that was to be found. Grandfather sat on at the end of the table, lost in daydream, his gnarled hands resting on the knob of his stick. I was washing up. I had traced the witch-mark on my forehead when nobody was looking, and now I found that my headache had gone.

'Well, well, well,' said Father, taking his cap off and sitting down. He laid a business card on the table before him, and after gazing at it a moment took it up again and began to turn it thoughtfully over and over in his hands.

'What is it, George?' said Mother. 'What did the man want?'

'He wants to buy our barley.'

'Buy our barley? Why, it hasn't even been threshed!'

'I know that, woman. But that's what he said.'

'A speculator,' said Connie. 'I hope you sent him away with a flea in his ear.'

'It don't pay a farmer to be hasty, Connie.'

Grandfather had turned his head, and sat gazing at Father with sightless eyes.

'How much, son?' he asked. 'How much will he pay?'

'Thirteen shillings a coomb.'

'But that's nothing, George!' exclaimed Mother. 'Surely you won't accept?'

'Haven't you women got any work to do? Allus in here gossiping and bothering a man.'

'But George –'

'Be *quiet*, Ada.'

Mother got up and left the room, but Connie sat on quietly. It was strange how Father tolerated her now, I thought, with a stab of jealousy. I filled the kettle, in case he should want tea, and fetched the pot and cups from the table. There were two coconut shapes left, and I set the plate down next to him, quietly, but with the side of his hand he pushed it away.

'This Turner – he judges it feed barley, then,' said Grandfather.

'No.'

'Malting? Why, that's less than six shillings a hundredweight. He must think you a fool.'

'At least it would be sold. He said he would advance me the cash – we could thresh in November, as we allus do. He would even pay for the transportation.'

'You'll get a fairer price in winter, at the corn exchange.'

'Perhaps; perhaps not. Who knows which way prices will go?'

'Thirteen shillings a coomb for malting barley's an insult – no two ways about it,' said Grandfather, and banged his stick upon the floor.

'That may be so,' said Father, the card, printed MR. A. TURNER, GRAIN MERCHANT, small and flimsy in his hands. 'But November is a long way away.'

XVI

All the barley came in, but the wheat was not yet dry enough, and we had a job keeping the farm's birds from it where it stood in yellow stooks in the fields. One bird, though, was missing, for although I called for him daily, Edmund failed to appear. It was still too early in the year for the landrails to have flown away for the winter, so I told myself that he must have found a sweetheart somewhere.

I don't know why I'd thought I would be allowed to go to Connie's meeting; because she had told me about it first, I suppose, and because we had spent so much time together that it just seemed natural I would be there. I think she had assumed I would be, too; but then, she was always blind to convention. The fault was mine for forgetting what I already knew: that in the evening – and even more so if there was going to be talk of politics – the Bell & Hare was out of bounds to a fourteen-year-old girl.

But not to Frank, of course. Watching him and Father help Grandfather into the trap that Saturday after supper, and drive away, I felt the gulf between us very keenly; that's when I really understood that we were on different paths.

I went back inside to begin the washing-up from supper. Mother was packing a basket to take to Doble; John sat on at the kitchen table, idly spinning his bone-handled knife on the soft, old wood.

'You want to go, don't you, Edith,' he said, without looking up.

I began to collect the dirty plates and dishes from the table. 'Of course. I hate being left out.'

'Perhaps it's as well.'

'I don't see how.'

'And what about you, Ada? Why did you stay behind?'

'It's my turn to sit with Doble this evening; in fact I should be there now.'

'That's not the reason.'

'Course it is, John.'

'Edith could have done that,' he said. 'Now, tell me why you didn't want to go.'

Mother sighed. She untied her blue apron from around her waist and folded it, then laid it carefully on the back of the chair opposite John and smoothed it with her hands.

'I've heard too much talk of politics lately, and that's the truth of it. I just — I just want to live an ordinary life, and look after my own family. Perhaps you'll say that I'm wrong.'

'Not at all,' he said, his voice soft. 'I don't judge you, you know that. I never have.'

'And why aren't you there, may I ask?'

'I didn't think I had the stomach for it — that's the truth,' John said haltingly. 'But perhaps I should go, after all. Some notions — well, it's like when a horse comes down with the farcy, or strangles; or when bindweed gets into a crop. Once things like that take hold they're terrible hard to shift.'

I went to heat some water in the copper, and when I returned to the kitchen both he and Mother were gone.

It only took me half an hour or so to decide that I would go to the Bell & Hare, and damn the consequences. Most likely I wouldn't be allowed in, but it was a warm evening and if the inn's windows were open I thought I might be able to linger outside and hear what was being said. Perhaps I would get a hiding from Father, but if there was free beer to be had it seemed likely that he would be incapacitated later, and I knew that neither Grandfather nor Frank would give me up. So once the washing-up was done I saw to the hens, ran upstairs to fetch a cardigan and set out.

Darkness fell a little sooner now than it had done on the night of the village fete, but as I hurried along the field path towards Back Lane there was still light left in the sky. A rich green aftermath had grown on Great Ley and over it a white owl floated, wings motionless, the disc of its face turned down to where tiny creatures doubtless crouched and shook. Home Field was invisible beyond a line of field maples and dog-roses on my right, but as I crossed into Greenleaze the view opened up to the stark corn stubble and the clump of alders, black as pitch against an opaline sky, that marked where the horse-pond was.

I stood a moment, my arms folded across my chest against the evening breeze, listening to a robin spill its plaintive song down from somewhere in the hedge. I couldn't have said why, but I wanted to see the pond again; I wanted to stand on the bank where I had stood two weeks ago in the moonlight, utterly possessed by the conviction that I had to go in. It would only delay me by a few minutes, I calculated; and the soil was dry around the shorn wheat stalks and strewn with flints, so I did not think the earth would cling to my sandals.

I can't rightly say what I was searching for there at the edge of the dark water; but what I found was Edmund's body, flyblown and stinking, his breast torn open and his heart removed from its bloody cavity, his once-bright eyes picked out by crows.

As soon as I emerged from the cut onto The Street I could hear Connie's meeting. The Bell & Hare was rowdy with voices and hubbub, and there by the green, Elmbourne darkening around me, the sound of it brought me up short. But I couldn't turn and walk home again, not now, for the discovery of Edmund's body had left my blood singing strangely in my ears. Compulsively, I traced a witch-mark on the goose-bumped flesh of my hip.

I took a breath and let it out slowly. I knew there was likely a door at the back of the inn somewhere, but I didn't dare try it; it seemed even worse to me to be caught trespassing in the private part of the inn than to risk making a spectacle of myself by going in where everyone could see. So, heart thumping, I crossed the road, thumbed down the iron latch and pushed open the door.

The air was hot and humid, and thick with the smell of hops and tobacco smoke. No-one turned to see me slip in, or seemed to feel the breath of night air I brought with me. I latched the door behind me and stood a moment to try to understand what was taking place.

All the tables in the tap-room on my left were taken, and men were standing between them, holding their mugs of beer; I had never seen the inn so full. I was glad to see some women at the tables: Elisabeth Allingham from Copdock, Mrs Godbold and one or two others. There was my father, red-faced at a corner table with Grandfather next to him, and my stomach lurched as I saw Alf Rose, laughing, on

Father's other side. Frank and Sid sat on stools with their backs toward me; none saw me, I felt sure, as I ducked back quickly and stood once again just inside the inn door.

The bar-room, on the right, had had its tables entirely removed, and all I could see at first were backs, so that for a moment it looked almost as though I had arrived late for church: jackets and waistcoats, shirtsleeves, a press of men. But unlike the reverent atmosphere in St Anne's there was a loud clamour of voices, and it was clear that this was where the meeting itself was being held – or perhaps had been held, for nobody seemed to be making a speech. I realised that in delaying at home I had probably missed it, and that I might as well just slip out again and walk home.

But just then I heard Connie's voice rising easily over the crowd and saw that she was standing in the entrance to the snug at the back, which was raised up a little by a step from the floor of the main bar-room. Six wormy, vertical timbers were all that remained of the snug's long-gone stud wall, and she stood in the gap where once there must have been a door. I craned to see her between all the men's heads; her height, and the step she stood on, gave her an advantage. She was wearing what looked like a shepherd's smock, but in silk, tucked into a narrow grey skirt; her hair had been set into loose waves and was held at the side with a barrette adorned with a yellow oxlip. She looked wonderful.

'Dear friends and neighbours, thank you again, and let me beg just one more moment of your time,' she called out. She looked happy, perhaps almost triumphant, and as the hubbub died down, she gave one of her dazzling smiles.

'You've been kind enough to listen as Mr Seton Ritter set out the great need in our country now for the Order of English Yeomanry, and explained a little to you about our beliefs and our aims. The Order is made up of honourable patriots, people like Hugo – like Mr Seton Ritter here – and myself, and growing numbers of farmers like your own George Mather, too: ordinary Englishmen who believe in progress and in fairness, who decry the enthronement of international money-lending, the centralisation of markets, and modern urban industrialism. People who are not afraid to question the high-handed edicts of the League of Nations or the P.E.P., and who above all understand the irreplaceable value of our rural traditions, and wish to protect the health and the purity of our English soil.'

There was a rumble of assent from the crowd. Connie was doing rather well, I thought; it all seemed eminently sensible, though I wondered what the P.E.P. was, and resolved to ask her later if I got the chance. It was a surprise to hear that Father had joined her club, or party, or whatever it was; I wondered if Mother knew.

'Many of you here belong to an agricultural union. The Order of English Yeomanry does not require that you give up these loyalties, for while there are important concerns to be raised about the evil of Bolshevism, we believe that the re-creation of a vigorous indigenous peasantry – one with a true stake in the future of this country – is by far the more pressing goal.

'Therefore, if you have agreed with our speeches tonight, I would ask you to consider joining your neighbour George Mather in this, the local chapter of our Order. The cost is a shilling; but tonight you need only give me your names. I shall be here until closing time – oh, and before I forget,' she said, holding up a copy of a magazine, 'I've more copies of our weekly publication here, *The English Pioneer*; it's usually a penny, but tonight they're free for you all to take away, so please help yourselves, if you haven't taken one already. I write a regular piece in each issue myself, and I think you'll agree it's a good read for all the family.'

She grinned at us, said 'Thank you' again, and sat down next to an elegantly dressed man in spectacles, who I presumed was Mr Seton Ritter; I recognised Mr Chalcott, her friend the photographer, in the snug too. But just as the roar of conversation began to swell again, a fair, stocky man shouldered his way up the step to the snug and turned to face the room. It was John.

'I have something to say to you all, friends, if you'll grant me a moment.'

Behind the bar the landlord folded his arms. There came a stillness now to the men's backs such as hadn't been there when Connie had been speaking, and again I was reminded of church.

'We've seen a lot of Miss FitzAllen at Wych Farm this summer, and heard a lot about her ideas,' he said. 'In fact she's become a regular fixture – out in the fields, too, where I'll allow she's been of some use. Now, you all know me for a fair man, and not one to speak out of turn. But I must say to you tonight that this woman is not all she seems.'

The inn was utterly silent; even the low murmur of conversation from the tap-room had stilled. I saw that Father and Sid Rose had got up from their seats and were craning to see through into the public bar. By standing on tip-toe I could just about glimpse Connie's face in the shadows behind John, wearing a fixed expression. I felt sick with embarrassment, and angry on her behalf.

'Mr Seton Ritter here has talked to you tonight of patriotism, and duty to one's countrymen, and the bonds of blood and soil. Now, I don't hold with everything he's said – not at all – but I believe him to be a man of honour. In the War he was Lieutenant-Colonel Seton Ritter, and he's had the D.S.M. and the Military Cross. To my mind, he has taken the wrong course since then, but I respect him nonetheless.

'Miss FitzAllen, however –'

Connie made as though to get up, but John simply turned and looked at her, and she sat back down again.

'Our Miss FitzAllen here spins a great yarn about her days in France as a V.A.D., but I've been asking around and from what I can make out she never even volunteered. Did you know that, Lieutenant-Colonel?' he asked over his shoulder. 'Or did she pull the wool over your eyes, too?

'And there's more!' he continued, turning back to us and raising his voice over the sudden hubbub. 'There's something else you should know before you decide to throw your lot in with this order, or society, or whatever it is. A few weeks ago Constance FitzAllen took it upon herself to evict a family of indigents living over at Hullets for no reason that I can see other than that they were Jews – them being to her mind responsible for everything that's wrong with the world these days. Well, I've news regarding that family. I was at a union meeting three days ago in Corwelby where all the talk was of a family called Adler not long arrived from our direction, the father carrying a girl by the name of Esther, four years old and no more than a bag of skin and bones. She were dead.'

I closed my eyes as voices roared and bodies surged around me. I felt as though I was floating; I knew I should find the door somewhere behind me and go out to get some air, but I couldn't leave. I took a deep breath but it was of stale pipe-smoke and men's sweat. John was wrong, that much was obvious. He was quite, quite wrong in everything he said.

'Now, I don't claim the right to tell you how to think, and so I won't; there's been enough of that manner of talk for one night,' he continued. 'All I'll say is this: we cannot set our faces against change: it don't do, it never has. Albert Mather is here tonight, the first and best man I ever took a wage from, and he taught me well. He allus said we *must* have change – we must have it! For the past is gone, and that's just the way of it. Change allus comes, and all that falls to a man to decide is whether he'll be part of it or not.'

'But it's change we're *wanting*, man! Have you not listened, have you not heard a word –'

It was Father, pushing and shouldering his way through the crowd. I saw men turn, grinning; saw them part to let him through. The tenor of their attention had changed, and I could sense it; this was sport now, master against man. I saw one or two jostle him on purpose, saw men nudge one another and crane their necks ready to see the confrontation. I wanted to get Frank, but he was in the tap-room with the Rose boys and Grandfather; I wondered if I should run home and fetch Mother, but I knew it would take too long. And then it was too late.

John stood his ground as Father approached, only folding his arms. Connie, behind him in the snug, was standing; I could not see Mr Chalcott or the other man from where I was, but it seemed they had stayed in their seats.

Father stopped a few paces away from John, his red face full of choler. With the advantage the step gave John, they were about the same height, and I realised, with a wash of horror, that they might at any second actually come to blows.

'Please God, no,' I said out loud, although I hadn't meant to. A big man near me turned; it was the wheelwright's apprentice, a lad I had only ever glimpsed before in his leather apron hard at work among the half-built wagons or forging their wide iron tyres.

'Well, if it in't the famous Mather girl herself,' he said now, and elbowed his companion. 'Look who's here!'

'*This* is change!' Father was shouting, pointing towards Connie. 'This, John, *this*! We must rebuild the country, we must put our own kind first!'

Despite the confrontation, more men nearby were turning around to look at me; I felt their eyes on me, probing and keen. What had the wheelwright's apprentice meant by 'the famous Mather girl'?

'This in't change, man, it's folly – dangerous folly, for all that.'

'You speak against me, John Hurlock?'

'In this matter, yes.'

'You think you know better, that's it. You allus have. And now you come in here, slinging mud about. Don't matter if the woman were in the War or not, to my mind.'

'No, I'll wager it don't – to a man who never served.'

Uproar then, the men rushing forward, something like joy surging through them and leaving me weightless and horrified and alone. I stumbled back a few paces, one hand seeking the inn door; I saw Frank, followed by Sid Rose, fighting to get to Father and John through the crowd; and then there on the floor was a discarded magazine, trampled by boots, an image of my face smiling idiotically out at me from the crumpled page.

Frank came out and found me. I was with Sally Godbold's mother and a couple of the other women; Elisabeth Allingham, when she came out, had strode off up Church Lane, muttering darkly about the foolishness of men. I'd wanted to run after her to ask her what she truly thought of Connie, for she had come to know her and was a shrewd woman who had seen a great many things. But Sally's mother had hold of my arm and was set on preventing me going back into the inn to see if Father was all right, and so I waited there, chastened and helpless, for all the shouting and ruckus to die down. I felt watched – not only by the people around me, some of whom were certainly staring at me strangely, but more distantly, too. It would likely be a crow somewhere, black in the darkness; perhaps the same one that had picked out poor Edmund's eyes, so that he could not see. I would have to gather my wits about me, that was once again as clear as day.

As the women shook their heads and began the work of dissecting and reassembling the night's events, work that would no doubt go on for weeks, I thought about the photograph of me in Connie's magazine, and wondered what words she had used it to illustrate. It must have been taken in Home Field the afternoon Mr Chalcott had arrived; I was holding a wheat-sheaf and shading my eyes with one hand, looking not quite at the camera but over to where Frank had been stooking, perhaps. It was both me and not me, and I thought about the possibility that hundreds of people might have seen it – had seen it already. It had been stolen from me, my own image pressed into the service of something I hadn't consented to and didn't understand.

That this could happen was further proof that I was not a real person, I realised; not real in the way that other people were real: Frank and John and Connie, for example. None of this would ever have happened to them. Perhaps I had made myself up entirely, and kept doing so every day; and if that was the case, what if I ceased all the work of being Edith Mather – stopped my body speaking and eating, for example? Once a little time had passed, enough for my grip to loosen, would I still exist?

There had been a time, not too long ago, when I had felt very powerful. When had that been? I couldn't quite recall. And now Edmund was dead, and it was my fault; he could no longer help me. Nobody could.

Frank came; he took my arm and led me away from the women. His face was grave.

'Ed, you shouldn't be here. You must go on home – quickly, now.'

'Why?'

'You know why. It's bad trouble that's broken out. Father and John have come to blows.'

'Should I fetch Mother? She can stop everything, she can –'

'No, but tell her – tell her what's happened, so she's ready. You must warn her.'

'Will you bring him in the trap, with Grandfather?'

'If he'll let me. I've got to find him first.'

'What do you mean?'

'Didn't you see? John bested him – well, he could have. Father landed him a blow, and then they were grappling – then John just pushed Father to the ground and stood over him, told him he were a better man, and a better farmer too. Then he spat on the floor and went back to where he were sitting, to finish his ale. Father picked himself up and took the back door out; the Devil only knows where he is now.'

Hot shame bloomed through me. Everyone had witnessed it – now everyone knew of our disgrace. It could never be lived down.

'Where's Grandfather?'

'Oh, he's all right, he stayed just where he was. Bob Rose is sitting with him now, and a couple of the old boys from Holstead.'

'And – and Connie?'

'Still in there, arguing the bloody toss with anyone'll listen. Look, Ed, will you get on home now? Alfie'll go with you and see you're all right.'

And there Alf was, at Frank's elbow, his eyes on mine.

'I – I can go by myself, Frank.'

'Ed, it's fine – everyone knows you two are walking out. Alfie even asked Father's permission earlier, and Father stood him a pint. Now, go on and warn Mother what's coming, will you? I must find him and get him home.'

XVII

I walked with my arms folded and without looking at Alf. For Mother's sake I knew I must take the quickest route home, through the cut rather than along the road, but I quailed to turn onto the secluded path. I kept my eyes ahead; I felt as though blinking was something I had to remember to do, for otherwise my wide eyes would surely dry out. I seemed to weigh nothing; I might have been walking a few inches above the ground. I don't remember any sounds at all other than that of Alf's voice, which came from somewhere very far away and yet was still too close.

'Take my hand, Edie, won't you?'

I kept my arms folded over my chest and let myself think it was so that he wouldn't see my ugly, bitten nails.

'Are you in a bate?'

I parted my lips so I might breathe silently, as an animal does, breathing very shallowly, one breath in for every two steps.

I said nothing in reply. The blood beat in my ears.

'You're upset about your father,' he said, his voice kind. 'It's only natural. Don't you worry, though. Frank will find him and bring him home.'

We were at the crossing over the Stound and I concentrated on matching my stride to the stepping-stones in the dim evening light. Alf followed behind me, whistling quietly through his teeth.

'It's nice to see you, Edie. Did you know I've been laid up? I took ill with a summer cold, else I would have called for you.'

We took the cut to Back Lane, goose-bumps pimpling the skin of my legs under my light cotton dress. It was a beautiful night, heavy with the scent of roses and night stocks from the village gardens around us. The moon was huge and low; 'Phoebe,' I whispered to her, under my breath.

'Slow down, Edie – what's the rush?' Alf said, laughing, and I felt his hand grasp my arm, where it was held tight against my chest. I shook it off – I wanted to run but I didn't dare to, and quickly I wrestled the feeling down.

'I have to warn Mother,' I said.

'You worry too much, that's what it is,' he said, an aggrieved note creeping into his voice. 'Your mother can look out for herself. And in any case, she's made her bed.'

Now we were between Greenleaze and Crossways. He was walking beside me, his face turned to scrutinise my own, and I could feel his anger, kept down for now – but for how long?

'Why won't you speak to me, Edie? Cat got your tongue?'

I was measuring the distance; I could see it was too far. I wasn't going to be able to reach home before he made something happen. Perhaps there were words you could say – to soothe, or ward off, or somehow contain. I didn't know what they were; I don't know if I could have said them, anyway. Mary would have known, and Mother, but I wasn't the right kind of person: I didn't know how to be in the world like that. I had thought that Connie could transform me into someone who was allowed to say yes and no to things, but it hadn't worked and now she was tainted anyway, tainted and perhaps a liar, or even worse, and although I loved her I knew that I should put her and everything about her far from my mind.

The truth was, I was useless and defenceless, and Alf knew it. He could smell it on me as a dog smells fear: the strangeness that had plagued me at school, that made me friendless, that left me always at the margins and I knew now always would.

He knew all that, and yet he still wanted to walk out with me, I realised suddenly; and everyone said he was such a nice boy, so funny and practical and kind. Yes, it was me who was to blame, after all; he had in the past called me cold and prudish, and I could see from the way I was behaving now that it was true.

I tried to drop my shoulders and slow my breath, but I found that I couldn't quite bring myself to uncross my arms. Dimly, amid the effort to relax myself, I became aware that I was very afraid.

'I'm sorry, Alf,' I whispered. 'I don't know what's got into me.'

'Well, it were an ... interesting night,' he replied, a little mollified, his voice less sharp but still with a petulant edge. 'I'll wager you're not the only one feeling upset. Your friend Connie has stirred up a real hornet's nest.'

'I think she meant well – I'm sure she did.'

'Oh, no doubt about that. I've a mind to join her little outfit, you know – well, we shall see how the land lies tomorrow.'

'Really?'

'Yes. That were a good speech that Seton Ritter chap made. He spoke a lot of sense about agricultural reform – and about the Jews, too. The cancer of Europe, that's what he said.'

Now something began to happen like the rising feeling before you vomit. I felt as though I must fight to keep myself from flying apart.

'You think that little girl, Esther – you think Mr Blum in the village – a cancer?'

'Oh no, Blum's all right. It's all the other ones I can't stand. They've no homeland, so no loyalty, you see; wherever they are, they only look out for their own, so they become a parasite – like that family at

Hullets were. There are hordes of them coming all the time – this country is being handed to them on a plate, Edie, and nobody high up seems to care. And if they're starting to spill out from the cities now –'

'But Alf –'

'Something must be done about them – that's all I'm saying. It's common sense.'

We were between Great Ley and Home Field with its stooks of moonlit wheat; in just a few more minutes the farm would be in sight. Relief began to course through me, and I felt for a moment that I might be about to faint.

'Stop, Edie,' Alf said then.

I closed my eyes briefly and kept walking, my legs weak. Now I really did feel sick, and suddenly cold. All the sounds of the summer night rushed back in: a breeze whispering like water in the leaves of the hedgerow elms and ashes; crickets chirping; a land-rail calling *crex-crex* from somewhere far away. The world felt very dear and close, and overwhelmingly acute.

He grabbed my arm then, spinning me around.

'I said *stop*, Edie. Did you not hear?'

And so we faced one another on the field path, my heart hammering. Here it was, then, and I must endure it. The fear fell away, and I uncrossed my arms and looked at him. For a moment – just a brief moment – everything was still.

He took a step closer, hips loose, eyes heavy-lidded.

'So pretty,' he said. 'You love me, don't you, Edie? Shall we have a kiss?'

He began to raise his right hand to touch the side of my face, and as he did so I felt myself flame into unalloyed rage so pure that he saw it. Rage: to feel it was like arriving in my body for the first time, entire and intact and beyond argument or doubt. I knew as I watched his hand falter that he could not touch me, for I did not wish it, and never again would I allow myself to be touched.

It was at that instant that it happened: there sprung up a bright orange glow on the far side of Home Field, vigorous and hungry and alive.

'Look – what's that – *what's that*?' I said, pointing, my voice rising to a shout as Alf Rose turned to look.

'Fuck me, Edie – fire! – *Fire!*'

I think perhaps you know the rest, but I shall tell it anyway. You will forgive me if I sound matter-of-fact. More than half a century has passed and I see it now like a newsreel rather than something that happened to me. And, of course, I have been made to go over it all many times since then.

I ran, my lungs straining, outrunning even Alf with his long legs and thumping feet behind. Strangely, I felt that someone was with me – Grandma Clarity, perhaps, or even Father's mother – and I felt so grateful, although of course it was far too late.

When we neared the yard I saw that our hay-ricks were both well alight, the heat like a barrier stopping me in my tracks. The barley-ricks, too, were smouldering, and the darkness above was filled with whirling flakes of fire as fragments of burning hay and barley-straw were sent aloft.

'The thatch, Edie! The thatch!' shouted Alf, and ran to the horse-pond, and in the orange glow I saw one or two tiny embers settling on the old, hunched roof of the house. I knew then that it was too late to save Wych Farm.

But then I saw Doble emerge from the smoke and flames: a small, slow figure, almost lost in darkness, his sunken chest bare, his too-big trousers held up with string. He carried a single bucket tremblingly before him, and I ran to him, the terrible heat calling to mind slaughter day when Mother would scorch the bristles from the skin of the pig.

'Edith! God be praised,' he said, and then his face folded into the maw of his mouth as he began soundlessly to cry. I took the bucket from him; it was only half-full, but I threw it uselessly in the direction of the blazing hay-rick all the same. Then I hooked the bucket handle over one arm and helped the old man haltingly away from the yard.

'The horses, Doble,' I said urgently as we reached the orchard, where the air was a little cooler, the roar of the flames less intense.

'At grass. Your father —' he gasped.

I went cold. 'Father?'

'He was here. I saw him.'

'Where?'

'At the ricks. Edith —'

'Where is he now? *Where is he?*'

'I can't rightly say, Edith. I'm sorry. Happen — happen he's gone.'

I left him under the trees, calling something to me that I couldn't hear, and ran back to the rick-yard, where Alf was flinging buckets of water onto the barley-ricks, one of which was belching smoke.

'Edie!' he shouted over his shoulder. 'You must run for help! *Go!*'

'You go! *You* bloody go!' I shouted back, thrusting the bucket into his chest as hard as I could. 'I'm staying — Doble says that Father's here somewhere.'

Flames were licking the side of the barn closest to the ricks as I plunged into its smoke-filled darkness, shouting and coughing. I fumbled my way around the reaper-binder and the tractor, calling for Father, my eyes streaming, my head becoming light. But there was no reply. Then I heard shouting outside, and stumbled out to see John leaping from the trap as Frank wrestled with Meg where she reared and bucked in terror at the inferno of the ricks and Grandfather held on tight to the seat of the trap.

'*Ada!*' John shouted, his voice anguished, as he sprinted for the house. 'Ada — please God — are you safe?'

And I remembered Mother then, too late, and my legs buckled under me where I stood.

I don't recall anything more of that terrible night, save for one thing. Some hours had passed, I think, and I was lying on a bed – I don't know where – and Grandfather was with me, holding my left hand in both of his and singing. I knew somehow that he had been singing to me for many hours, and that he would continue for many more yet.

I wanted to tell him that my rage had lit the ricks, that I had used my powers to save myself and so it was my fault that everything, everything, had been lost. But I couldn't bear for him to stop singing, and so I stilled the words and just listened to his clear, resonant voice as at last my grandfather gave me the songs passed down to him through all the forgotten generations, tears seeping out from the corners of my closed eyes and into my hair:

The spring she is a young maid who does not know her mind,
The summer is a tyrant of a most ungracious kind,
But the autumn is an old friend that does the best he can
To reap the golden barley and cheer the heart of man.

All among the barley, oh who would not be blithe
When the free and happy barley is smiling on the scythe!
The wheat he's like a rich man, all sleek and well-to-do;

The oats they are a pack of girls, all lithe and dancing too;
The rye is like a miser, he's sulky, lean and small
But the free and golden barley is monarch of them all.

All among the barley, oh who would not be blithe
When the free and happy barley is smiling on the scythe...

Epilogue

I have had such a happy life. This place is truly wonderful, even though some of the other women staying here are – and there's no kind way to put this – not quite right in the head. The food is tolerable, I have been given plenty of books to read, and everything is very clean. For the last few years I have even had my own room.

Mother came to see me once a week at first, but I think that it upset her in some way. I do recall clearly the last time I saw her, though. We were outside in the grounds, and it was spring: I remember the green smell of it, and the wild cherry blossom like confetti drifting down. We stood on the petal-strewn grass and she held both my hands and made me look at her, and she said that I could go back home with her if I wanted – but I shook my head. She told me that she loved me, and made me promise to send for her if one day I changed my mind. I never have.

Frank and Mary came too, of course, and Miss Carter; even old Elisabeth Allingham from Copdock

Farm – unless I am misremembering that. I dimly recall talking to Sally Godbold's sister Anne, too; I think she might have been staying here when I came. She wasn't well at all.

It is good that I was brought here, I can see that now; although it was only to be a short stay at first, I'm glad to have remained. I am very powerful sometimes – it waxes and wanes – and it is better to be here where I am prevented from doing any more harm. It hasn't happened for some years now, but I am given to understand that it may return at any time.

When I was a child I believed that what I wanted mattered so little that it wasn't even worth me discovering what it might be. And I thought, too, that I was helpless – and that is a dangerous belief to hold, for it makes one susceptible to the influence of others, for good or for ill.

I often wish I could go back and help the child I was somehow, but the truth is there is nothing I could say now that she would understand.

They tell me, when I ask, that I am seventy years old now – but I don't feel it. They say that a woman is now our prime minister; they say the country has changed beyond all recognition. But there are times when that summer seems only just to be over; when 1934 could have been but a week or two ago.

Frank told me in a letter that most people in the village believed Father torched the ricks, so deep in debt was he; Frank, though, was of the opinion that they simply heated and caught fire from being damp and badly made. Of course, I confessed at the time that I had set them alight with my powers and so caused the farm to burn. I told anyone who would listen, I told them over and over, but they merely hushed me, and then began to look at me strangely, and after a while I came here. I don't insist any more on my part in it all, for I have found that it frightens people, and I have no wish to do that. The truth is, though, that I caused the fire that moment on the field path with the Rose boy, and everything that happened afterwards is my fault.

Father's body was never found amongst the debris, and I do not know whether he perished in the blaze or got away. Mary told me that someone had been seen living at Hullets, and a watch was kept there for a while; but he would have been far from the only farmer out on his uppers in those years, so goodness only knows if it was him. I don't think of him very often any more; although for a long while I did.

Doble lived for only a few weeks after the fire. I knew when I left him in the orchard that he would be gone soon; it was very clear to me. I would like one day to visit his grave, if he warranted a headstone; if only to find out his given name. Constance was right about one thing, perhaps: for with him died a part of England that will never return.

The farmhouse survived the fire, though the barn burned to its brick foundations. Having returned from visiting Doble, Mother, it turns out, had climbed out of the dormer window in Mary's room and onto the thatch, where she sat beating out any sparks that landed with a wet cloth. She had been hidden from us in the dark, I suppose, by smoke, and the pitch of the roof.

There was some insurance money, and she took over Wych Farm after the fire and ran it with John; when Grandfather died, some years later, I'm told John moved into the house. I feel sure – though I couldn't quite say how – that Frank and Sally now farm there, Mother and John being long dead; and I have written a letter addressed to the farm, to find out. I hope someone will reply soon.

Frank and Sally married, of course, and took up one of the new council farms somewhere quite distant, near a little village called Milton Keynes. He stopped coming to see me then, though he wrote for a while – well, it was Sally's hand, but Frank's sentiment, I'm sure of it. But after some years the letters dwindled, and at last they stopped.

Of course, I was not able go to Frank's wedding, or the christenings of the children Frank and Mary had. I wasn't even told when Granfer and Grandma died, or where they are buried; I can only assume that they're gone. You might have thought I'd have known when Clarity passed, but I felt nothing. Perhaps it was the pills they used to give me; they interfered very strangely with my thoughts.

I have no idea what became of Constance FitzAllen. I know she left the district, and wasn't seen in our parts again; I don't think she ever came to see me here – though there is much I cannot remember about the very beginning of my stay. Perhaps she visited; or perhaps she simply vanished back to London and became something else entirely. She was good at that.

I was pleased to discover, some years ago, that her ideas for the country did not catch. I have had the opportunity here at last to grow up, and read, and formulate some opinions of my own, and while I never did manage to leave any mark on it, I have perhaps come to understand something of the world.

Nothing stands still, and nor should it. I think of John, and of Grandfather: 'Change – we must have it!' they both would say. This place is closing down, for reasons unclear to me, and I am being returned to the world. They have been preparing us for some time now, with television programmes, classes on how to use electrical kettles and pop-up toasters, and afternoon trips by motor coach. And they have said I can take any books I like from here, and the framed pictures of rural scenes that hang on the wall of my room, which is kind.

I will be cared for in the community, they say. I asked which community, and they said my own: I am to go back to Elmbourne to live out my days, along with a few of the other people here. I can't quite picture where in the village they plan to house us. I only hope it isn't the row of old cob cottages Constance and I cycled past one sunny afternoon half a century and more ago, for they were very damp.

I used to dream all the time about the valley I grew up in. Asleep, I'd find myself by the horse-pond in Greenleaze, or at the circle of oaks, or on the sunny, green bank of the river where Frank and I bathed. Awake, I would picture in loving detail the valley's fields and farms, its winding lanes and villages, conjuring up a vision of a lost Eden to which I longed to return. But at last I came to see that there is a danger in such thinking; for you can never go back, and to make an idol of the past only disfigures the present, and makes the future harder to attain.

Alfred Rose became a soldier and wrote to me once, from Egypt. I still have his airgraph letter here, on thin Forces paper:

October 15th 1942

To Edie,
I thought you would be pleased to have a letter from your old friend Alfie. I am here with Sid in the desert of Africa a place I never thought I would see. We have moved up to the line and are waiting for orders. We get enough to eat and soap sent by the Daily Sketch but no baths to wash in for water is in short supply. All of us very sun-burnt but cheerful enough.

Well I must tell you that when all this is over I plan to marry. Her name is Iris Barker, a great girl, I hope you will not be too much upset.

Edie I hope you are recovering your strength and do not dwell on things past. You are a great girl but it would not have worked out for you and me. Lately I have found myself thinking I should not have done as I did but then I think of your ardour and know that you would tell me that we were both 'just kids'.

Please write back with news of home if you have it.

Your friend,
Alfie Rose

I never replied to his letter, God forgive me. I do not know whether or not he came home.

It is December now, and cold. Dusk falls earlier every day, and the trees in the grounds here have lost all their leaves. At night, if I open my window, I can sometimes hear the birds Grandfer called windles calling to one another, high in the darkness overhead.

This morning my friend Aisha took me in a silver motor-car to Market Stoundham, for tea in a café, and I wore my red winter coat. The town was both different and the same, and I felt at every moment that I might be about to glimpse myself as a girl, hurry-ing down Sheepdrove or entering the corn exchange with Father, holding his hand. But of course all that was many years ago, and that child is me now, something I know to be true but can't quite believe all the same.

I didn't choose my red coat, but I like it. Everyone has been so kind.

Aisha is from Ipswich; she is some kind of volunteer. She's been coming to see me for some weeks now; we talk about my grandmother, Clarity, and John's horse magic, and what little I know about witch-bottles and poppets and the ballads and songs we all used to sing. She even brought me a copy of Constance's book, *This Happy Breed*, which she had found in a library; but I told her I had no wish, no wish at all, to read it now. I gave her a corn dolly to thank her for her friendship; she asked if it was from the olden days, but I had to confess that I'd made it in one of the craft classes they put on here.

Aisha has promised to help me settle in to my new lodgings, and to come and see me often. They say I will be in by Christmas, and that everything I need will be taken care of; I only hope someone has thought to season an ash faggot for the fire. Perhaps the person on hand there will have done so – for they tell me someone will be available in case anything should happen to me, or to one of the others. In case I should need help.

I was somewhat apprehensive about leaving here when they first broke the news – we all were – but now I am so looking forward to going back to the place where I grew up. It will only appear strange for a moment, I'm sure of it; and then it will seem quite ordinary, and I shall be part of it all once again.

Historical Note

The Order of English Yeomanry is an invention, but in febrile, depression-hit 1930s Britain dozens of similar groups, large and small, sprang up in town and country, many with openly fascist agendas and beliefs. Some were little more than crank outfits, but others wielded real influence, both locally and in press and parliament. These complex, fragmented groups differed from one another, sometimes slightly, sometimes profoundly; but all drew from a murky broth of nationalism, anti-Semitism, nativism, protectionism, anti-immigration sentiment, economic autarky, secessionism, militarism, anti-Europeanism, rural revivalism, nature worship, organicism, landscape mysticism and distrust of big business – particularly international finance. Fascism in Britain was not a phenomenon solely of the far right; it proved attractive to some disaffected socialists, some veterans of the World War One trenches (most famously Henry Williamson, author of *Tarka the Otter*), and some suffragettes.

The British Union of Fascists claimed that 10 per cent of their candidates were women, a higher proportion than for any other party.

In 1945, the year Auschwitz was liberated and the horror of the Nazis' Final Solution revealed, George Orwell published an essay called 'Antisemitism in Britain'. He began by recording instances of anti-Semitic speech he had encountered in the previous years, among them:

> Middle-aged office employee: 'I generally come to work by bus. It takes longer, but I don't care about using the Underground from Golders Green nowadays. There's too many of the Chosen Race travelling on that line.'
>
> Young intellectual, Communist or near-Communist: 'No, I do not like Jews. I've never made any secret of that. I can't stick them. Mind you, I'm not antisemitic, of course.'
>
> Middle-class woman: 'Well, no one could call me antisemitic, but I do think the way these Jews behave is too absolutely stinking. The way they push their way to the head of queues, and so on. They're so abominably selfish. I think they're responsible for a lot of what happens to them.'

'Something, some psychological vitamin, is lacking in modern civilisation, and as a result we are all more or less subject to this lunacy of believing that whole races or nations are mysteriously good or mysteriously evil,' Orwell wrote.

A final note. In the early 1990s, when I was studying for my A-levels, I began spending an afternoon a week at one of the last of the big psychiatric hospitals (or 'mental hospitals', as they were known), then earmarked for closure. With other volunteers, I helped with occupational therapy classes, the aim of which was to ready patients for deinstitutionalisation as part of the 'care in the community' programme which had begun in the 1980s.

Many of the elderly patients had spent their entire lives in the hospital, or had been transferred there from county asylums at a young age. Most had diagnoses ranging from psychosis and schizophrenia to Huntington's chorea, but several of the elderly women, I was told, had been committed after becoming depressed, falling pregnant as teenagers, suffering trauma of one kind or another, or simply behaving in a way that was somehow troublesome to those around them. They had never been allowed to leave.

Acknowledgements

I learned an awful lot in the process of writing *All Among the Barley*: about the interwar years; about East Anglia; about farming; about storytelling; about myself. I learned the most, by a long chalk, from my agent, Jenny Hewson, and my editor, Alexa von Hirschberg, two brilliant women without whom ... well, I dread to think.

This book was lucky enough to have several early readers, and their feedback was very valuable. Thank you, Matthew Adams, Saskia Daniel, Sarah Ditum, Peter Francis, Lewis Heriz, Helen Macdonald, Paraic O'Donnell and Peter Rogers.

I am once again grateful to the writer and psychotherapist Martha Crawford (www.subtext-consultation.com), who helped me understand what a psychotic episode might look (and feel) like, and how it might be represented on the page.

My copyeditor, Silvia Crompton, was a dream to work with. I will be eternally grateful for her eagle eye when it came to continuity, as well as for the sensitivity of her edit.

Thank you once again to David Mann, Bloomsbury's jacket designer extraordinaire; and to Neil Gower, whose heart-stoppingly beautiful maps made the world of the book real, and brought it to life.

Thank you to the Museum of English Rural Life (MERL), and the University of Reading, for illuminating 1930s farm life and agricultural practices for me. In particular, thanks are due to Dr Paddy Bullard, Dr Jeremy Burchardt and Dr Oliver Douglas.

Thank you to all the people who put me up, looked after me and gave me the time and space to write: Anthony Young; Jo, Tom, Matilda and Anstice Ridge; Ted Ridge, Lauli Moschini and Sukey and Xander Ridge; Joanna Walsh; everyone at Gladstone's Library; and Elizabeth and Michael Evans.

Thank you to Sam Lee, who gave me the timely gift of the book's title.

And thank you, finally, to Marigold Atkey, Jasmine Horsey, Rachel Wilkie and Ros Ellis at Bloomsbury; Jessica Boak and Ray Bailey, authors of *20th Century Pub: From Beer House to Booze Bunker*; Ian Brice; Mike Burgess of www.hiddenea.com; Brian Clist; Susan Golomb; Jonathon Green of www.greensdictofslang.com; Sjoerd Levelt; John Lewis-Stempel; Jamie Muir; Andrew Roberts, creator of studymore.org.uk/mhhtim.htm; Matt Shardlow of Buglife; Adelle Stripe; the Suffolk Horse Society; Pip Wright (pipwright.com); and Louisa Yates.

Note on the Author

Melissa Harrison's debut novel *Clay* won the Portsmouth First Fiction Award, was selected for Amazon's 'Rising Stars' programme and chosen by Ali Smith as a Book of the Year for 2013. Her second novel *At Hawthorn Time* was shortlisted for the Costa Novel Award 2015 and longlisted for the Baileys Women's Prize for Fiction 2016 and the Encore Award. *Rain*, a work of non-fiction, was longlisted for the 2016 Wainwright Prize. A nature writer, critic and columnist for *The Times*, the *Financial Times* and the *Guardian*, she lives in London and Suffolk.

melissaharrison.co.uk / @M_Z_Harrison

Note on the Type

The text of this book is set in Bembo, which was first used in 1495 by the Venetian printer Aldus Manutius for Cardinal Bembo's *De Aetna*. The original types were cut for Manutius by Francesco Griffo. Bembo was one of the types used by Claude Garamond (1480–1561) as a model for his Romain de l'Université, and so it was a forerunner of what became the standard European type for the following two centuries. Its modern form follows the original types and was designed for Monotype in 1929.